Exile according to Julia

CARAF Books

———

Caribbean and African Literature
Translated from French

Carrol F. Coates, Editor

Clarisse Zimra, J. Michael Dash, John Conteh-Morgan,
and Elisabeth Mudimbe-Boyi, Advisory Editors

Exile
according to Julia

Gisèle Pineau

Translated by Betty Wilson
Afterword by Marie-Agnès Sourieau

University of Virginia Press
Charlottesville and London

Publication of this translation was assisted by a grant
from the French Ministry of Culture
Originally published in French as *L'Exil selon Julia*
© Éditions Stock, 1996

University of Virginia Press
Translation and afterword © 2003 by the Rector and
Visitors of the University of Virginia
All rights reserved
Printed in the United States of America on
acid-free paper

First published 2003

1 3 5 7 9 8 6 4 2

Library of Congress Cataloging-in-Publication Data

Pineau, Gisèle.
    [Exil selon Julia. English]
    Exile according to Julia / Gisèle Pineau ; translated by Betty Wilson ;
afterword by Marie-Agnès Sourieau.
        p. cm. — (CARAF books)
    ISBN 0-8139-2247-X (cloth : alk. paper) — ISBN 0-8139-2248-8
(pbk. : alk. paper)
I. Wilson, Betty, 1940– II. Title. III. Series.
    PQ3949.2.P573 E9513 2003
    843'.914—dc21

2003011722

Random memories, inventions?
Everything is true and false, emotions.
Here, the essential is side by side with casual
    reminiscences.
There are neither heroes nor minor players.
Neither good nor evil men.
Only a hope in better tomorrows.

Contents

Translator's Note

I would like to thank the following people for their helpful advice and suggestions at various stages in the preparation of this translation: Jeannette Allsopp, director of the Caribbean Multilingual Lexicography Project, University of the West Indies, Cave Hill; my colleagues at the University of the West Indies, Mona, Kingston, Jamaica: Steve Gadet, Grace Rookwood, and especially Marie-José N'Zengou-Tayo; Gai Constable-Reyal; Marie-Agnès Sourieau; Pam Mordecai, who kindly proofread the entire manuscript at very short notice; Carrol Coates, professor of French at the State University of New York, Binghamton, who guided the work; and, finally, the author, Gisèle Pineau, who generously responded to my requests for clarifications and explanations.

The translation attempts to be as faithful as possible to the writer's language, structures, rhythms, and registers. A glossary has been included to help with some of the terms that might be unfamiliar. There is a great deal of variation in Caribbean Creole/French/English terminology, as well as in the orthography of Caribbean words. (For example, within the text the narrator uses both "pommes-Cythère" and "prunes-Cythère," which can be translated into Caribbean English/Creole in several ways, including "Jew plums" or "June plums," "golden apples," or "pommes-sitay.") This is reflected in the translation, and the glossary indicates some of these variations. At times I have kept the original French/Creole words, italicized, and sometimes I have used common equivalents from the "anglophone" Caribbean. Sometimes sentences written in Creole are repeated or paraphrased in French in the original text. I have followed

Translator's Note

the author's lead and rendered all the Creole speech appearing in the text in English also. I hope that the English version will convey to anglophone readers some of the joy and the pain of Man Ya's beautiful story.

Black
and White

Goodbye Until We Meet Again . . .

Nigger
Négresse à plateau
Snow-White
Bamboula
Coal Black
and company . . .
Those names track us everywhere. Eternal echoes, devils hopping about in puddles, they splatter us with dirty water. Lost arrows, long and poisoned, reaching to the heart of a brief truce. Spitting on pride. Raining rocks on our heads. Suddenly our souls slip, crumble . . .
Sometimes we start suddenly. Our clenched fists begin to dream of one-two faces smashed, teeth broken. But to tell the truth, fighting is not our style. Ears trained in this music, prepared for the worst, some feeling always holds us back. It is enough to pretend as if those words were not burning our eyes. As if our tormented hearts were unmoved. As if our black skin was cast in bronze. "Don't pay any attention!" Manman would cry. "Don't pay any attention! Those words have no weight! You must not cry, above all you must not let them see they have hurt you, you mustn't give them that satisfaction, you mustn't draw attention to yourself."
"You," that is, my brothers and sisters and myself. Apart from Man Ya, my parents, and a few Caribbean army friends, there are only white people around us. Imagine, the middle of the sixties. A housing project in the middle of Ile-de-France. Our soldier friends are the only people my parents see. Together they unreel the threads of time, dreaming endlessly of the lives they had lived elsewhere, of the roles they played in bygone days.

That way, shaking off the dust of their humdrum everyday lives, they escape the numbness of the winters. They plait the sorrow that spreads its roots into their pretense at well-being and puts out its leaves in the carnival of savoir faire. They quell the doubts that keep springing up in them like weeds along a deserted path.

Our Pater, Maréchal, dearly loves those brave men, survivors, like him, of the Second World War. Veterans from French colonies, these men risked their lives in the mines of the same campaigns. Comrades, sharing the same barracks, brothers in arms, they ran desperate, ahead of enemy fire, suffered side by side on a hospital bed, in Indochina or in Africa. A spirit of almost mystical loyalty led them, in former times, to perform heroic deeds, etched indelibly in their memory. The army is their credo, France and her et cetera of colonies, their world. On Sundays, between the roast and the rice and peas, they tell the stories of their adventures, going over the numberless times when, helping out each other, they conned death. Saved, they have a good laugh. Make grand epic gestures. Their stories go from anecdotes to cheap army jokes. Sometimes bygone days come to jostle words from the present. Then they stutter, all choked up, stumbling with emotion over words that will not come. While these fragments of history come tumbling out one after the other, we children are only allowed to keep quiet and admire. Well trained, we sit up straight, our hands quietly on the table, our embattled feet fighting fiercely underneath.

Somewhat bored, the women listen, heads tilted, leaning on one hand. Mechanically they agree, smooth their hair, yawn behind their napkins. Without much effort, I can see them before me: widows in veils and black dresses, walking in procession behind a coffin draped in the flag, blue, white, and red, mourning for the unknown soldier cut down in his prime. How many times have they heard these stories, fascinating no doubt, but which, repeated over and over, have lost all their sparkle and now fizzle out miserably, like damp fireworks set off by forgotten heroes? Behind the screen of simple fraternity they know only too well that these men are also keeping close secrets sealed in male honor. So, the delight of the early days is no longer with them. I am how old . . . ten, eleven, perhaps. I can sense, without being able to express it, the feeling of derision that smiles at these heroic tales. The efforts the actors expend to rekindle the embers of past gallantry are only half-effective. Everything now is mere show, a great arsenal of words to dazzle and to disturb. I sense that one must not laugh, however, even behind a hand. For me, each life is an illustrious story that deserves a patient hearing because its mere evocation cuts the thread of time and builds tomorrows. Lives are throbbing in those stories. Unfortunate lives of the nation's minor players, returning on their knees from trenches where heroism, its deeds and its medals, lie rotting. Anonymous heroes who have given their entire youth to France and who have been accorded only grudgingly the leaven of glory.

Fulfilling their wifely duty, the ladies compel each other to be sympathetic. They discover they have things in common, speak about children, sewing, knitting. In order to show that they too belong to this exciting whirl of adventures, they tell stories of their lives in Congo Brazzaville, Zimbabwe, Cameroon, Chad, or Madagascar. Often, the ritual of doing the dishes catches them comparing their colonies, recalling the markets in the African quarter to which they ventured, black wives of black junior officers in the service of the French army. I like to listen to them. Drying the dishes, they also dry up their secret sorrows and speak cryptically, in very confidential tones, because of importunate ears—mine on this occasion—of their bitterness as wives and of the military regime that they sometimes endure. Late in the evening, after dessert, cake made by the lady of the house, they let slip nostalgic couplets about the faraway islands where they grew up, just before being carried off by the prestige of a uniform and the carefree freedom of youth. They were sentimental young women who read romances, love stories filled with rose water, orange blossoms, and the cypress-lined pathways where lovers stroll. How did they get to where they were? They are still asking themselves that . . . One day they had said Yes to the chance that stationed a man in uniform on their path.

Black and White

Yes to all the reasons love laid out, to a tomorrow filled with travel on the arm of a hero with bars and stripes. Yes to exile, which seemed as easy as changing blouses. They saw themselves becoming grand, free women. Over there in France, saved from the paternal yoke, relieved of the duties of seniority, spared from the fate of old maids whose only ecstasy now was to be found in God. These soldiers had landed like prophets, with the word in their mouths: France, the great promise of romance, beautiful dresses, balls, patent leather shoes, and furbelows . . . Alas, the sighs they now utter betray all their dreams. And the "If I had knowns . . ." evocative of the sunless beds in which they pass their existence, are evidence of the broken dreams they have already suffered. When their eyes meet mine, round and greedy with questions, their faces once again fall back into their ordinary mold, and I turn away my head.

My grandmother, Man Ya, does not join in these disillusioned laments. Her spirit floats above the melee. There she is, not troubling anyone, like an old outmoded piece of furniture, carved in a hard wood. A kind of cumbersome chest of drawers relegated to a corner of the kitchen generations ago. The cracked doors with peeling varnish squeak and the hinges need oiling. *Poulbwa*, wood ants, cockroaches, and mice eat and sleep inside. You can do nothing to repair it again, but you will never throw it out. You keep it, lovingly and with respect, telling yourself that, perhaps, the world's great secrets have seeped into the veins of the wood, have been written in the debris that it still holds in its drawers.

Man Ya is getting a big stomach. The skin on her legs is dry and cracked, just like the black crust on the puddings made from stale bread, taken out of the oven on Saturdays. Her calloused feet have nails that are dark and hard, so hard that before any attempt can be made to cut them, they have to soak for a long time in a basin of soapy water to soften them a bit. We children supervise the procedure. An array of scissors, files, nippers, graters proves to be imperative for this operation. We lay out the instruments in question with the slow, deliberate gestures of pretentious surgeons. And the one who starts shaping the nails, cutting and scraping the thick shell, is sure to have memorable shivers. Man Ya does not resist. She grimaces if the clippers cut into more tender skin. She has the wide-spaced teeth of those who, long before their birth is announced, have cracked open the dry shell of the good-luck nut. Yet, she rarely smiles. Hardly ever laughs. She didn't learn how, or else she has forgotten. Her body stays there, with us; her spirit wanders tirelessly between France and her Home Country, Guadeloupe, where every day she hopes to return. Unimportant as we are, we rejoice for her, and no one tries to lift the shades that cover her gaze, which is far, far away. Meanwhile, waiting for the great day of her return, she takes care of us, is always at our disposal, and we find all that quite natural. Her ways are rough. Her caresses more like vigorous rubs. Her words go straight to the point. She says life has one end and two destinations. Those who want to take the wrong paths get there quickly, but fall into ravines and savannahs where light does not penetrate.

Back Home, she said she used to cross over raging rivers and scale steep *mornes,* carrying on her back her load of misery, and the misfortune of having been born female and black. Her husband, Asdrubal—nicknamed the Torturer—used to kick her violently and then wore out his whip on her back. In a whisper, she confided that he was pursued by the ghosts of the dead who had fallen in the trenches in 1916, when he was fighting in France. In her youth, she had lost children in the sad waters of miscarriages and the hell of colics . . . She tells us stories—nobody admits that they believe her—about how in Guadeloupe, friends of the Devil have the power to fly, to turn themselves into dogs, to halt the course of rivers, and to dismantle life. She has already been chased by *diablesses* with cloven hooves and twisted fingers. She has seen night in broad daylight and day breaking in the middle of a moonless night. We shiver at these frightful memories. But she continues to tell these stories and to linger at ease in these nightmares, proclaiming all the time a thousand reasons why she wants to go back to the beloved country she has lost. She speaks of hordes of jealous men, of torture in the early dawn, of devils' brews and sorcerers' marinades. Terrorized, we feel weak, surrounded by Lucifers in shorts, by damned souls in tail coats. But all at once, she takes us back to her garden, and we escape from the bad men. Even more than her house in Routhiers, she misses her garden. She pictures it for us, a wonderful place where all kinds of trees, plants, and flowers grow in abundance in an overwhelming green, an almost miraculous verdure, dappled here and there with a silver light that shines nowhere else but in the heart of Routhiers. She conjures up an everlasting, flowing spring, gushing from a rock, hurled onto her lands by the great Soufrière. She lets us see her river, which comes down from the mountain to flow through her woods and wash her clothes. She sings us the song of every bird; afterward she names the foliage and fruits. Then she hoists us into the branches of her trees, just so we can see the horizon better, the horizon with its little bumps of islands bending under the weight of their smoking, spitting, pot-bellied volcanoes. We see it all through her eyes and believe her as one believes in Heaven, wavering endlessly between suspicion and deep conviction.

Of course, she does not feel at home in Ile-de-France, in the narrow confines of an apartment. But it's either that or death Back Home, they tell us in a whisper.

Long ago, in the war years when General de Gaulle was saving the mother country, Man Ya had urged her son, Maréchal, to join the dissidents. To stop him from raising his hand to his Papa, she had told him: "*Foukan De Gaulle! A yen pé ké rivé-w!* Go join de Gaulle! Nothing will happen to you! You will come back alive, crowned in the glory of the Lord . . ."

Maréchal came back in 1950, in one piece, victorious, decorated, with ribbons and stripes. That was when he fell in love with my manman Daisy. A dark-skinned black man from Routhiers, he had in his favor his good education, his flawless French, and as a guarantee of honor and nobility, the uniform of his country, which he wore easily. He courted her, faced her parents, and ended up marrying Daisy, to whom he had promised Paris.

Eleven years later, just before returning to France once more, destiny brought Maréchal back in the meantime to Guadeloupe. He had known various parts of the world and learned to love the Mother Country even more. He had seen wars and countries born at the same time. Everywhere he had met men, arms in their hands, seeking peace. He had lived, loved and hated, defended women and children in Africa, in France, and in Indochina. In that year, 1961, already blessed with a lovely family, Maréchal had the feeling that the Good Lord was giving him one last chance to save his Manman. Perhaps, if he delayed any longer, he would never see her alive again, he told himself, and he would be haunted with remorse for the rest of his days. I was five years old in 1961 and for me . . .

First there was the time in Africa. From '60 to '61, I think . . . I remember very little of the time spent in that land. I see huge almond trees, slow to move like crippled old bodies that don't move a hair for fear of waking a pain. They cast amber patches on a terrace bleached by the sun. Columns as big as elephant's feet.

The seaside was far away, the bush as well . . . Apart from the snakes, which kept us out of the jungle of the cassava field spread out behind the house, African animals never came near us in the military compound where we were quartered. To frighten each other, the grown-ups would tell the story of some lion that massacred a village. Some tiger that devoured a whole family, down to their teeth. As children, we would only gather the exciting side of these stories. Combined with our picture books, paid for in CFA francs, they grew and grew in our imaginations and took possession of our dreams, which changed them into great adventures, wild expeditions filled with unforeseeable animal life. Elephants, roaring lions, great monkeys, zebras, and giraffes wandered in herds through scorched savannahs. Tarzan could appear and disappear at any moment on an indistinct track leading to sleepy villages. There, women in *boubous* pounded millet. Ivory hunters and seasoned English explorers pursued Pygmies in the midst of an impenetrable jungle ruled over by warlike tribes who aimed their poisoned arrows. There was such a thing as "Africa," which competed, with its colorful representations, which passed through and passed away in our minds, seeping through all the ramparts of the French army quarters.

There are still photos from that time . . .

I leafed through what is left of our family albums. It was the age when I was turning over lots of questions in my mind. I wanted to put names to faces. I wanted dates, I wanted to put colors on the black and white photos. Moods. Words to express the ethereal and the elusive, the insignificant and the forgotten. Manman was very reluctant to indulge in reminiscing. I could feel that she was still resistant, that she wanted to keep all her treasures for the corners of her heart. I had to soften her up before asking questions. After a long breath, as if extricated from the trammels of her memory, she would bring back past times. Then her reticence would vanish, and her words soon outstripped her thoughts, burning her lips. Thanks to her, on glossy paper, I would recover the splendor of the Africa where we had all lived, all except Suzy, who would be born in 1963 . . . Manman used to say that Africa had nonetheless always kept us at a distance, as if skin color alone was not enough to make family . . .

For a long time I have had the feeling of having lost something: a formula that once upon a time would unlock jails, a sovereign potion that would release knowledge, a memory, words, images. I have nourished within me this loss, weighing me down like a bereavement, an indefinable emptiness. Hungry for knowledge, thirsty for an authentic essence, eager to find the very foundation of the world, I loaded my shoulders with a bitter burden. Africa left the weight of this cruel baggage . . .

Once upon a time I wandered in deep woods where all the paths looked the same. I always found myself embittered in the face of death, which closes in its darkness the trunk of memories and then consumes the body of times past. I spent the days of my life gathering scraps, old bones, stale food, damaged documents, yellowed photos. I knew for sure that I would have to fish for words in traps, catch them in seines, haul them in, spike them on hooks. I wanted to tread in ancient tracks, gather ashes, dust . . .

Goodbye Until We Meet Again . . .

I wanted to grab hold of each saying, stuff it, turn it inside out, and then bite into it. A hunger that cannot be imagined . . .

1961. Guadeloupe awaits us.

For eleven years our parents have not set foot in that place!

Eleven years since they went away to see the color of other lands. Has their country changed? They themselves, are they still Guadeloupeans?

Having left as an innocent young bride, my Manman Daisy returns to her country with five children. Maréchal has earned other stripes. A kind of intoxication grips them. The crossing lasts ten days, and as the island gets nearer, they are shaken by a force from within. Their fingers fastened, they return together to other waters, crazy, rough, which wash them. The waters of a river mouth where ocean and river join. They bathe their bodies and wash off the marks of life. We children wet our lips and lick that salt which heals wounds. We run up and down madly on the deck of the steamer, our hearts filled with an inexpressible joy. Guadeloupe! Guadeloupe! Soon, soon we shall see her! Three days. Three short days. Tomorrow! Tomorrow! One more night and the country will come into sight. *Cap Est!* Head East! Land! Land! the captain will shout. What is that vast country—surely a hundred times Africa and France together—which leaves gold specks in their eyes? We don't know anything about it, but we laugh with them. The happiness of the heart is a feeling that comes in easy and disappears like quicksilver. What is that country? . . . "It's my Country," Manman repeats. "That's where I was born. My whole childhood is there. Near to rivers and cane fields, *mornes* and woods. At the seaside, Sainte Claire beach. You are going to see Pa and Man Bouboule, my sisters and brothers, my uncles and aunts, my whole family. It's my Country. Mangoes, breadfruit, fresh fish. It's Guadeloupe! Goyave! Capesterre! . . ." The unknown Country seems infinite to us in the black of Manman's eyes.

These eleven years that have passed.

What has become of the beautiful Daisy and her Maréchal?

The excitement of their wedding day lies far, far away . . .

We must not dwell on that time. We must allow all that to fade away in the depths that no one is willing to plumb. What is down there? Rusty tin trunks filled with tears, fireflies watching over love's casket, a menagerie of years stuffed with straw, old earthenware pots with holes in the bottom that could not hold the broth of youth? . . . Daisy and Maréchal still believe that a new life can begin with each journey. In that photo, they show themselves off, don't they! Their faces have a look that says: "Ladies and gentlemen, we were right to set out for the Metropolis. We are handsome, well-dressed, wearing new shoes. We have worked hard and have a fine family." Three boys, two girls, who would ever have thought . . .

Maréchal comes from Routhiers, Cacoville, Capesterre de Guadeloupe. Routhiers is a place . . . how can I describe it . . . Woods! At the foot of the Carbet Falls. Interminable mist and drizzle. Rich black earth. You throw a seed, and from it grows a forest that holds wicked zombies and witches' magic. You have no desire to risk yourself behind dark thickets, or to be attracted by the flame of a gray candle that tempts your eye from the darkness of a house. There you encounter distress, love, rapture. Forehead creased, arms swinging, mouth twisted, provocative, austere women climb the hills in bras, children clinging to their skirts. Disoriented men philosophize about life beneath their caps. Others, who have been tirelessly forking the same earth for centuries, smile gently at their dreams of harvests. Birds of paradise, huge extravagant flowers, open their orange beaks along the path. You ask your way of mocking spirits who linger in these lonely places, appearing and disappearing. Normally the folk who lived there, under the shadow of the back of Soufrière, didn't seek their destiny anywhere else but in the perdition of the cane fields. But Maréchal loved school. He won a scholarship. A boarder in the Lycée Carnot, he managed to get his elementary school-leaving certificate in '41. He could have gone further. Alas, France had gone to war. Young, brave, so filled with honor, he joined the dissidents in '43. As a volunteer. In the army, that was how he became a career soldier.

Goodbye Until We Meet Again . . .

Daisy is from Goyave . . . Her papa, an overseer on the Sainte Claire estate, owned a line of buses. Her mother kept the largest shop in Goyave. They lived, resigned as it were, in a shrewd prosperity that nothing seemed to trouble, or so they thought. Alas, the papa signed as a guarantor for a false friend, a con man who, in order to disappear without a trace, faked his own funeral. According to reports, there was a widow in full mourning and orphans weeping at the burial. Flowers, wreaths, a funeral service, and, at the grave, the black earth of the cemetery thrown onto the coffin as a seal of truth. Farce! Plot, masquerade, blasphemy . . . because in reality the coffin had been closed on a banana tree. While my grandfather was selling all his possessions to pay the rascal's debts, collapsing into bankruptcy, from which he never recovered, the said gentleman was leaving for France on a steamer, with his fat packet. While my poor grandmother Bouboule was going to beg the bailiffs and the Good Lord not to take her shop away from her, the wretched man, hidden behind aliases, was opening big shops in Marseille and Paris. More than one person saw him here, there, and everywhere, without being able to catch him. One day nothing more was heard of the crook. But he must have died badly, that's for sure, in mental anguish that rotted his guts, dislocated his bones and dried out his bone marrow. That is how my Manman's family ended up in Capesterre. There, fate crowded them into a dingy little house, across from a savannah where people who had no land came to tie out their cows, goats, pigs.

. . . November '49. Every afternoon, her face shaded by a parasol, Daisy leaves the dry goods store where she works, and walks down the main street, straight ahead, without looking either left or right. Because the saying goes that you can't read on people's faces whether they are communing with angels or devils, she does not look for any company on her way. She has seen how man can climb high, fall, and be broken as easily as a toy. At present, because of the family's ruin, she also knows that rogues often have handsome faces, aristocratic smiles, neckties and papers to sign.

Black and White

Maréchal has just spent a period in Senegal. He is freshly landed, on leave at the end of the campaign. It is three or four o'clock by the sun. Manman is nineteen, beautiful, a proud mulatress. That day she is going to meet her future. She doesn't know it yet. What, who, which admirer is she thinking of? Their eyes meet at the ball, and Papa Bouboule changes into a wall when the time comes to ask permission to go dancing. How can the rocks of that fort which resists all assailants be scaled? At that time dances are rare and good prospects even more scarce. Manman walks a little faster. She is going home, to finish sewing a blouse. Perhaps tomorrow her day will come. She has faith in God. She has patience. The stories she reads in novels always end happily. Love and marriage go hand in hand. Fanned by the wind of boredom, her thoughts break free and crisscross wide blazing waters. She is dreaming of being swept away, of romances, of serenades. She walks on, her forehead smooth, her eyes lost in a night of illusions . . .

Suddenly a small boy is in front of her.

"Manman!"

"Who are you?"

"Paul. My name is Paul." The child is clean, well dressed.

"You aren't by yourself, all the same? Where do you come from?" She raises her eyes. A very black man dressed in a military uniform is standing right in front of the sun, which makes him so tall, so dark. Blinded, she shades her eyes with her hand.

"Manman!" Paul takes her other hand and gives her kisses and his most beautiful smiles. Then as if they were entangled with their tomorrow, the young people yield before the child and together fall into the same net. Each one is thinking: "It's my destiny." She, a creamy beauty with fine skin, flesh like ivory, with the thick silky hair of a mulatress, little treasure trapped in her mother-of-pearl shell, knows nothing beyond her native Guadeloupe, which she loves with all her heart. But she knows, she has always known that she will not remain there, to tread no other land but this. In the setting sun, the *mornes* of the colony are like the broken wings of a bird that will never soar. She wants to travel the world. She needs winter landscapes, swallows that herald summers, russet autumn dawns, summers in Paris. Sometimes she sees herself on a steamship that is taking her far away. To somewhere else. To France. Daisy shudders suddenly. Maréchal tells stories. He has traveled the world. Dominica, America, Africa. His words skip from one continent to the other. A lion roars at the bend of a word, while a nation of zebras takes flight. France flashes past before her eyes. He speaks so quickly, urgently. On leave, but he is leaving again soon. Paris appears, then fades, in the story of his life intertwined with Paul's. A real drama! No, the child is not his! A freak accident killed his real father. Poor child . . . Kindness personified, that man! His Manman lives in Routhiers, Man Ya, a saint! Bombs from the war explode in her eyes. Daisy sees him beside General de Gaulle and then under enemy fire, parrying bullets with his two hands. He is brave, she says to herself. Already he promises all the magic of Africa, France, centuries of enlightenment. He lifts a single corner of the veil, and she begins to build, she crosses oceans. She weighs and weighs up the prospects. Already won, she makes a single sauce out of his words, her feelings, and intuition as well, a flight of enthusiasm and haste, those fickle friends. And then, he speaks French so well, so well. He has diplomas, certificates. He is a sergeant in the French army. Paul wants a Manman . . .

Everything is done according to proper procedures, even if very quickly: request for her hand, ceremony. Papa goes away a month after the wedding. Manman joins him in May 1950, just enough time to get some things together for her trousseau.

Grown-ups, discreet and secretive about their love affairs, don't want to stir up that water which no longer flows in them. How can I tell about everything since those nine moons, the first cry at daybreak, since my memory worried about gathering together all the facts, since time was time and my life was placed on this earth. Tell my how, my why, my thoughts, my words, my actions . . . My life began in that very place, even if I didn't yet exist. Before going any farther I must describe this first encounter. No, he did not force her. She could have looked him up and down contemptuously, squared her shoulders and given him her disdainful back, her corseted waist, and her outraged hips to gaze at. She could have smiled at him sidelong and said: "You are a black man, sir! Go your way! My skin is too light for you!" She had the right to shower all those words on him, a man who was begging for a Manman for his orphan and who was bold enough to want to put a mulatress in his bed. Without even taking a little time to get to know each other better, they both rushed into it together, young people filled with expectations, with shared desires . . .

Why did she say yes so quickly? No doubt too many stars were shining before her eyes . . .

Why did he believe that a child's word came straight from heaven? Very likely he wanted to see in every flash of life a heavenly sign . . .

Why did they link their destinies to the idea of exile?

Everything begins there, with this questioning hurled like a rock into a calm pool, which ripples into silent circles, chuckles of water.

Why did they leave?

Once Over There, seven thousand kilometers from Guadeloupe, it seemed I was calling, as would a soul standing alone in a savannah. A horn, blowing till it is out of breath! A horn to awaken the surrounding hills!

Why did they leave their land?

Landings and sailings.

Comings and goings.

Flamboyant departures for France, the Homeland.

Returns never permanent to this summer camp.

. . . "Children! There is nothing, absolutely nothing good for you Back Home," the grown-ups would say. Long ago it was a land of slavery, which no longer has anything good in it. Don't ask about the past! Take advantage of France! Take advantage of the luck you have to be growing up here! Back home, children speak patois. Take advantage of the opportunity to learn French French. . . You have no idea how many blacks envy you. There is so much jealousy . . . It isn't easy to escape Poverty,

Malediction, and Witchcraft, those three breeds of Evil that rule over there. The blacks sweat in the cane fields and never see a single sun rise over their lives. The children go to school without shoes. They don't know fashionable clothes, nor licorice candy . . . But as for digging up these stories about slavery, it's not worth it. And let white people tell their own stories! Don't bother yourself! Just count your luck . . . No, there is nothing good Back Home.

They list all the ugly things about it as if to reassure themselves, and to convince us too. But sometimes, thinking of the island, wonderful lights glint in their eyes. All the fine things France has to offer: beauty, liberty, ease, paths to success, cannot uproot the love for their Guadeloupe. Without really wanting to, they let a loose cord hang between them and the land of their birth. A sturdy line from which to unhook the bait of nostalgia, stories of witches, the windfall of one or two attitudes and tones, the godsend of Creole speech, sparse news, Man Bouboule's parcels: vanilla, nutmeg, rum, and cinnamon. Treasures wrapped in a sheet from an old local newspaper that they smooth out for the nightly reading. Riches that Manman would use sparingly and keep tightly shut in the bottom of tins. To tell the truth, the grown-ups wavered constantly between the rapture born of each return and the rebirth that they say accompanies exile. They spoke of Back Home with love, nostalgia, and resentment . . . They loved their country, yes, but with an ambivalent love, like a love from one's youth that one cannot manage to forget even though it bore no fruit.

Deliverance

At the time "Deliverance" was the grand word that was used to describe my grandmother Man Ya's departure for France. According to our way of seeing things, we were her saviors. We had delivered her from the Torturer, the name with which we had permanently labeled her husband, my paternal grandfather, Asdrubal, behind his back.

In 1961 when we landed in Guadeloupe, for four months' leave at the end of the campaign, Maréchal wanted to forget that he had joined the dissidents in order not to pay back his papa for the blows Man Ya suffered at his hands. Alas! Nearly twenty years later, the poor woman was bending her back under the very same blows. She had said "I do" to *Monsieur l'abbé* for better or for worse. And the "worse," a demon that was consuming every day of her life, harbored under his dirty, sharp fingernails, the scum of old hurts, never forgotten, the bleeding memory of an old cut in the middle of his life, the rusty remnant of an iron saber slicing at him every additional day that God and the Devil give him. So Maréchal comes back as he had left, furious with the Torturer. Man Ya holds his hands and stops up his mouth so that he wouldn't say anything openly against his papa. She implores him to leave the sword of justice to divine law, which always rewards with a crown those who believe in the Good Lord. In order that he might accept continually seeing her under this yoke, she tells him that life here below is not life and that the great hope of Heaven lies ahead for the humble, the meek, and the lowly of this world. She speaks with anxiety, watchful of her surroundings. The Torturer terrorizes her, but she does not plot any vengeance against him, she never dreams of pouring hot oil into his ear one evening as he sleeps. She does not try to find some ingenious recipe for poison, instead every single day she cooks the meat or the fish that he buys to fill his belly. She eats after he has belched, if there is some bone to suck left over, or some fat in the bottom of the earthenware pot to dip a piece of bread in.

Two, three days before taking the boat for France, Maréchal gets up one morning with a plot to kidnap her in his head. His sleep is disturbed. General de Gaulle has appeared to him, clasping a stone Marianne, symbol of the French Republic, rescued from Hitler's curse. Maréchal himself has become the little black boy from Routhiers-Capesterre, Guadeloupe, once again. He is ten years old, or perhaps twelve. The strange thing—he is watching it all as if from behind a great veil—is that he is already dressed in military uniform. Chained, gagged, beaten, humiliated, Man Ya is a Marianne too, or rather an African statuette—because she is black and carved in an ebony wood like wood he saw in Senegal. Changed into a liberator, he is about to assail the Torturer, when he wakes up, saved from the unthinkable by the cry of a turtledove. His head resting on his hand, one after the other he calls up the images from the dream, until the Good Lord writes his first words in the sky. That man they call his father has no feelings, he tells himself. He, Maréchal, has traveled. He has seen how people live. He is a decorated soldier, congratulated by the General in person. He is a man on his own two feet. And all thanks to Man Ya!

But Asdrubal allows her to go down to mass . . .

As she does every Sunday, Man Ya gets up before the sun, the clouds, the cocks, and all the animals in Creation. She washes, plaits her hair, and gets dressed, praying in the silence of her heart. That night the dead from the Filthy War had again come to visit Asdrubal. He cried out like an animal. His body wept death on the mean bed. Now he is pretending to be asleep. Man Ya knows this. She knows all his tossing and turning, his sly tricks, his monkey gestures. He is watching her from below, his eyes half-closed in the darkness. His gaze weighs down on her . . . "Dear God!" she prays. "Let your love emerge victorious! Lord, send Satan back to the depths without pardon! . . ."

Black and White

She puts her household under the protection of the Most High and pulls the metal door behind her. The Torturer will get up in a minute. Poor thing, bed is his enemy. As soon as he falls asleep, the past assails him. He struggles all night long. A freshly brewed coffee is waiting for him on a little shelf in the kitchen. He loves Man Ya's coffee. He loves the way she browns meat, the way she cooks rice and peas. He loves to wear the shirts she washes, starches, and irons. He loves everything she does, all her little tricks to make something good from very little, her great thrift, her accommodation to the harshness of life. The only thing he reproaches her for, in fact, is being there, being around. Meeting her eyes, hearing her breathe. Knowing that she is breathing the same air. Having to put up with the sight of her dresses hanging in the house. Hearing her sing praises to God. Finding her always at her work, her spirit free, her back breaking, her hands busy. He would like, just once, to know the thoughts of this black woman, Julia, when sleep is carrying him off, across the battlefields of France, and when he is crying out, pursued by his dead comrades in the trenches. He endures her presence.

Man Ya walks some five kilometers, praying all along the way, for the repose of the soul of her manman, for her children, her friends, her enemies, and the sad master who has reestablished slavery, just for her. Sometimes a family of white rabbits gives way to her. A suspicious-looking bull stares at her defiantly. Man or beast, she does not trouble herself to solve this mystery but goes on her way, just making the sign of the cross to render herself invisible to malevolent spirits. On Sundays she feels a little of the Lord's benediction running down her back. She receives like a blessing the fact of walking from here to there, at this hour, in the heart of these fragrant woods. Then she greets the coming of the sun and each branch and each blade of grass. Nose wrinkled, lips pursed in order to better breathe in the nature of things, she goes on her way, listening for the noises and the comings and goings of the Good Lord's little creatures, carrying their food or the four leaves from a nest dismantled by the rain. The wind picks up the green skirts of the

———

Deliverance

torch lilies that line her property and then rises and goes to shake in their slumber the *pommes-Cythère,* the mangoes, and the guavas dangling over the metal roofs in the neighborhood, and even the breadfruit hanging among the branches. Melted into the darkness of the pre-dawn, the Carbet Falls and all the rivers falling hard onto rocks urge her to hasten her steps. While the *mornes* groan, suffering under the weight of the clouds, she whistles with the birds and watches out for *diablesses.*

What time is it then? Here time is not a matter of the clock. Time is written in the sky, the early morning darkness, the fickle sunsets. The days lengthen or shrink according to the seasons. Men's time is borrowed time. And the day unwinds quite naturally if you listen to time trickling within you like grains of sand in an hourglass. Time settles on time, and if you wait for evening, one hand under your jaw, you will not see anything passing. No, Julia is not late. She is going down to the village to meet the Lord and to pray to the Lamb who redeemed the sins of the world. Mass will not yet have begun. Often she meets spirits who have lost their way in the early dawn, *soucougnans,* furtive and malefic shadows. All these creatures fly quick-quick in the air. They have to go back before day dawns fully and pokes them in the eye with a blinding ray of sunlight. You have to hurry so as not to be condemned to beat your wings in the eternal despair of these poor unlucky souls. So Julia goes down the hillside quick-quick herself and does not pay them any attention. She always gets there for the first mass, and if it is too early and closed doors bar the way to her faith, she simply waits patiently, with no resentment in her heart.

That morning as she comes out of church, Maréchal is waiting for her with his last brother. They are standing in front of a green car. In those days you could count the number of cars. Proudly, Man Ya gets in, without suspecting a thing, and disappears inside the car. She doesn't know as yet that she is also disappearing, and for six years at that, from the life of her husband Asdrubal. Two days pass. An I.D. card, French nationality, comes for her. An X beneath her photograph. There? Yes, here! Make an X to sign. Maréchal is taking her away to France;

he has made up his mind. She is going to live far away from the Torturer, far away from the blows. There is nothing to be said. He is spurred on by a combination of filial duty, good intentions, and a series of ominous dreams. He is doing it for her own good, because on this earth—in 1961!—people have no right to be living like animals still. This savagery, all this misery is over! Soon there will be no more empty bellies, no more suffering on this earth! It's not for nothing that Schoelcher delivered blacks from slavery! Maréchal himself is sick, and his heart bleeds when he thinks of the hell she is enduring in Routhiers. He no longer wants to see her on this way of the cross. Leave, that's the only answer to this torture.

Maréchal recounts all the comforts of France. Man Ya begs him to leave her to her destiny, falls on her knees, and hands clasped, swears that her sufferings disappear in the sweetness of prayer. Asdrubal is the man whom the Lord has sent her, she says. Maréchal shakes a bell made of glass, and eternal snows fall on an Eiffel Tower. Man Ya tells him that she was married in the church, the Good Lord will not be pleased to see the sacrament undone through her fault. After that how could she receive communion and say: "I am Madame Asdrubal!" And her things, her linen? Her four dresses, her blouses, her skirts, her petticoats that she had made little by little by selling coffee, chocolate sticks, castor oil, cinnamon, nutmeg. Maréchal has an answer for everything, he promises a wardrobe, fine cloth, fine silk. Too bad for the Torturer! He will see, but too late, that he has lost the treasure of his life . . . "And my garden?" cries Man Ya. "Who will take care of my garden? And my two hens, and my pig?" "Don't distress yourself, Manman. You have already worked hard enough . . ."

Man Ya stays, hidden, for three days, in Ilet Pérou, in a house made of wood and stones. In the evenings the neighbors hear old Asdrubal prowling around. He curses the woman, his treacherous son, and all the blacks who come from France with their heads scoured by the ideas of the whites and their so-called just world. His old overseer's whip flays the night. Once, he even fires a shot in the air with his old gun from the First World War.

The eyes of the neighbors detach themselves from the shutters only when Asdrubal's ranting and twisting are no longer heard on the stony path. They suppose that he ends his night out there on the savannah, where the disheveled heads of the dragon's blood hedge form in the west a sort of zombie army under the command of Governor Asdrubal.

Legs weak, her back stiff, eyes shut tight behind a veil of terror, Julia embarks on the transatlantic steamer, *Colombia*. We are there too, clustered tightly around her, fearing at any moment to see the abandoned rascal rise up before us, stick in hand, feet shod in the stiff leather boots that he habitually employed on Man Ya's sides. My God! Let not the mere evocation of his name cause him to materialize or take him to France in the dark hold of the *Colombia*! These visions are frightening. Even after ten days' crossing, all the expanse of sea stretched out between her and him, Julia still has anxiety in her heart and every sound of boots makes her start.

When her foot touches the soil of France, she makes the sign of the cross, genuflects, and then weeps uncontrollably. Why have they forced her to leave the man who is her husband in the sight of God? No, she does not lift her skirts to dance as she should have. She does not laugh, does not sing. She is not delivered. She is barely disembarking in a land of exile and five cable lengths of chains have just been added to her existence. She weeps for her lost country. She is already missing her rough life. She does not understand why they have brought her to France. She does not know how long she will have to remain there. To do what? For what purpose? She tells herself that perhaps behind Maréchal's long speeches are hidden other reasons . . . The children. But she has so little to give. A great bitterness for such a tiny hope.

Walking over a land that has bled so much, breathing continually the stench of the sufferings of slavery, which did not blow away, just like that, on the wind of Abolition, sucking the bones of despair, one is forced to understand the rage, and also the fear. And to ponder the insignificance of laughter, the flashes of courage, the jealousy. One cannot judge. Julia is already used to all that. Her beloved land has cast her down how many times, and then picked her up again. That is exactly where she wants to live, in Guadeloupe. She supposes that a curse hangs over blacks. This race has been cursed since the time of the Old Testament. She herself prays and believes. The promise of a better tomorrow lives in her heart. So, she could have suffered for five more centuries the Torturer's beatings. The Good Lord beside her lights up her life. She asked nothing from anyone. And she weeps over Asdrubal left alone in the house with his ghosts and his nightmares, his loneliness and his torments.

Who can track the indecision in women's hearts? In this country of cold where time in a hurry dominates man, Julia does not believe that her good angel has abandoned her. Even if she senses in the air over here something that makes smiles false, that eats away at you inside, and that saps and tears down, she assumes that she is not there by Maréchal's will alone. So, she tells herself that her crossing must serve a purpose. Papa assures her that we have come to a country of great civilization. "You are coming from a long way," he says. "Delivered from hell and damnation." And he makes her understand that she ought even to consider herself miraculously saved. Defeated by these words, Julia says yes, so as not to vex him. But her look has suddenly changed, hardened. For one brief moment, she seems like a warrior fitted out to conquer France. She measures the heights of the concrete walls, the arms deployed, looks over the ships oozing with ancient rust, the path that cuts through the fields, the long path, and the sky that has disappeared. The time that is coming holds nothing to worry about, she says to herself. The days present themselves one by one; all you have to do is to take hold of them one after the other, one after the other, one after the other . . .

The time in Guadeloupe! Such a short time.

I was five years old before this return to France with Man Ya. We, the children, spent those four months with our maternal grandparents, Manman and Papa Bouboule . . .

The memories are faded or replaced by other memories. Only

the frozen photos open onto pools of light. The past lives on the other side of the scalloped frames. There, kids who will never grow up continue to run, to laugh, and to cry. They wear little red and blue striped training pants. Arms and legs covered with scrapes, poor. The mosquitoes gorge on their sweet blood and devour them constantly, especially at night. In the mornings, Man Ya gives them a bush bath that soothes the bites. Look at Élie and Rémi! That's me there, with my black doll. Even today, I easily reach over time and immediately fall back into the comfort of my five-year-old self . . .

Content yourself with a single image, even if it is blurred, spoiled, torn.

Reconstruct the hours that have passed.

Reinvent the sun on that day.

Shape the images that come.

Defy the times, mix them up, break their course.

. . . Holding his cane, Pa Bouboule, a big *chabin,* with a round head and white hair, is sitting on the verandah. Behind branches of croton with green and yellow leaves and the red flowers of a gnarled hibiscus, he sits there the whole blessed day, thinking about old times . . .

After the bankruptcy, the loss of the shop, the fake burial, he stopped seeing anything clearly except the viciousness of the world, and his existence fell into unrelieved darkness. One morning half of him stopped living. And for the rest of his days, he found himself dragging along this dead side, like a soldier struck down by a bullet in the war, a sort of brother in arms he could not resign himself to abandon by the roadside.

Papa Bouboule is bitter and seems exasperated with us children, who have a new life before us. He understands neither the sky nor the clouds that quite suddenly darkened his existence. So he shouts at all the kids who run around near him. He terrorizes us, and we torment him. He watches us, but we are watching him too. His favorite game: pretending to be dozing with all the business of snoring. One finger to our lips, we walk by one by one, on tiptoe in our bare feet. The old man is never asleep. He has no other distraction: spying on the movements of each of us. Then he hooks our legs with his cane. We fly off in all directions, and too bad for the one who is caught and who—as the price of his freedom—has to stammer a long explanation, looking Papa Bouboule in the eye. We are little birds that he takes pleasure in scaring off. We are no more than the mad ants that crawl along the length of his trousers and that he brushes off with slow gestures.

Manman Bouboule, on the other hand, shows herself to be a strong woman. Constantly, she says that her Émile is too soft and that his kindness has messed him up. She looks like one of those old Sioux women from America that we will see later on in films about cowboys and Indians. A mulatto, her skin is polished to a copper red. Her hair reaches as far as her ankles when, head tilted to one side, seated in her rocking chair, she combs and plaits it for a while making two endless braids that she winds around her head and holds in place between the teeth of four mother-of-pearl combs. On the backs of her hands flow green rivers that mingle their waters and wander off between the stiff bones of her fingers with their gray nails. She stands upright, squarely facing the life that blows over her.

She has lost countless children . . . Her Joseph, in the war. Philogone, from an unnamed illness. And her eldest daughter also, following right after her husband, who was too interested in politics. Those two left three orphans. She lost her shop in Goyave, half of her Émile, her manman, her papa, but she has never lost her mulatto's pride and her faith in God. She is raising her grandchildren, the children of a poor relative, and also the brood belonging to an unfortunate neighbor worn out by poverty. Like Man Ya, she goes to church every Sunday, not in Capesterre, where mass is over too quickly, but in Goyave, her beloved district.

She had advised Émile not to compromise himself, not to sign on behalf of that fellow who made them see the belly of hell and then went off, in a pretend coffin. But men are impressionable, and they don't take the time to listen to the reason that comes out of women's mouths. One day, while Émile is waiting for the bailiffs, she walks straight ahead, a girl child in each arm. The midday sun was blazing high in the sky. She asks: "Lord, what are You giving us to eat this day?" She sits on a rock at the foot of a tree. Raising her head, she spies a branch offering its single bunch of green mangoes. At that moment, a young fellow appears, a pole on his shoulder. She hails him. And, without a word, he picks lunch, just like that. But what's the use of thinking about that time . . . She is going to give Papa Bouboule his portion of breadfruit and call to Daisy's children.

In normal times, walking in front of Papa Bouboule is like an expedition. But at this hour, he no longer frightens us. His mouth opens, closes, beats air, then closes over the spoonful that Man Bouboule offers him. His cane is resting between his legs. We walk confidently, like soldiers in a victorious legion. He looks at us surreptitiously but will never dare to hook us in front of our grandmother. She does not laugh whenever he catches us, predicts broken arms and legs, bloody poultices, disfigured faces. She sees a confraternity of doctors, hears ambulances wailing, and smells the ether from the hospital at the slightest sign of tears.

For dinner, she is preparing a custard for us with Man Ya's chocolate sticks . . . "Don't stay in the kitchen, children! Fire is dangerous. What will I tell your manman, if you come out of here with the skin on your back burned and your insides exposed! . . ." She only agrees to let us come as far as the door. So, in order of size, our heads one on top the other, leaning on the doorway, we watch her hands, which proceed with a deference mingled with certainty. She measures out without weight or scale. First she takes down a saucepan without a handle, with a blackened bottom, a bit of zinc pierced with holes, rusted, black. She grates the chocolate, adds a trickle of water, and then slowly stirs. An old biscuit tin holds cinnamon, nutmeg, vanilla. She breaks a piece of this, sprinkles a pinch of that. With her sharpened old knife, she peels a lime, drops the peel into the mixture. When she lights the fire, casting glances in our direction that speak to us without words, we take a step backwards. Too little, we know nothing about what is being prepared in the saucepan. But a kind of attraction forces us to remain there all the same, mildly intoxicated by the aroma of the cocoa, looking at Man Bouboule's hands and the height of the flames that form a ring around the rounded bottom of the poor saucepan. Sometimes one of them shoots up suddenly, reaching for a finger. Man Ya neither cries out nor jumps, but continues, imperturbable, stirring gently with her big wooden spoon, adding little by little water, French flour, until the cream thickens. At last she taps the spoon gently on the heel of her hand, tastes with her tongue, and then bends over to put out the fire. This last gesture gives us permission to take one step into the kitchen. Stunned by the strong odor that fills the house, we assemble on the table earthenware bowls, jugs, china cups, mugs, goblets, tin cups. She gently pours out the steaming chocolate. No two bowls are alike, but we are confident. Man Bouboule has a secret measure in her eye. She gives to each according to the size of his stomach and not the hunger in his eyes. After this operation, we are on our best behavior. She looks us over from head to toe. And the one who has been good all day long earns the favor of scraping the bottom of the pot. Man Bouboule gives it to him or her solemnly, like a real monstrance, holding the sacred host. Invested with glory, the angel of the day thanks her, then retires with the precious booty. Fierce, sitting on a stool, not far from Man Bouboule's eyes, he hugs his saucepan. If greed gets the better of pride, some dare to beg the good one for a scraping of cream. Out of Christian charity—and because Man Boule is watching—the chosen one furiously spoons into bottomless mouths a scraping of the delight, so that he can be left in peace. Only, you don't beg twice. At that point you have to be content with the provoking odor. Each spoonful seeks out and brings back life in a burned morsel that sticks to the teeth, and dislodges from the crevices a coil of quivering cream buried under our watchful eyes. The attachment to scraping out the saucepan does not proclaim a longstanding daily hunger on the part of the heirs of slavery. Earning the right to scrape the bottom of the dessert saucepan—corn, vanilla, or chocolate custard—shows that life can satisfy itself with simple pleasures. This one, you cannot weigh in gold or in silver, at best you may be able to trade it against two coconut sugar cakes, a share of *doukunnu,* the first steps in a sweet dream. The scraper of a saucepan cannot operate in haste. He stretches out the duration of his happiness until some grown-up is tired of hearing the scrape-scrape of the spoon and seizes the saucepan to put it to soak. Thanks be to God, glory does not last forever. No sooner is he relieved of his treasure than we consider the so-called paragon a greedy fraud, a usurper. Later on, thinking about it by chance, pain suddenly clouds our eyes, regret takes hold of us. Until we are resigned, the feeling of having lost a tiny bit of this happiness disturbs our thoughts. For, when all is said and done, the custard chilled in bowls, that everyone—big and small, ignorant and wise—eats at dinnertime cannot be compared to the exquisite *crème brûlée* at the bottom of the saucepan.

Night comes via the sea. Sitting on the gallery of Man Bouboule's house, we wait for it, eyes already fluttering. On the other side, the sun is hanging on in the *mornes.* Every evening, the sun swears that he will not lower his eyes; that he will suffer for eternity the gaze of the big forest trees that live in the recollection of the Caribs and the Maroons. He does not want to disappear and resists, under the pretext of a last salute to the sugar cane flags, he laughs like braggarts do, shouting that he will rain more and more blows on the backs of the women working bent over in the midst of the fields. While he is losing his first rays in a ravine, he is still struggling. And just like these proud people who don't know how to say sorry, he rails in agony, then suddenly sinks down, pushed by the dark sky.

I remember the end of a day.

I am standing between Man Boule's thighs, begging for a story to satisfy my dreams. The day is dying, swallowed up by the *mornes* and the blades of the sea. Man Boule announces— and I shudder—that Guadeloupe will one day suffer the same fate. ". . . A wave from the sea will end it all for her, my child. Just one big wave. For a while, two or three centuries perhaps, people from other lands will lose their souls searching for her, lifting up every wave, every rock, the tiniest grain of sand. Ancient shells will whisper words: promises of a city under the waters, secret routes with no return, the marvelous kingdom of an African king. Little silver fish will send up bubbles that will tell of the Creoles' struggle and their combat in the heart of the turbulence. Learned men, sent specially from France, will unfold old maps belonging to the late Christopher Columbus. They will hunt for light in the broken pieces of Carib pottery and for hope in the calabash gourds and all the dead fires. It is certain that, from the bottom of the seas, they will bring up slave ships and quantities of old bones of slaves who did not understand why they had been brought there, and who did not want either to live or die on a Caribbean land. The Antilles! They are not lentils, no! They are like brothers and sisters, different, but from one same family. They are Guadeloupe, Marie-Galante, the Saints . . . and also Saint Lucia, Martinique, Haiti, Dominica, and still others yet, of all different sizes. Small countries where they have put a little of everything: damnation and holiness, rascality and goodness, jealousy, beautiful women. Evil paradises, where love is destroyed by sorcery. Lands without front or back, without right or wrong side, upside down, capsized. The Lord assembled every color, language, religion, nation, to see how people were going to behave. Living there is like traveling the whole world without moving!

"I love this country, even if it raised my Émile up high like that and then dashed him down to the ground. It was jealousy that threw him down. But there is rise and fall . . . I am not weeping. There are those who frequent sorcerers and Maliémin, others who implore nameless gods, beg for gold, for glory; I, I pray to the Good Lord and his saints. The only mystery: Why are we here, on this earth? And why are we going to die? In this life there is rise and fall, over and over and over again, endlessly. So take courage and be patient . . . You know in a dream, I saw Guadeloupe going back to the belly of the sea from where she came. And the sea, which has no memory, was smooth once again. With no beach, no shore, no coconut tree. Look at those *mornes* disappearing into the night! Perhaps one day they will no longer see the sun setting on their sides, and it will be the darkness of the bottom, the silence of fish, the salt of man's tears. Only the honey bees that have tongues long like that will be able to talk about the height of the wave that will cover this country. But who will understand the language of those creatures? My daughter, there will come a century when the people of this world will no longer lift up their souls. Their gaze will seek to go even beyond the horizon without taking the slightest bit of time to rest on what is nearest to them. Ears will have lost the ability to hear the signs whispered by creatures that are on the earth just to alert and to forewarn. People will not see the little leaves falling and rushing away too quickly in the river. They will not feel the earth coming apart under their feet. They will not even hear the passing of the mad ants. No, it is not enough to chatter. You must nurture yourself with the teaching of the years and learn to read the pages of the clouds, the sun's moods, the sky's round sketches . . . One day, believe me, this Island, which bears us at present, will no longer be anything but a canoe lost on the open sea, tossed about, mast broken, a lost country, that will live on only in the dreams of whites, in the memory of Creoles, who have escaped to France or to America. Who will remember the rest of us?"

"I, I will remember, Man Bouboule!"

"Yes, perhaps you will be among those who escape . . . Oh, but then everything will begin again elsewhere, in other lands, among other faces, after great upheavals. But, I myself, assuredly, will no longer be there . . ."

. . . For the moment, before the fulfillment of these terrible prophecies, the Good Lord simply commands night to fall on the earth. Then the sky fades all at once, grows dark, setting free all the shadows that during the day hide their bodies far from the fires of the sun. While the houses close their doors one by one, the sky sleeps with only one eye. It guards our sleep from devils and spirits. It puts out the stars and summons the moon. Tonight, the moon is full. She is carrying life in her belly. In spite of her failing eyes, Man Bouboule insists that Ti-Jean is there in the moon . . . "Oh, yes! My daughter, he is carrying his bundle of clothes on his back. Look carefully! Listen! He is calling out and asking the stars the way." Sometimes the moon represents the smile of a black in the dark night. "See," Man Boule explains to me, "blacks have already been enslaved, they have already been trampled on, their hamstrings have been cut, they have been made to understand that they were no more than animals. In spite of all these tribulations and heaps of bad treatment that your ears cannot hear, blacks have survived. And that big smile that adorns the night, it is as if to tell the world that the spirit is stronger than the flesh. And that the laughter of blacks in the midst of torment is the strength of the spirit over the pains of the body . . ."

But you must not stay out late, nose in the air, defying those who, when night falls, utter words from hell, remove their human skins, and change into flying spirits to lay the eggs of the worst evil in the depths of houses. Man Bouboule jumps up, closes doors and windows, murmuring an Our Father, who art in heaven . . . My God! May the creatures from hell spare those who truly believe! My God! Protect us from _soucougnans_! . . . On tables and sideboards, the yellow lights from gas lamps flicker in columns of black smoke. The grown-ups set out on the floor the seven mattresses that sleep one on top of the other all day long, on Man Bouboule's rosewood bed. We throw ourselves down and fight in the sheets made of flour bags. Sleep is already in our eyes . . . Go and pee, children! One by one! And say your prayers! And say goodnight to Pa Bouboule! And to sleep please, ladies and gentlemen! . . . In bed, we give each other one or two soft taps, pull the sheets and plot, yawning, the intricacies of a maneuver that will allow us to escape Pa Bouboule's cane the next day. And then our jawbones relax more and more between sentences. The words fall like beads from a broken necklace. The words roll and disappear between the folds of the sheets and the cracks in the floor. Lips begin to drool a little. A mosquito taking advantage of the situation alights on a forehead. I resist sleep. I don't want to give in already. Sleep is stronger than death. It transports you to an unknown world brooding within you. It unearths and reawakens forgotten eras, old wounds, and faceless fears. It makes you a spectator, mutilates you, bleeds you, tears you apart.

Armed with her candle that cuts through the darkness, Man Bouboule goes to put out the big lamp on the sideboard. At this hour, her feet drag a little. "Thank you Lord, that the day has not seen any misfortunes!" she thinks. Her shadow stands out on the half-open door of her room. Sitting on her bed, she takes out her combs and arranges her thick hair. Her smock that collects diaper pins, her dress, then her chemise, fall on the bed one after the other. She puts on a nightcap, decorated with crinkled lace, and her head bowed devoutly on her breast, makes a sign of the cross that ends in a sigh.

It's never fully night in Man Bouboule's house. A candle on a bedside table defies the darkness. Its light guides the steps to the chamber pot that they uncover and cover again very carefully. While all around ordinary things become nameless shadows with long faces and clenched teeth, the slightest noise brings with it diabolical assumptions. No, night never passes in the midst of an undisturbed silence. The adults' whispered speech clothes the shadows that become a movie. The cries of a child's bad dream encounter the creaking corrugated iron roofs. Two fingers of a little breeze tap on the barred windows. The clock, tirelessly, marks the time. In the kitchen, a mouse family dines on the remains of a forgotten meal. Cats chase each other on the roof. A pack of stray dogs roams up and down the street yapping solitude. The rain comes down suddenly, hammers on the corrugated iron roof, and the din it makes, above our heads, causes us to grip the bed sheets tightly and huddle more closely one against the other. We are safe, thank God. Behind the door, *soucougnans, diablesses,* flying spirits have the right to wander, fly about. Outside, evil's great wings can cover the world. And men who call on Beelzebub are free to change themselves into dogs, oxen, or horses. We ourselves are under the protection of the Good Lord, of his only son, of the holy apostles and of the angel Gabriel, the kindly ones. In gilded frames, immortalized in images hung on the walls, they are there, love. They stop in their tracks black demons with long hooked nails, cloven feet, horns on the forehead, and a tail stuck on behind. Not a single fallen angel will be able to force Man Bouboule's door. Not a single one of Satan's army will be able to overcome her prayers. I fall asleep in this assurance.

In the morning, at the hour when the unspeakable creatures are going to resume human form, Man Bouboule feels for her sandals with her foot. Her head is already covered with a kerchief. She goes to the bridge to empty the contents of the chamber pot in the waters of the canal. Shadows go by, pass each other without greeting, furtive, bent over, loaded down with their stinking buckets. Soon it will be broad daylight. Before she returns to us, the smells are already blown back by the breeze from the sea; they wake us. That's how it is every morning . . . and even worse if a late rising has surprised a household. In full sight of everyone, a miscreant is obliged to run, nightshirt in the wind, hair unkempt, to tip his chamber pot under the bridge. A signal shame accompanies his return, for the odors that we will be forced to endure even later in the morning hours, already precede him. Pestilence.

Man Ya's
Five Ministries

The Army

She does not understand why they have brought her to France.
  She does not know how long she will have to stay there.
  To do what?
  For what purpose?
  The task is tough, uncertain. And France, for Julia, is more than anything else, Tribulations and Damned Nuisances Associated . . .

  She says: "My God, the cold gets into your flesh and goes to your very bones. All these whites don't understand my language. And this way they have of looking at me as if I were a creature who came out of Lucifer's side. You have to see it to believe it. When I go back to Guadeloupe, I will tell Léa that Over-there, France, is a country of desolation."
  She says: "The trees have no leaves and the sky no color. As for the sun! It's no better than a fat, lazy pig that gets up grudgingly. What do you want to do in a place like that! Why didn't they leave me in Guadeloupe? No, I didn't ask for anything. At times there are people who skirt fate. But, my God, You are my witness, I never wanted to abandon Monsieur Asdrubal. I only prayed that peace should come over his soul and that the dead from the war should not come and pursue him even in his sleep. And even if I screamed Torturer. And even if he gave me nothing but blows. Did they have to put all that amount of sea between us? How many days crossing . . . Seeing only the sea. Sailing like any Noah in the deluge in search of dry land. My God! What day am I going to go back? So many seas that one cannot imagine it. I saved a coffee jar, only that. A jar of green cof-

fee. No one has told me when I am going to go back. But it is certain, one day I am going to go back home. Seeing nothing but the sea . . . Wondering if there really is a land that can bear humankind, so far away, behind the Good Lord's back. Who is going to split open my vanilla, who then Lord . . ."

Before getting to Paris, the family lives in a village in Sarthe. The winter is harsh that year. In Aubigné-Racan, in our stone house, our stove neither sings nor hums. It devours buckets and buckets of coal, but its warmth is pathetic. We circle around it, under our pullovers layers of newspaper that are supposed to keep the heat in our bodies. Alas, all the tricks in the world cannot get the better of this cold. In the evenings they stuff hot red bricks wrapped in the same paper at the foot of the beds. That winter I am my manman's only daughter—Lisa stayed behind in Guadeloupe and Suzy is not yet born. I sleep with Man Ya in a big wrought iron bed, under two sheets and three blankets. My body driftwood fitted against hers, which is heavy and makes the mattress sink, my feet glued to her warm legs, head burrowing under her arm, in the only place where heat unties its bundles. In spite of all these precautions, cold governs my gestures and holds my flesh in its claws. On the frozen tile near my slippers, behind the pane of glass, which gets paler and paler, in the air, the water, the stone walls, the cold is everywhere. If I don't budge, it forgets me for the twinkling of an eye. Then sleep, lying in wait, suddenly gallops up to me, like a black horseman who has escaped from satanic troops—those that the archangel Gabriel is fighting against above Man Bouboule's door. He casts me into a bottomless pit. I am losing all my strength. I am hurtling down the sides of a ravine. I am rolling, tumbling, slipping, spinning. I can't stop falling. So I scream, silently. I am going to die, and it will be all over. One, two tears, powerlessness and resignation, wet my face. I cry until Man Ya enters into my confusion, shakes me to bring me back from where I am, and says: *"Pa pléré ti moun! Ou ké sové! Pa pléré!"*—"Don't cry little one! You are safe! Don't cry!"

The Army

Rémi, Élie, and I are all enrolled in the village school . . .

There used to be some photos from that time long ago. No one was interested in them. If Hurricane Hugo had not blown them away they would still be there, under the zinc roof, gathering dust in a garret, among heaps of outmoded clothing, yellowed cloths, old trunks with metal hoops, bundles of faded copies of France-Antilles. I was the only little black among all those little whites in gray smocks. On the black slate one of them was holding you could read: School Year 1961–62.

It is good to go back over these old paths even if they have been trod a hundred times. At the beginning, when you walk along, everything is enchantment. And then suddenly, you go back into unknown, oppressive woods that block out even the gaze of the sun. In one brief moment, you understand that you have never known the person you were, what you came to seek on this earth. You hang your life on the thick lianas that the trees throw to you. You run, you keep going. Dead leaves cry out under your feet. You pick up stones in order to get back to your house, your lost family. Have they abandoned you? You don't know. A river is calling you. You want to go back up it, walk in its waters encumbered with rocks. Fall. Get up again. And then let yourself be carried away.

First day of school. I don't cry when I get there. I have come to learn. I sit up straight, I listen. To read and write is to enter into the world of books, catalogs, postcards, and shopping lists. In the afternoons Manman knits or reads novels. She smiles at the rows of lines. At the end sometimes she sheds tears. The letters arranged in a certain way have power over her. And even when it is shut, a book is never an object like any other. She thinks about it with excitement. Disturbed during her reading, she looks at us as if she were engaged in worlds where living and dying send you into raptures or drive you to despair in an exhilarating way. I am hungry for the same emotion. I can already recognize some letters, but a number of others are still steeped in mystery. I want to learn. Like Rémi, who acts like someone important. Every evening, he assaults our ears, hurling chopped up words. No one understands a thing from these stories he haltingly recites except Manman, who lifts him in triumph.

Sitting in the third row, I am listening to the teacher. She smiles at everyone and then offers us the keys to success: WORK and DISCIPLINE. Now two lines crease her forehead. Her arm rises and falls. Her hand goes round and round. And letters appear, little by little, at will, in loops and circles, mysterious upstrokes and downstrokes, up and down. Each shape has a name. When the ruler points to one, the lady's mouth immediately takes hold of it. The letter springs from her tongue. First she spits out little bits of it: *buh-buh-buh!* As many as are needed for all of us. We repeat with her: *buh-buh-buh!* The letter has the flavor of knowledge. Each sound is an evocation . . . *ba*-teau! *ba*-lloon! *buh-buh-buh! bou-bou*-le! Manman *bou-bou*-le! . . .

But the bell is ringing already. Manman is waiting for me in front of the big school gate. She has brought the snow with her. Rémi is holding one of her hands. While our footsteps write in the snow, I tell her feverishly about letters and the whole art of saying them. I explain to Manman that at every moment she herself IS SAYING letters. Letters are everywhere . . . Manman is in raptures. I am not hungry, except for letters. Quick, I want to set off again, brave the cold, cross the church square, and get back to school. And two days pass like this caught up in the magic of writing. My pencil is even more eager than I am. It is shaking between my fingers.

"Open your exercise books!" says the teacher. "Write *luh-luh-luh!*"

Over and over she makes the same loop, going up slowly, slightly slanted, turning, turning, and then comes back down, pressing on the chalk. *Luh-luh-luh!* We have to imprison the *luh* behind the bars of a jail, behind the big blue lines stretched out on white paper. Not a single hair of the *luh* must go outside the lines. The children are struggling, tongues stuck out down to their chins. Ruler in hand, the teacher walks up and down the rows. I am getting ready to begin a second line of *"luhs"* when

The Army

she gets to me, takes my exercise book, looks at me, looks at my writing, looks at me again, and then exclaims: "Children! The black girl has already finished! So you can do it too!" Her fingers pat my plaits while I swallow the praise, which caresses my throat like a barley sugar candy. She sends me to the blackboard. I believe that I have gained her favor. Eyes shining with gratitude, I can already hear myself telling Manman how, out of the entire class, I distinguished myself. I am smiling at the sweet joys of life. Around me, hair untidy, blue eyes dulled, the children are waiting in blissful insignificance; it is said that in the mornings they drink cider instead of a bowl of milk. My hand is a little animal that I have very quickly tamed. I can do what I want with it. Up, up, turrrn, and back down. One more *luh*. Up, up, turrrn, and back down, *luh luh luh*.

And now the moment has come when my eyes, my mouth open wide, when my brow creases. In that moment, I understand that grown-ups wear masks and that friendly taps on the head are often a prelude to raps on the fingers with a ruler. The teacher has changed into a wicked fairy, straight out of one of those picture books that Manman hands out to brave children who have not shamed her, those—as rare as good thoughts—who were able to keep back tears and screams in the face of the monstrous vaccination injection. The lady advances toward me. The children's interest is aroused a little. She snatches a duster that she shakes, outraged. Chalk dust flies about my face. She rubs the blackboard to permanently erase the vile design. What have I done wrong? ...

In other places, at this hour, surely there are children who are dancing in the rain. Children who people call *"Ti moun"* and who go barefoot for the pleasure of feeling the soft earth under their feet.

At this hour, far from here, perhaps there are kites that are cleaving the sky and the clouds. Children who are drinking water straight from the coconut, who are chattering away around a paper cone of roasted peanuts.

Far from here in the little town of Capesterre-Guadeloupe, Pa

Bouboule must be watching over the movement of the world and disturbing the mad ants to fill up time that drags on.

In the little town of Capesterre-Guadeloupe, the day must have come to a standstill at the height of this afternoon. One or two straw hats are moving about all the same in the sun. A beautiful young miss is walking along, swinging her hips, shaded by a parasol. Her dress is red and green. In front of the church, stray dogs lick old wounds. Fishermen throw flying fish into proffered baskets. In the market, the market women are gathering up chives, batches of peppers, vegetables, and ground provisions. At the Amédée-Fengarol School there is perhaps a child like me, waiting . . .

Behind the windowpanes, the snow keeps on falling. If only the bell would ring . . . Dear God, please make the bell ring!

"In the first place, we are not among Arabs here," storms the teacher. "We do not write from right to left! Secondly! That hand, that left paw, is not the hand for writing! You must keep it flat on your exercise book! And so that you don't forget, hold out your hand! No! The other one! Take that! And that! . . ."

My skillful hand pulls back twice before being touched. It closes and escapes, burnt by the fire of the ruler. I won't tell you that my fist, clenched behind my back, gave back to the teacher all her blows and then hit out at the indifference that clothed all the children assembled there. I kept it closed tight until evening.

Manman listens to the whole story: *The left-handed black girl in the Arabs' country and the torment of the blows from the ruler.* She sighs and promises to go and clarify the matter the very next day. She makes me know that Arabs live in deserts and that to be black, and left-handed too, is not serious, it's not serious . . . To conjure these two conditions, there was only one remedy: to be first in class.

The next day, Manman speaks to the teacher, who smiles and acquiesces and then does not give me another thought until the end of the year. I become the invisible black girl. Too bad, I learn to write all the same, from left to right, doing the whole silly business of upstrokes and downstrokes. Too bad if she looks me over without seeing me, if the children keep me at a distance. I can read, and I read everything I come across. Papa buys all the sales agents' books: thirty-odd volumes of the Encyclopedia, ten bound collections, heaps of complete works and softcover novels. The books and all the characters who live in them speak to me, let me take part in their conversations. At the age of seven, I am reading pages from Madame de Lafayette's *The Princess of Cleves,* from Baudelaire's *The Flowers of Evil,* from *Dangerous Liaisons,* from Edgar Allan Poe's extraordinary *Tales,* from Daudet's *Letters from my Windmill . . .* and a lot of other titles that have left their indelible mark in my memory. These books are not lying about in the sight of everyone. They are sitting in the attic, some in boxes, others shut up in a special case, locked with a key. The key is on the door. My Sunday afternoons are exhausted in reading these books. Manman is knitting for the winter that is coming. I go up into the attic. I don't understand everything that I read. But I smile at the sentences, I feel as if I am treading a path of forbidden writings, frequented by strange characters. The smell of old paper fills the attic. Sometimes I read anxiously. My heart beats fast and jumps at the noises made by the floorboards, at the silence, which is oppressive and strangles me all at once. I steal the words. I peruse the books. How many eyes have plundered these pages before mine? I steal stories. I extract confidences. I rack my brain to penetrate the secret of complicated letters. I read, frantically.

I smile when the teacher lays her indifference on my shoulders. I don't need her gaze to live and to grow. I say to myself that the Marquise de Merteuil and the Princess of Cleves have et cetera of time to live. Even if the paper gets yellow and stained from age, these women will remain beautiful. They could care less about those who don't give their lives a single glance. Death is nothing to them. So, even if this teacher doesn't see me, I do believe that others will see me, will hear me, will love me. I leave my body on the hard bench and my spirit takes flight. I am a closed book, stuffed full with adventuresses, with witches, where gold, love, and beauty are conjugated in every tense. A book that would open worlds as phantasmagoric, comic, and cruel as life. I am a huge bird, I am flying toward a country where all kinds of people are living together: Left-handers, Arabs, blacks, Chinese, whites, Africans, Marchioness and Princess, Right-handers, Cowboys and Indians. People from town and country . . . I am a honeybee buzz-buzz! I fly around the head of the wicked lady. I promote myself to commander-in-chief; the dictation written on the blackboard is under my orders. At my command, the words fall apart. Each letter becomes a weapon, an instrument of torture. The *l*s are lassoes. The *i*s fire their dots like canon balls. The *t*s are sharp knives. The *u*s, latrines that have not been emptied for a century of time. A band of *a*s, holding each other by the hand, form a chain around the witch's neck, haul her in, and then cast her into the filthy waters of the *u*s.

I don't remember very much about Man Ya during these winter seasons. She suffers from the cold and remains prostrate, next to the huge stove, all day long. Her head buried in her neck, arms crossed over the vest, which presses down her large breasts, she says very little. Far away in thought, her eyes remain fixed elsewhere, without seeing us. We scarcely know her. We think of her as a creature from another era, so old, with abrupt manners. In Guadeloupe we had been left with Man and Pa Bouboule. As for Man Ya, we had seen her two, perhaps three times before coming over. Man Bouboule used to speak to us in French, Man Ya only spoke Creole. She does not know how to laugh and speaks to us so little.

She says: "My God! You have sent me over here, Thy will be done! I am your servant. You are my witness, I have never asked anyone for anything. I never wanted to leave Asdrubal. And my house and my animals, my garden, my vanilla. I only implored You every day that the Torturer would change from being an animal, that the spirits would grant him the favor of getting his night's sleep. I am not a woman who weeps, You know that very well. You have put seas and seas between him and me. I don't know why. These children look on me as a strange creature. The whole blessed day they speak with RRRR in their mouth. I don't understand their language. And there are only whites in France. And I don't understand why blacks go to lose themselves in that country."

She, who has never known how to waste her time in idleness, is obliged to remain sitting down, shut in, until evening. In the same place, like the old women here, condemned to muse over their lives, to reflect on their frustrated destinies. As punishment for what, Lord! For what sin! They would eventually reveal it to her. She knows nothing of this country. So, she does everything as she is told: Wear khaki socks (like the French army) and brown furry slippers. You mustn't catch cold. Stay beside the stove to rest from years of labor and poverty. Drink. Eat. They want to do everything for the good of her body. But they don't nourish her spirit, which never stops turning over thoughts and foundering in sorrow. And waiting. Waiting for this question of good weather half wears her out. Daisy has promised her: the sun here will soon give the same warmth as at Home. So Julia waits. She has already stopped believing it when buds appear on the branches of the trees.

Spring takes her out of her depression. She believes that her purgatory is over. She looks at the sky, sees that it is blue. The sun on her skin whispers warm words. She thinks that it will be there all the days to come. No doubt one has to go through this time of cold, live through it like a time of trial. She thanks the Good Lord for this favor. And, since from now on she is obliged to stand upright in this land, she takes us in hand and suddenly throws all her energies into a grand spring-cleaning. She would like to see us showing the same contentment at this forced labor. No one is spared. Put the mattresses out to sun. Pour buckets and buckets of water in the house. Brush, scour, shine everything you come in contact with. "The sun is shining, thank God! "*Sé ti moun la, travay!* Come on children, work!" She says. The sweat from working pleases her. Her passion overwhelms us.

Cleaning, scrubbing, washing, tidying are the four corners of her universe, the solution to every ill. Seated on a stool, in the middle of the yard, a wash pan between her legs, she washes and washes interminably. She likes to spread the washing out on the wooden doorway and bedeck the branches of the trees. And it is useless for Manman to repeat that here in France, that's not what is done, that the washing is hung on a line; Man Ya does not listen. She loves to see the shirts flying, to see dresses and trousers billowing with the wind. Her joy increases even more when she sees the garden. It is sighing and weeping under the suffocating heat of three heights of weeds. Two feet in military boots, body bent in two, as if she were at the bedside of an important patient, Man Ya weeds, sows, waters, and watches over the growth of the young plants. Handling the earth, turning it over, feeling it between her fingers, delights her. She makes that earth hers. The features on her face express serenity. She forgets her fingers swollen by the cold, the icy cotton wool falling in winter, the cold piercing her bones, the red brick in her bed. She reaches another dimension. The tree of life growing in the middle of her stomach to hold her heart like a nest in its branches smiles and puts out flowers. Carrots, lettuces, beets, tender peas, tomatoes grow prodigiously. Tilling the soil gives her life, sustains her.

She says: "You have created all these lands, my God, and the heavens and the seas. And all the creatures that live in the hope of the resurrection. Well, if it was Your will to bring me to these places, I give You thanks. You know Your reasons. Only, remember Asdrubal. Spare him, Lord. And consider also these children who laugh to see my two hands in the earth. I do not ask anything for myself, except the strength to understand this country. Only the strength not to give up before returning . . ."

Up in the early hours of the morning, she never stops going until the sun has set. Sweeping, preparing soup, scouring an earthenware pot, polishing, washing, ironing. As for us, we yawn and stretch out in the shade of the work that Man Ya persists in unearthing, in every place, at every hour. Time, however, teaches us to know her better. Her Creole speech seems less obscure to us. Her ways, a little rough, her comical expressions and her gestures become familiar to us. She constantly astonishes us by the way she has of balancing each new day on her shoulders, like a load that will have to be carried, whatever the cost, and borne until evening, without groaning.

She says: "Lord, you have given me two hands to glorify you. I am not afraid of work. I am not afraid of wearing out my body, no. You have brought me here. I have seen that there is sun in this country also. Well, I am pretending as if I were there, in Routhiers. Crying is not a solution. I am in good health, thank you, Lord. I ask You only to take Asdrubal under Your protection; do not allow Satan to put obstacles in his path. Here there is neither vanilla, nor coffee bushes, nor cocoa trees. But I am not despairing. The soil is here all the same, no different. And there are these children to bring up, for Daisy and Maréchal."

Little by little, we understand that Man Ya is not an ordinary person, weak and lukewarm and staid, like those we see here. She gives the best part of herself with each word, thought, action. And, she reveals herself in all her glory when it comes to great, heroic maneuvers . . .

It is still spring. Rémi and I now go back and forth to school by ourselves. That day, Manman has gone to Mans, in the car, with Élie and cousin Emma. Man Ya is sitting by the kitchen door. She is peeling vegetables for the evening soup.

In thought, Man Ya is already back at the door of her house in Routhiers. A sack of green coffee on her head, she is thinking of her sad master. Out of spite, perhaps he is gambling his entire pension in a bar at this very hour? Man Ya's spirit is used to going back and forth like this between Guadeloupe and France. For her, it's nothing big. Even if her body is condemned to remain here, that does not change anything. She only has to go down into the depths that she is cherishing in the midst of her soul. She sees Asdrubal again, on his return from France, in 1928, the same year as the bad hurricane. Handsome in his military uniform, tall, a mulatto with light eyes and wavy, pasted-down hair.

During his campaigns, the rascal sent letters in which the ardor of his love flattered Julia's heart. He proclaimed a life of delights, walks arm in arm. He promised a new house in which to nestle their embraces. Monsieur declared that he dreamed of her, his Julia, adored above all women, a black woman without scales or sharps, nor *do re mi* flats. He was asking forgiveness for the old days, when he used to beat her, out of youth and ignorance. Fine words, my Asdrubal! You were always able to twist and turn and make French shine on paper. And I stayed there, the biggest and grandest of fools, listening to all those untruths and that nonsense being read to me. And I dreamed of your return, Asdrubal. I waited for your coming. But when you came back your look was sharper than a saber, and you cut me into pieces. And your breath passed over me like the cruel wind, which had just devastated everything that the country bore. That is the husband who came back to me! The honey and the sweetness, the Torturer, his blows, his displays, his deeds, his curses . . . What am I going to cook with these vegetables? It will not be enough for Asdrubal. I am going to parch this coffee in a little while. Before that I have to feed the hens. Afterward, I have to pick the ripe soursop that I saw this morning . . .

The rain comes suddenly.

At that same moment, Man Ya puts down the thought of Asdrubal, folds the vegetables into her skirt and goes into the kitchen. The children will soon come out of school and meet the rain. They will catch cold while she is hiding her body. But what time is it then? Deep in her thoughts, she did not count the strokes of the bell from the Aubigné church. On the buffet, the hands on the clock are showing the hour. Julia knows numbers, change, paper money. But she can't tell time. The rain is pelting down furiously, and Daisy isn't there. If the children come back without a coat, they will be completely soaked, with a cold on their chest. And there is nothing to treat it here, neither papaya blossoms, nor honey, nor rosemary. She saw Daisy packing the coats in the trunks, which will go ahead of them to Paris, where the army has given them accommodation. She runs to gather them up, puts on her son's heavy military overcoat and on the way puts on the black kepi with its gold braid.

She charges across the square. The rain lashes her face. What time is it? The sky over here does not tell time. The streets are empty. Windows with small panes cut up the pale, wrinkled faces of old peasant women who have nothing else to do but watch the rain falling, chewing on their worn-down teeth. Man Ya greets them with a nod. She does not speak French, but she knows good manners. It does not matter if they don't return her greeting, if people look at her strangely. A car passes her, splashes her. The driver looks her up and down, like a damn idiot. Man Ya greets him all the same. She is well brought up. In any case her spirit is not troubled by whites. She has already noticed that this race is very odd. These people like to touch each other . . . They kiss each other on the cheek four times, then compliment each other, smile at each other, then sit down to chat endlessly. Two white ladies come to visit Daisy sometimes. Man Ya listens to their incessant chatter, which sometimes resounds in her head like chant from Holy Week. They talk and knit, knit one, purl one, and this and that, garter stitch and stockinette stitch, and so on and so forth, and really, exactly, what nice weather, isn't it . . .

The rain is flowing in little streams into the drain. There is no one near the school gate. Man Ya waits. How long will she have to wait? It doesn't matter. It's better that she rather than the children catch a chill. She will open the big overcoat and take them under her old mother-hen wings. How long has she been standing there, all alone under this kepi, which doesn't really cover her plaits? A tractor passes. Two boys on bicycles. A van like that of the neighbor who goes from farm to farm selling underpants, bras, panties, and trousers. His wife has a shop. Daisy buys wool and needles there. She is knitting for the winter. What a winter, again! thinks Man Ya. Umbrellas arrive. Bikes. Cars. And even the police van. The coat, which reaches her to her ankles, is beginning to feel heavy when the rain suddenly stops. Man Ya shakes the water from the kepi, then puts it back on, just so as to keep a somewhat martial air. The sun has come out again, just like in Routhiers, for true. In the rainy season, rain and sun used to fight each other in the sky. Man Ya would not gossip with either one or the other. The garden needs the anointing of both.

Man Ya's Five Ministries

Rain and sun
Like two hands
The right and the left in the sky
One washes the other
One holds the other fast in prayer
One holds the stomach
The other holds up the head
You need the sun, the rain
Like you need your two hands.

The whites were looking at her insistently. Their eyes spoke to each other. Some were mocking her. But others were wearing sheepish expressions, as if France had just been invaded by one of her eternal enemies, as if the honor of the Fatherland was being trampled on, right there, before their very eyes, as if war had already entered the village, and as if they in turn must take out their extra-special guns and brandish their forks in order to "let the impure blood water their furrows." But Man Ya did not stoop to their level.

When the school bell rings she finds herself between two gendarmes, in the middle of a gathering of people. She calls out and struggles. Her Creole speech derails the French of the representatives of the law. She, who suffered the blows of the Torturer without daring to utter a single word, forbids these fellows to take hold of her. She knows that nothing is weighing on her conscience . . . except having left Asdrubal. But perhaps he has written to the attorney general of the Republic, she says to herself, to de Gaulle, to the government . . . It is possible that they have been looking for her from forever ago, on French soil! Her photograph must be in police stations! No! She will not go to jail! Not like a criminal! At the end of her tether, she implores the Lord Jesus Christ and Our Lady of Perpetual Help. She calls on her manman, her grandmanman, and the holy apostles. And seeing us at last, she cries: "*Sé ti moun la! Mi yo ka pati épi mwen!* Children! They are taking me away." Given the rarity of black people in the area, one of the gendarmes supposes that Rémi and I have some blood ties with the accused. The entire school is there. The whole village is staring at us. Lots of eyes, alarmed. Why the police? Because of the army cap, the military overcoat? Why these solemn faces, these grand outraged airs? Man Ya did not intend to insult France, only to keep off the rain. She did not see what wrong there was in walking through the streets of Aubigné in a military overcoat. She only did it on account of the rain. It was raining, that was all there was to it. The rain. The cold in the children's bones. The cold on their chest . . . Alas, the law is not concerned with good intentions. Let it be said: there are coats and Coats!

"Children, is this person related to you? We asked her to identify herself. To give an explanation for being dressed in military garb. We do not understand her language. If you speak French, FRENCH!, tell us how she comes to be in possession of this overcoat and this kepi belonging to the French army?"

"They speak the way we do!" cries a voice. "They live in Madame Bourrasseau's lane! They are not bad children . . . Their manman is down there."

"Show us the way, children!"

We cross the square in front of the church, leading the procession. From time to time, we turn around. Man Ya is well treated. Her kepi on her head—no one was able to take it away from her—she seems to have surrendered her arms and is going along, shoulders hunched over. Resigned to her fate, she believes that jail is awaiting her, for a period that no one will be able to count. Back Home, she has never had any dealings with the law . . .

"Who desires respect, must earn it! A black woman must atone for the sins of her race. A black woman must show the whiteness of her soul and do good. A black woman, who is ugly with nappy hair, must merit, more than any other, her place in heaven. Do not disrespect yourself," her manman used to like to say.

Man Ya no longer has any desire to struggle.

Very well! Too bad if it is Asdrubal who has sent in search of me, she says to herself. Glory be to God! I will be going Back Home. And everything will be as it was before. My house, my coffee plants, my cocoa to hull, and also, in the ravine, the spring that gives water to drink, the river where I bathe my body when I leave the garden. What month are we in? Is it time to plant the yams, to reap the peas, to fertilize the vanilla? How long have I been languishing here, under the white sky of France? And, perhaps the Lord, in His great mercy, has given Asdrubal a heart, or even an ounce of charity. Perhaps he has mended his ways, repented . . .

Deep down, the gendarmes are not really proud of themselves. They are holding an old woman while a band of Gypsies, chicken thieves, and pillagers of farms are a law unto themselves over the countryside. They can just feel that this lady is no longer there, with them. Her eyes are looking inward to another world. Her spirit is brooding over thoughts of another time. But the law is the law! And contempt for the French army, something that cannot be tolerated . . . This is not carnival, after all!

Rémi and I quicken our pace. The gendarmes are at our heels, as if we were going to hide some piece of evidence, one, two medals for a general, one cross of Lorraine, a collection of rosettes, boxes of grenades. Man Ya walks along like a zombie, eyes staring straight ahead. She does not walk like someone who knows where she is going. She puts one foot in front of the other mechanically, while her spirit floats about, like debris from a shipwreck. She is going to disappear like one of the characters from Routhiers, whose epic stories she regales us with, isn't she? It is very possible she possesses that power too . . . She must be keeping it in reserve for the day when she is truly exposed to the forces of evil—perhaps these two gendarmes. In her stories of Guadeloupe, the initiates always wait for night time to venture their magic. They utter magic formulas and smear their bodies with a golden oil, take off their skins and then fly away, from roof to roof, *"yole vole de tôle en tôle."* Back Home, she says, there are people who change into dogs. They can speak, of course, because they are people just like us. So they chat to you. Take care not to throw a rock at them, or they will make you pay dearly the next day, when they have regained their human form. Also, in the wee hours of the morning, your path may cross that of a beautiful black woman. Make the sign of the cross, without her seeing you. The others in her sisterhood are not far. They are young hussies who are recognizable from their raucous laughter. They are really *diablesses,* and animal hoofs are pawing the ground under their three hundred petticoats.

Manman, who is a lady who speaks French French, declares that her husband is an officer in the army, a brave veteran. She gives a million explanations and promises the gentlemen that from henceforth she will oversee the proper use of the military uniform. Man Ya suddenly looks like a scarecrow made of dry sticks dressed in the garb of a conquered soldier. She does not move a hair. It is as if they are speaking about someone who does not concern her. Flesh that they can put in jail or in irons. A body that they can hang from any tree.

Imprison and then hang.

They used to do that long ago. Who worried about it? It was the law.

The law no longer allows it. In former times, everything happened inevitably because of the curse.

Yet, these were the same men.

They had crossed the sea as well, long expanses of sea.

It was the law, written in black and white. Who was disturbed about it?

When the gendarmes leave, Man Ya comes back to us—that is, her eyes see, movement comes back to her face, her body is inhabited once more. She takes off the overcoat and kepi, which had allegedly been desecrated, hangs them up with feigned respect, and goes back to peeling her vegetables. Going to bed that night, I look at her differently. She is praying, kneeling on both knees. I listen and watch her intently: her words, her sighs, her hand, which passes over her face. I tell myself that some day very soon, she will not be there when I wake up. To escape from life's woes, she will have asked the Lord for two great wings and flown away.

Religion

1963. We know now that Man Ya is our ally. She wipes away the traces of all the foolish things we do: broken dishes, burned cooking, wet beds. She never allows us to be deprived of dessert and wakes us up at night to slip us apples, which we eat sleepily, under our sheets and in the dark. She always promises to punish us but never raises her hand to anyone.

1963. Manman is in the hospital. Life in the Kremlin-Bicêtre apartment bumps along mechanically, but it is as if the mechanism needs oil. The food has no taste. Our ordinary discussions don't ring out with the same sound. Our laughter overflows, of course—children always find some pretext to laugh—but it subsides weakly. A brief silence casts a shadow on the horizon, breaks up in glimmers of light and then forms again when one or other exclaims: "And what if Manman never comes back?" Man Ya repeats that we have to learn to be patient. "*I ké viré épi on dot ti moun* . . . She's going to come back with another little one." A brother—or better yet—a sister, would soon join us. Nobody knew whether the baby would be a boy or a girl until Manman came home at last with the baby—Suzy—wrapped up in white. It proved to be urgent to untie the strings of this marvel. Our thirst to know changed into colics and stomach aches.

In the past, all these things were surrounded in great mystery. Where did children come from? To ask questions was insolence . . .

Paul, our last resort, is bitter. Monsieur is grumbling all to himself. By way of reprisal, he twists and turns around the cradle without casting a single glance at Suzy. He cannot accept that an old woman like Manman—she is at least thirty!—could still be having children. We little ones are already won over. I am seven, I suppose that Suzy owes her birth to some tangle of improper kisses in the darkness of sheets. Alas, when Paul decides to open our minds about the facts of life, he carries us off in high-sounding sentences, which run out of steam at the first sign of raised eyebrows.

To us, Paul is distant and close, authoritarian and gentle. If he threatens to punish us, twirling a strap over our heads, a slight smile belies his intentions. He is struggling with the metaphysical problems that affect him at that age. Deeply conscious of his role as big brother, he tries hard to guide our steps, to give us his example. In '64, when Papa goes to French Polynesia, he helps Manman and suddenly becomes the man of the house. He is growing up before our eyes. His chin is beginning to sprout hairs. His voice deepens permanently. Asserting little by little a measure of freedom, he goes out in the evenings, very late. Sometimes, Manman worries . . . "Be careful, eh! Be VERY careful!" Paul goes out with white girls. According to him, he uses no clever devices to attract them. They just fall into his lap like that. He only has to snap his fingers. It's all because of his natural looks and his deep spirituality, he says. The blackness of his skin makes them imagine exciting things. They imagine an animal power or something of the kind. Sometimes we pass him in the street. He is with imitations of Sheila, Sylvie Vartan, or Françoise Hardy. We look at him stealthily. He has asked us not to giggle like the damn idiots we are, not to show ourselves . . . "Those girls don't need to know that I have so many brothers and sisters, you understand!" Is he afraid to be lumped in the same calabash as those blacks who never finish counting their brethren? Some whites are like that. Seeing too much black at the same time frightens them . . . Immediately they imagine the whole of Africa landing in Paris, villages from the bush, vast families, tribes without beginning or end. Show them one relative too many! Their minds immediately unreel herds of polygamous brothers and sisters, wives in brightly colored cloths, car-

rying bawling babies on their backs, colonies of marabout uncles, dealers in charms, black magic merchants, aunts who have
been excised or infibulated, cousins who are drummers, little girl
cousins with tribal scars . . . All these people one on top of the
other, with rams, sheep, and goats in a poor little apartment
meant for the Typical French Family. Naturally, we don't hold
it against him. He is protecting his interests and pursuing reali-
ties the vital nature of which we can't yet imagine. Even so,
when he passes us without seeing us, it is as if, all of a sudden,
he were denying us.

At that time, we were like the branches of a single tree. Each
one often found himself alone facing the wind, but strong, nourished from one and the same sap and bound to the others by invisible fibers, by a solid bark. Whites scratched us with the claws
of their looks. Words corrosive as ammonia continually flew
about. Caresses of gall left us as if with wounds on our skin . . .
The same evils afflicted us all more or less violently. How could
we escape? Each one, according to the toughness of his body,
felt the sting. Each, according to his spirit, withstood the burden. We had a duty to sustain one another, to cheer up the
thoughts of the poor soul who was losing his illusions like leaves
before the season. Of course, there were one or two whites who
said they liked us well enough, who maintained that we were
not like other blacks. Girls and boys in our classes who, in the
street, seemed to walk beside us without being ashamed. One or
two for so many others who saw black skin as a stain. One
or two . . . I remember especially this strange annoying habit
they had of touching my braids, soft as wool, fleece. I remember too that they were surprised at the light color of the palms
of my hands. At that time you could count the number of blacks
in a school. The white children stared at us for a long time, as
if to get used to our color. Sometimes it took until Christmas before they realized that I was a person who could speak, read,
write, just as they did. Sometimes we tried to hang up our jer-
seys, just to play. But the moment a little childish squabble
broke out, they would take out the cannons and fire . . .

Négresse à plateau!

Religion

Bamboula!
Go back to your own country!

Man Ya is getting used to the city, to a life even more restricted than in Aubigné. She walks along in the shadow of high buildings, on sidewalks laid out along the sides of clearly defined roads, which belong to cars. Be careful! You must not walk in the middle of the road! Don't go too far, at the risk of getting permanently lost. Cross in the pedestrian crossing. Don't leave the apartment without your ID card. Don't talk to strangers; it will frighten them. Don't speak to anybody, because here no one understands Creole. Don't go out without your coat. Don't trust the sun that is laughing behind the windowpanes . . . It is also forbidden to walk on the grass, to pick flowers, to break branches. Man Ya knows her rights: she can sit on a bench, both hands on her lap, and take a bowl of fresh air. She loves to go for walks with the children who read the names of the streets. In the afternoons, she is authorized to push Suzy's baby carriage in the neighborhood park. She nods at everything they say to her.

The only thing that she openly criticizes is the door. That one single door to go in and out of the apartment. One solitary door that has to be kept locked all day long, even when the sun is shining bright. Do not rush to the door when the doorbell rings. Before opening the door, always put your eye to the glass eye that looks through to the other side. Inspect the landing from top to bottom, taking careful note of the number and gender of the persons who are waiting on the other side. For your safety, always look through that eye. And only turn the key afterward. You never know what is lurking behind the doors in this country. It seems there are stranglers of old ladies, child murderers, thieves in hats and Sunday best. One solitary door . . . And when you go out, don't slam the door, leaving the key on the inside; you may not be able to get back in. And the windows, too, always closed; we are on the first floor. Always closed because of the cold and the burglars who are lying in wait in their thousands. And the gas, always turn it off. Check three times. Forget just once and the entire building could burn, explode, and see all those whites who live on the upper floors burned to a cinder. And if this misfortune should occur . . . My God, they would say that blacks have murdered whites. Jail would be the final result of this sacrilege. All those whites, who live above our heads, do not have the slightest idea that their life only hangs on a thread of folly. There are even some who live for days and days without their feet ever touching ground. Man Ya whispers that these whites, who go about up there in unimaginable disorder, turn the night into bacchanal, more noisily than the *soucougnans* on the corrugated iron roofs in Routhiers. Observing their comings and goings: bland faces, eyes as blue as the angel Gabriel's heaven, those people, you would give them the Good Lord without confession . . .

Man Ya says: "Yes, yes, *an konprannn* . . . I understand!" We thought her docile. Yet, she shows, a little more each day, that she does not trust our erudite words. "Yes, yes, *an konprann,* I understand." But in reality our values are not hers. Apart from God, her only guide is the voice that speaks to her conscience and separates Good from Evil for her. And too bad for Mesdames Propriety and Appearance, those two town garfish who have hearts of stone. Man Ya accepts her lot because she has faith in divine justice. She knows that she will once again see Routhiers, where her garden is waiting for her. She embodies, without words, the idea that strength lies in the mind, not in the body. That you cannot tell the worth of people just by seeing the way they look and their color alone. That it is risky to give credit to facile arguments. There are those who shout and fight, who plunder, snatch, murder. They fear the world's rout, its outcome. Earth is their jail. They love it and hate it and want to live there for all eternity. And then there are those who use their persons as a shield, heal wounds, clear mines from the minefields of existence. Those are the ones who calm fears, dry tears, give hope. Julia thinks of Asdrubal and guarantees that she would have been able to endure for a long time more with him and with the spirits that pursue him by night. Life on earth is but a brief moment to pass. She misses her river so . . . But what do you want, she is here, in France, with all the rest of us, held up as intrepid saviors.

We children are blind, and deaf, and damn idiots at that time. We speak French, a beautiful language. We understand life, so-called. In spite of the knocks and the rough patches, we want to believe in our privilege of growing up in France, of having escaped the cane fields, Creole, the house with no television, no water, no electricity, without a toilet, a bidet, or a bathtub. We want to believe in our evolution, in the good fortune of living on a continent. And all the educated people who come to the house, officers with two stripes, scholars with their primary school diplomas, pledged to be French French, look at Man Ya without seeing her, with a hint of compassion. In their eyes she represents a former state, the long distant past, when one did not know the town, its turns of phrase, its polished high-heeled shoes, its fine clothes, all its bright lights, its cosmetics. She is a poor old lady from the country, illiterate, with calloused heels, roughened legs, a big stomach. They cannot admit that they too come from there, and gazing at each other, they measure how far the black man has come. Man Ya, in her self alone, represents all the thoughts of slavery that come to them from time to time and that they stifle and repress like the Creole in their mouths. They are infinitely indebted to France.

We ourselves, the children, see Man Ya as an anachronism. From another century, from another time, as if from another country. The dimensions of her very own time, which is not that of France, disconcert us. She imposes her measure on this time over here, which is estimated in paper money, in four seasons, in length of words. Her own time stretches out to infinity. She can walk in the paths of her youth in the morning and sit in the middle of her garden at noon. If her flesh remembers the Torturer's blows, her mind sets her free; she abandons her body and goes off to bathe her soul in little moments of joy, in her stream, in Routhiers. When her heart weeps for her house and her church, she leaves us, buries herself in visions of tomorrows that take her back home. And when she whispers to us the stories

Man Ya's Five Ministries

of slavery that her manman told her, shivers start to come over her soul. Just for us, black men emerge from former times where they walked with feet in chains. Desolate lives go back up ravines of forgetfulness . . . Lengths of seas crossed. The whip. The wretchedness of the cane fields. Poison. Tongues swallowed. The whip. The drum that beats like a heart in the night. Despair. Chains. Fear. Cunning. The whip . . .

Often she astounds us with an idea whispered by her logic. If the lost sheep could find its way in the pages of the Bible, Man Ya too can find her way in Paris. The streets of Paris cannot be more tortuous than the unfathomable ways of the Scriptures. Every morning through the kitchen window, she contemplates the Sacré-Coeur, the Basilica of the Sacred Heart. The first time that she sees it, emerging gradually from a halo of cloud, she believes that the Kingdom of Heaven has just appeared at the world's horizon. These clouds are not gray like those of the ordinary sky. They blind the sinner, force you to lower your eyes. A dazzling white, wads of light cotton, they muffle the noises of the world. That is the way that she has always imagined the house of the Lord, the heavenly Paradise where she will go to spend her eternal life. She would like to go there as soon as she can. So she cries out to us all: "You must see the wonderful sight! There, under the clouds! A Kingdom!" Daisy smiles. She is beautiful and has just had her hair cut in an urchin cut, like Petula Clark. While we try vainly to go into ecstasies, to experience the same wonder, Daisy explains that the phenomenon is only a big earthly church. "One day soon, I will take you there in the car. It's a promise . . ." she tells Man Ya.

The days pass.

Man Ya waits.

Another spring is already putting flowers and buds in plenty on the branches of the trees.

Man Ya is patient. Every morning she stations herself at the window to see the basilica emerging from its sheets of light.

In Guadeloupe, she could walk for kilometers. From Routhiers to the little town of Capesterre. To go to mass, she would set out before the first cockcrow. She would walk and

walk. Her legs never faltered. Here, you have to wait for a car,
as if walking was a sin. Maréchal has gone to the Pacific, leaving Daisy alone. Each day she puts off the visit to Sacré-Coeur.
Man Ya waits . . .

She says: "Six children for one mother, that's a great deal of
trouble! I myself have brought up only three. I carried angels who
did not survive. How many? . . . I've forgotten; those calculations
are a matter for another judgment. Maréchal's brood is not dis-
agreeable, but they love to squabble and to fight. These children
chase each other around the table like animals. This one forbids
anyone to enter her room. That one spends the day making fun
of the other, who has wet the bed and pays back the mockery
with punches. Miss Marie screams as soon as anyone goes near
her. Mr. Paul needs extra quiet to sing in English and to pluck
at a guitar with a friend. To keep that whole crowd in order, you
need to shout or to take down a belt. But Daisy does not use
leather on their backs. We are in France. Must imitate civilized
whites who correct kids with a little strap. These children laugh,
hide the strap or pull out thong after thong until what is left is
no more than a soldier's stump from Asdrubal's war . . ."

No, she is not going to bother Daisy. She must make up her
mind. She can walk there. Sacré-Coeur is within arm's reach,
nearer and nearer day after day as it were, just for her. This
morning the clouds form the face of a holy woman. The forehead, the eyes, the nose, and the mouth, which gradually fades
away in a virgin's smile. How long is this spring going to last?
What will there be afterward? Snow, bare trees, cold, and pains
all over her body . . . She is getting entangled in the quatrain of
seasons over here. No doubt Sacré-Coeur will never be so close
again. "Today!" a good spirit whispers to her. "You must go
there this very day!"

Man Ya follows her own mind. She neither seeks to please
people nor to imitate those from here who think they hold in
their hands all the light in the world. The belly of Paris does not
frighten her any more than the little town of Capesterre. She sets

Man Ya's Five Ministries

off, her mind free, as if she knows the way. Élie, my little brother, goes with her. He is seven. How long will they walk for? The basilica, which to the eye seems so near, recedes the nearer they get. Élie is mentally weighing up the audacity of the expedition: Man Ya cannot read. She does not speak French. Does not know the streets. Man Ya is old and black. She does things that whites do not understand. We are going to get lost in Paris, he thinks. Repeat the name of the housing estate in order to tell a policeman. Repeat the name so as to get back home. So as not to remain lost one's whole life long, walking through the streets like that, so far from home. The Surfs' tune comes back to him. He hears Claude François and begins to sing, to banish fear.

In Trinidad, lived a family,
In Trinidad, down there in the Caribbee,
There was the Papa, the Mama and the eldest son
Who at forty will still not marry.

While Élie is thinking that he may never again see Claude François's Caribbean, Man Ya is walking along, her eyes shining. She is not worrying about anything. A smile smoothes out the bitter folds of her face. She is walking toward the light of the Heavenly Kingdom, saying to herself, that soon, the two great doors of the Sacred Heart of Jesus will open for her alone. Does she still feel Élie's small hand in hers? . . . She goes along. Time can go by. The setting sun can give up the ghost if it wishes. She walks along. She knows that she will get there, with a deep conviction. What! The mysteries of Paris, criminals who kidnap children and snatch old ladies' purses! She has met worse crews in Guadeloupe. She knows the face of the man who can change into a dog. She has seen the soles of the hooves of three *diablesses* on the run. Malevolent spirits have come in tens to blow out a votive candle in her house, which was shut up tight against the wind. She is not afraid of these wicked men over here. They have narrow faces and soft teeth.

"Man Ya, let's go back!"

"*Pa pè nou ké rivé* . . . Don't be afraid, we'll soon be there."

"Man Ya, let's go back!"

"*An di-w nou ké rivé!* I told you, we'll soon be there!"

"Man Ya, Man Ya, let's go back to the house!"

"*Pa pè ti moun, légliz-la tou pwé!* Don't be afraid, child, the church is very near!"

And indeed, the dome is there, just two steps away, it seems. Alas, they keep on walking, one hundred, two hundred steps. Yet they can see the basilica, so near.

"Walk pilgrim, stray sheep, sinner! Go to meet your Lord! Don't falter! Think of the suffering of Jesus Christ, of his crown of thorns, of the Cross that he carried! Remember Golgotha! And you will see that your pain is slight!" her guiding angel is whispering to her.

"We are lost, Man Ya! Let's go back!"

"We are not lost! *Asé pléré!* Stop crying."

Élie is thinking about his manman who he will never hug again, of his brothers and sisters, of Zorro, of Steve McQueen, Thierry La Fronde, Belphégor, and Tarzan, who will be having a thousand adventures while he will be trying to find his way home, going round and round in Paris, or, worse yet, praying for the rest of his life in the Basilica of Sacré-Coeur. He hears Henri Salvador's laughter rolling out: "Ha! Ha! Ha! Ha! Ha!" And he understands that he is the hero of a nightmare. "Ha! Ha! Ha! Ha!"

And then? And then? And then?
Zorro appeared-d-d!
Without being in a hurry-y-y!
The great Zorro!
Handsome Zorro!
With his horse and his great lasso . . .

"Man Ya, Man Ya, let's go back!" he exclaims.

"*Asé pléré kon sa!* Stop crying like that!"

"But Man Ya, it is going to be dark soon!"

Man Ya has already understood that at this time of year, day sits up very late. Today, time is of no importance. She is walking towards the Kingdom. To Sacré-Coeur de Paris!

Repeat the name of the housing project. Say it over and over again until the words are imprinted on his tongue. Élie's head fills with letters, and then suddenly, is totally empty. He is afraid to forget where he comes from. His name, yes, he can tell his name. My father is in the army. He has fought in the war. Infantry. Repeat the name of the housing project. He should have marked the way, so he could go back. Unwind a reel of thread between the house and the church. Next time, he will know. No! There will not be a next time. Always remember the way you came. Don't walk with your head in the air. On the contrary, look around you.

"Man Ya, let's go back!"

But what can stop Man Ya? Tell me . . .

Tiredness? . . . Up at four o'clock, in bed at ten. Her body is used to enduring.

Lack of faith? . . . Her faith in God, in the Virgin Mary and her son Jesus Christ is engraved deeply in her, right there in the middle of her heart.

The blinding vision of the folly of her expedition? . . . Her spirit is drifting in joy, filled with hymns and with a passage from the Latin mass.

Deo Patri sit Gloria
et Filio, qui a mortuis
surrexit, ac Paraclito,
in saeculorum saecula. Amen.

Glory be to God the Father,
and to the Son, who rose
from the dead, and to the Holy Spirit,
for ever and ever. Amen.

Man Ya walks. Her gaze looks right through the faces that stare at her strangely. An old black woman and a child. A black woman who chants in Latin and smiles as she walks along. Mad, for sure. How long have they been walking like that?

"Man Ya, let us go back!"

Man Ya does not answer. She has just lost sight of the Sacré-Coeur. Her hand tightens around Élie's. Left or right? Go up this road or that one? Her mind tells her that the church bench where she will be able to sit down is not very far away now. The air is less oppressive. She can sense those things. Devils do not frequent people from this place. Too many crosses. Too many prayers recited. The Holy Spirit dwells in these places, she knows it. Abruptly, she crosses the street and calls out to a group of nuns who are walking in twos, veils flying in the wind.

"*Siouplaît, Masé! Masé! Kí koté an dwèt pwan pou kontré Sakré-kè-la?* Please, Sister! Sister! Which way must I go to get to Sacré-Coeur?"

Seeing right in front of them all of a sudden this black woman, speaking an African language and making large gestures, which threaten their immaculate veils, the good sisters quicken their pace.

But the Most High is a shepherd and man a lost sheep. At the end of a little street vibrant with vendors of religious objects, Sacré-Coeur reappears at last, in all its majesty. Even Élie is dazzled by the marvelous sight. Man Ya makes the sign of the cross three times then climbs the first steps. Already, on the church square, where all types of flowers grow, a foretaste of Paradise is waiting for her. There, birds eat from men's hands and then fly away, and their wings go "Flap, flap, flap" as if to applaud this enchantment. A bell rings. People of all colors and all generations come in together to bow their heads and to pray to God.

Man Ya weeps over Asdrubal. She says: "Lord, I am in torment. Asdrubal is neither dead nor at war and is consuming his solitude all by himself, over there in Routhiers. Without anyone to take care of his health or his clothes. He took the trouble to marry me, me, Julia, an ugly black woman. *Bon Dyé! Ka an péfè pou réparé tò an jà fè-y?* . . . My God, tell me, how can I make reparation for the wrong that I have already done him? . . ."

During these long conversations with God, Élie does not interfere. He is admiring the great statues in gold and plaster, the immense stained glass windows, the candles that burn to give hope, the paintings of Christ in his Passion. For a moment he forgets his pagan idols on French television, Josephine Baker's spangles, the magic of "Star Trek," of Albert Raisner's

"Têtes de Bois" and the *yéyé* singers of Mireille's Little Conservatory.

When Man Ya has prayed to her heart's content, she is neither hungry nor thirsty. Having placed her life's troubles in the hands of the Lord, her sins having been confessed and forgiven, nothing bad can happen to her now. She is going to let life go by for a while, waiting for her time to come. The Virgin Mary has even assured her that she would see Asdrubal again, before long . . . before great debauchery takes hold of France. Kneeling, she makes a last sign of the cross and sets out for home with Élie. They are greeted by a flight of pigeons.

"Man Ya, we are lost, aren't we?" Élie asks once more.

"*An pa ka pèd kon sa, ti gason!* I can't get lost like that, little boy."

These children have no respect, she says to herself. Is she so careless as to walk in a country she does not know, without taking note of her way!

In the housing project, we are anxious. We have already been around the grounds and the buildings three times. Nobody has anything to tell us. Nobody has ever seen this old black lady who pushes a baby carriage or goes for walks with black children. A black boy? How old? Seven. Don't know him . . . Call the cops! someone shouts.

"We have to wait a bit longer before calling the police," says Paul, foreseeing a terrible sleepless night. While the soup is getting cold in the plates, the basilica fades in the setting sun. Daisy is thinking of tragedies. In consternation, we construct the worst hypotheses, drawing straws for who will have to send a telegram to Tahiti to tell Maréchal about the disappearance of his manman and his third son, Élie.

When they came back, in one piece, without having asked anyone the way, Manman wanted to lecture them. But a strange light was shining in Julia's eyes. A light that said: "I believed, I overcame! I am ready for other trials . . ."

Schooling

JULIA. J.U.L.I.A. Just one little word, misery. Two syllables. Five letters, full stop, new paragraph. Three vowels and two consonants, alleluia! And nothing else! Nothing more . . .

Easy to say, but to write . . . The road to perdition, without even the little light from a firefly to light the trembling hand that is struggling and getting lost on the schoolboy's slate. Up. Turn. Down, again! Up again. Down again. And stop, there, at last! Breathe.

What goes on in the mind of an old woman who finds herself in her grandchildren's school? First of all, how to hold a pencil? Man Ya has held a pencil on very few occasions . . . For birth certificates, for notarized documents. The last time was back home, for her I.D. card. She marked an X on the spot that was shown to her. An X. No one told her the meaning of that X, a little wobbly, placed beneath silent writing. She could see very well that in their eyes, they considered her an ignorant woman. So she didn't ask anything. She just made the X. Perhaps that meant that she agreed with the words set out there. She complied, humbly, but remaining dignified in her gestures and her look.

She wondered how much time she had signed for.
For what function?
For what purpose?

During the writing sessions Julia remembers her childhood . . . Her manman said that she could not send her to school. Have to stay home to watch over the younger ones. She just had a baby and is going back to the fields. There is no other solution. Edu-

Man Ya's Five Ministries

cation is not for me, Julia thinks. If Manman says so, there is no
other way. Must stay and clean the house. Cook the cassava and
the yams. And not cry over school, recitations, songs that tell
about spring, stories about France and geography. Her manman
is struggling in the cane fields, which are devouring her. Must
struggle with each day, that's the daily lesson. Don't run away
when day comes. Load and pull up the days one after the other,
stronger than cart oxen. Pull them along until evening. Don't let
your heart cry when this one or that one goes off to school.
School is not for everybody.

Your name did not come up, Julia. If it were necessary for life,
like your two arms, the Good Lord would not have abandoned
you by the wayside. You look at writing from a distance. You
can't tackle it. Ink stains. The things that they call letters come
from France, according to what they say. Your manman has not
needed writing to live honestly and even to find one of those
good black men who don't wreck themselves with drink. How
did it happen that Mr. Asdrubal chose you, you! He didn't find
you at a dance, you don't know how to dance. We don't send
you to dances. Would you have liked that? Dancing. Carnival
neither, you did not have the opportunity to play mask on
Mardi Gras nor Ash Wednesday. The drums have never called
you. They were beating there, deep in your heart. You did not
feel good, without knowing why. They were beating for pain
and sorrow and your heart took up the melody. Feelings so
mixed that you can't tell where they come from. Work like a
beast. And haul each day until evening. Forget the beating. Forget all the faces that the drums are awakening. Take joy in the
garden. Plant, sweat, reap.

When Asdrubal was in his youth, sowing his wild oats, because of his pale eyes and his wavy slicked-down hair, all the
young hussies would go to bed with him. When he came on his
overseer's horse, with his white colonial helmet, his whip in his
hand . . . from a distance, you would have thought him a local
white. He was not liked on the plantations. Perhaps because of
his light skin, he thought he had rights over the black or Indian

workers, and over the women, too. He was threatened how many times? During his inspections, there was more than one look that expressed the desire to kill him. He wanted me; he had me. It is said that he looked for the ugliest of the darkest black women in order to offend his papa and to bring shame on him. He never loved me, or so abominably, if he did, in a very ugly way. I was like an affront, an outrage . . . his slave. Afterward, he went off to war, to fight in the trenches. It is from there that he brought back his ghosts, all those young faces astonished in death. I know he was sowing his seed all over Guadeloupe. My neighbors' bellies carried his fruit. As for me, he would kick and kick me. I never fled under these blows. I would say to myself: "It is the Good Lord who has placed me in the hands of this Torturer. One day, He will tell me why."

What readily goes into the hard head of a child goes into reverse faced with white hair. Julia wants to learn. She does her work willingly. She wants to believe—as we tell her—that learning is a lifeboat, a way to get out of ignorance. Alas, reading and writing find no place to attach themselves to in her. So, she tells us that her head is like a dry savannah. The earth has become rock. It is useless to scatter seeds. It is a waste to water. There is no more hope of green. She says, too, that the bones in her fingers are too stiff to hold the chalk, to move it here and there, up and down, at will. Begin again. Again. Again. *"I ja twota sé ti moun la! An ja two vyé!"* she says by way of excuse, "It is already too late children, I am already too old. The letters don't want to let themselves be known."

Nevertheless, she applies herself, begins all over again when we tell her to. Her letters are so deformed, so big, unable to keep straight on the lines on the paper. They wobble, knock into each other, grimacing. J.U.L.I.A. J.U.L.I.A. We vainly set out for her ten small letters, even, neat, delicate upstrokes and downstrokes, with capitals chiseled like the handwriting of a schoolmistress devoted to the cause of hopeless cases. Man Ya only produces awkward, misshapen, clumsy letters, which exacerbate our anger. Sometimes the chalk breaks, and with it the hope of writing, all at once, without hesitating, the five letters that name her to the world.

The apprenticeship goes on and on. Difficult times, when despair, renunciation, and enthusiasm are woven together. Times when I storm, showing more impatience than an embittered old schoolmistress. Times of dry anger, which see us treating her like a rebellious and wayward child, whereas she is merely powerless, completely defenseless before the pretentious little letters lined up in front of her. Sometimes there are sudden flashes of light, fleeting and blinding, and on these, dreaming, we happily construct pages and pages of miraculous dictations, and—why not—the total eradication of illiteracy. Alas, they are always followed by periods of disenchantment. At these times, the words on the paper rise up like malevolent shadows that one swears to strike down at all costs.

She says: "When the '28 hurricane passed over Guadeloupe, he was far away, Asdrubal was, in France, I don't know. He asked for forgiveness for all the blows. He sent cards, shaped like hearts, sprinkled with sand speckled with gold, letters with the scent of roses, on which he had stamped bouquets of flowers and figures of white people kissing each other. Such letters! Love letters, if you please! A child from the neighborhood would read me the beautiful sentences . . . "Love of my life. My heart is beating for you alone, my beloved. My kisses fly towards your sweet lips. Love is a fire, which will never go out between us . . ." Asdrubal, I thought that the colonies had sorted out your feelings. Foolishly, I believed that you had learned to live because of the French uniform. I waited for you, Monsieur Asdrubal. I even tried to learn the alphabet, so as to read for myself your words of love, and to savor in solitude the scent of the paper. Alas, when you came back, you were the same Torturer that the Lord had given me for my life on earth. I did not run away under the blows. But I no longer sought to understand the writing. I no longer caressed the letters from France. I no longer dreamed of hearts or of love. I waited for your mouth to tell me why you beat me like that, why you did not think me any better than if I were a slave that you had bought, why you liked to defile me and to whip me before turning me over without a word. No, I never again caressed your beautiful letters, Asdrubal. I did not throw them in the fire; I buried them at the foot of a nutmeg tree. Just to see if they could produce beautiful living things, fruits, or else monstrous flowers, never before seen in this world.

Words of love never came from the mouth of the loathsome fellow, only from his spirit, from his fingers. All the lying words on the paper had only softened Man Ya's soul the better to tear it apart. Because of that she kept an instinctive mistrust of all that was written. A corner of her memory refused to harbor this farce of signs. Monsieur Asdrubal was an educated man, but that did not prevent him from being a savage. He had brought back from his campaigns Congratulations from this one and that one, Rank, Honors, Merit, Gratitude from France to her son from Guadeloupe. All these Distinctions framed and placed under glass were like rectangular glassy eyes. Hung on the surfaces of the house, cocooning extravagant upstrokes and pompous downstrokes, they looked at Julia with great contempt, spied on her on behalf of Asdrubal. And every day she had to pass in front of this writing that recalled the grandeur of the feats of arms overseas, made the cannon roar in the house and mourn the souls of the soldiers. While Asdrubal went about his business, Man Ya peered at the engravings, sometimes with her finger she traced the letters, which, placed end to end, certified that the soldier Asdrubal was a model of bravery. Fine capitals, beautifully molded letters, drawn in violet ink. Lies! And all this prestige, this war pension, came from France, which had commanded him to kill men for her three-colored flag, for four or five territories conquered somewhere in the world, for the Fatherland and the Nation and for time-honored glory.

She sighs: "Yes, the angels are my witnesses. I told that to the Sacred Heart of Jesus. I have never prayed to leave Asdrubal.

He is my husband before God. It's the truth: I have taken blows. But I don't believe Asdrubal was seeking my death, only relief for his soul. Those children were following good inclinations, taking me from beneath his boots. They can't understand . . . He is more lost than I am, Asdrubal is."

After years, Man Ya succeeded in being able to write a little and to sign her name. Such a fragile victory, barely snatched. Bitter pride. She has time to see six winters Over There before returning Home. By dint of eating French apples and strawberries, *béchamel* sauce, potatoes, warm croissants, and *clafoutis* . . . By dint of seeing the snow as a miracle and the seasons as a favor from heaven, Creoles come back to life new people, quite different on the old soil of France. But Man Ya rejects these stories of four seasons. The first winter, she puts up with it, thinking it was just a matter of a necessary tribulation for all new arrivals. But, when she understands that it comes back again every year, she lives in the hope of summer alone, confusing the order of the coming of autumn and spring.

Back Home, she has known hard rainy seasons with end-of-the-world-hurricanes, come just to crush and to derail human beings who were already trying so hard to come to terms with poverty. The rain, the flooding! Behind her house the river would suddenly swell and carry along rocks, tall and big as oxen. Julia would watch entire tree trunks going by, upside down. It could just as well have been bodies, half-dead; she could not have done anything and would have stayed there watching them pass. The zinc roof crackled under the gusts of wind, and the boards creaked. Her old house never gave way. A hurricane takes delight in dismantling the houses that hardships and determination have put up the previous day, knocking down beams and planks, sending flying the new corrugated iron that swaggers and bets the first person to come along that no, never will rust tarnish its silvery waves. After Carnival comes Lent, the dry season that finishes with the avocadoes in July. Lent means drought, a time for not eating meat and for sending up to heaven prayers to ask for two little days of rain on the scorched savannahs. The plantations are dying. Lent gives mass a different feel. Fanning, sweat, silk dresses that stick to the thighs, dry mouths. Rain or sun, Lent or rainy season, day or night, Julia loves time that goes along like that, easily, arranged into two seasons. For her, time in France unfolds according to a music that is too highbrow and that she does not want to keep in her head. She does not like this time torn apart, precisely just so. Is it spring or autumn, this season where the trees are in waiting and weep so much over their foliage? . . . The children have told her so many times. She has forgotten, as she has forgotten the little letters of the alphabet that call her an idiot. In France, she prefers to stay in her Guadeloupe time, which swings between rain and sun, between going and coming. She says she is too old to change horses.

Man Ya does not understand French very well, nor does she practice. But, when there is nothing more to be done in the apartment, except to stretch out on a couch, she sits in front of the television. We adore *Thierry La Fronde, The Little Conservatory of Song, Belphégor—the phantom of the Louvre, A Tender Age* and *Hard Headed* by Albert Raisner, and loads of other black and white programs that, at the time, we thought very interesting. Man Ya does not laugh, does not go into raptures, hardly reacts. She watches white people gesticulate. Sometimes, she is overcome by sleep in her chair, hands clasped between her thighs, petrified by the flow of the words. She shows interest only when there are one or two black faces on the screen. She asks the name of the person, the reason for this favor. The Reverend Martin Luther King, His Lordship Henri Salvador, Josephine Baker, and, of course . . . Sylvette Cabrisseau.

Sylvette allowed us to measure the two seasons of glory: Rise and Fall. Applause followed by booing. First of all, we felt stupefaction. Admiration followed. Then pride. Then fascination. A black woman, a Martinican, the first ever, announcer on French television. Beautiful Sylvette, chosen from among hundreds of thousands of white women . . . We could not manage to admit it, even by forcing ourselves to the extreme. Getting used to the idea that you were going to speak how many times a day on the small screen, announcing white people's programs, seemed to us out of this world. The first time, we watched and waited for you with the same fervor as Christians hoping for an apparition of the Virgin Mary. You were the most gracious. Your smiles were for each one of us, and your presentations, going right to our hearts with a painful joy, had us in raptures. Sylvette, know that our devotion to you never faltered. A black woman on TV! At the time, this race was very rare on the ORTF, French National Television. Moreover, it seems, you resembled a young black woman, a distant cousin, who used to come to Routhiers to visit her old godmother, Erzelie. "The same gestures, the same way of raising her eyes and batting her eyelashes," said Man Ya, who made you our relative.

Alas, the state of grace did not last. You had gone into the lion's den. An old demon began to shake certain people who were witnessing this nightmare: "A black woman, an announcer!" First, there were letters from anonymous viewers: "I am not a racist, but this Sylvette Cabrisseau does not speak correct French, and that is dangerous for the purity of the French language and harmful to young children who are learning to speak . . ." Or: "I have nothing against blacks who stay in their own country, but the black woman who is presenting programs frightens my granddaughter. To each his own country!" And again . . . "The ORTF is dishonoring France by putting on *bamboulas*! There are enough beautiful French women in our provinces to spare us this ugly face . . ."

Sylvette, all that you suffered, we endured with you: insults, threats, slander . . . Like you, we were torn apart, trampled upon, shattered. You disappeared from the small screen, pushed out, whisked away with our illusions like a chaplet around your neck. And we lost you forever . . . You were our glory, a beacon in the night of France . . . *Your tongue, the tongue of those unfortunates who had no tongue; your voice, the liberty of those who foundered in the dungeons of despair.* We were bitter, furious with our powerlessness. At the thought of the storm of protest that had been unleashed just because of your color, tears came to our eyes. Nails clawed at our stomachs, and without being hungry, our guts were in turmoil. Mad ants crawled through all our dreams and devoured our insides, even the bones. We were still standing, but it was a sham, pure show. In one fell swoop, we had become old trees, half dead, eaten by termites. At that time, the shadow of the tiniest bird, resting on one of our branches, could shake us. When Man Ya worried about not seeing Sylvette on television any more, Paul told her that she had gone away to Martinique, but that she had had time to get bags of money, enough to go into business in a big way.

Bamboula!
Négresse à plateau!
Nigger!
Dirty Nigger woman!
Coal Black!
Snow-White!

I am twelve. TV ceases to fascinate us. RACISM becomes the only word, which subtitles our favorite shows. *Zorro, Sergeant Garcia, Thierry La Fronde,* and *The Last Five Minutes* suddenly seem suspect to us. It now becomes obvious that their world ignores us. And we watch for the appearance of One of our complexion—just one!—who would erase The Word on the screen of segregation. Sometimes a slave suddenly appears in an American film. A black porter following an explorer becomes significant, getting himself devoured by a lion. An enormous black maidservant with a white apron says "Yes, ma'am . . . "; a manservant polishes shoes, singing about his love of life. A Satchmo blows us the hope of imminent racial equality. We admire those—resourceful geniuses!—who have won small parts or who—exceptional virtuosos!—enchant the ears of whites. Josephine Baker and her adopted children, of all different races, become unreal; we refuse to believe in this fairy-tale chateau, of shared, manufactured happiness. And when she appears, old, powdered, eyes dull behind her heavy false eyelashes, with feathers and sequins, singing: "*J'ai deux amours, mon pays et Paris . . . ;* I have two loves, my homeland and Paris . . . "; we waver between admiration and mistrust. Unconsoled about our beautiful Sylvette, we assume that one day Josephine too will experience disgrace. We are satisfied with so little: Henri Salvador singing "Our ancestors the Gauls," the Surfs from Trinidad all the way over there in the Caribbean, Claude François's black Claudettes, Tom Jones, Nancy Holloway . . . we loved them all, just because of their color.

While we are constantly criticizing French television, Man Ya acquires a taste for the images, becomes interested in the newscasts, which take her to every continent and span oceans with supernatural ease, to show parts of the world, pieces of living history. Africa, Biafra at war and her starving children. Pope Paul VI. A Kennedy assassinated in America, Pandit Nehru mortally wounded in India. The war in Pakistan. Floods in Italy. De Gaulle in Moscow . . . TV produces random images that proclaim that the world is really very small, quickly traveled, but most of all torn apart, fragile, strewn with hate. The lengths of the seas are no longer anybody's business but hers, Julia's. The earth is like a great body with peaks and valleys, exposed areas, facets little explored, peopled with living beings, who—it is believed—will never get in the way of the great march of technological worlds. The earth harbors flesh that is sick and flesh in apparent health, so many wounded parts, gaping and purulent, ravaged through and through. The world's navel is everywhere and nowhere. And all the catastrophes that the TV brings threaten to alight anywhere on earth like flies that are a sign of gangrene. Guadeloupe would not be spared. The Last Days seem nearer at hand every day.

Man Ya is an Edith Piaf fan. She runs to station herself in front of the TV as soon as she hears three chords. Even if she does not understand the words she knows that this woman sings about love and denounces suffering. Her tormented hands, her eyelids heavy with old sorrows, cast a spell over Man Ya. Moreover, Edith has so few weapons: her cross on her black dress, her voice that wells up from her stomach to cry: "My God, my God, my God, leave him with me for a little longer . . ." Then Julia thinks even harder about Asdrubal whom she has abandoned, all alone, with his pain, in Routhiers-Capesterre.

Schooling

No one has ever been able to untangle the threads of the feelings that tied Man Ya to her Asdrubal. In France, every day she prayed: that she would go back to him, under his yoke, that he would keep healthy, that he would have enough to eat . . . Asdrubal himself, according to the rumors, was suffering in his new solitude. Why did she want so badly to go back to him? No one ever found out . . . Only *Gone with the Wind* gave me some idea of the explanation. I concluded hastily that adults were people who understood nothing about feelings, compared to children, who knew how to love and hate and to categorize these two extremes in two opposing abodes. Big people could love a creature who did not love them. They managed to love and hate the same person at the same time. They were also capable of loving, then hating, then loving once again and so on, until death . . . So Man Ya was a Vivien Leigh, and Grandfather Asdrubal an arrogant Rhett Butler on his horse.

She said: "Monsieur Asdrubal was a boastful type. He never spoke to me like a person. Always like his slave. Everything he told me to do, I did. I have never said no. When he spoke to other people, it sounded just so, beautiful French. Whenever he was tired of seeing me he would shout: 'Get out!' Asdrubal was good at reading and writing, but he would also put his hands in the earth. Ink stained his fingers, as well as banana sap. Even if I called him Torturer behind his back, I have always respected him. He gave me his name and three sons. Perhaps he was sorry he married me. Perhaps when he looked at me with my nappy hair, my broad nose, he felt he would have killed me, I was so different from what he liked. A dark-skinned black woman, with big feet. Perhaps that is the reason he beat me so much."

Every Thursday, we sit down around the table in the dining room to write to Papa, who is in Tahiti in the Pacific Ocean, where the army has posted him. Our letters take a good twenty hours before getting to Papeete. Armed with five dictionaries and ten encyclopedias (letters that are badly written come back to us corrected in red ink), we always tell the same tales, promise to be good and to get the most wonderful marks in order to honor him and to be able to aspire to a good job later on. Without being able to read or write, Man Ya supervises us . . .

"*Pa fé pon fot sé ti moun la! Papa zot pé ké kontan!* Don't make any mistakes, children. Your Papa won't be pleased! You have to work, work! Go to school so you won't become an idiot, with no education, like me, who doesn't even know A."

If these words happen to come at a time when our frenzy to teach her how to write has waned, we promise ourselves to begin to teach her again, to draw over and over on the slate the five letters of her name.

Julia, miraculously you write your name the day we tell you Edith Piaf has died.

Some time goes by.

And then Edith is back singing on the television, as if nothing has happened. Alive, in her black dress, all frail and vibrant with suffering. With her same cross of Jesus Christ, her tormented hands, her song: "My God, my God! . . ." It is Christmas. Man Ya did not understand the marvel of television, which has the power to resurrect indefinitely. She is convinced that we invented her idol's death. She almost insults us. For a long time she believes that we made fun of her because she can't read or write. Not even A.

———

Training

Obedience

Listen to glances
Weigh silences
Understand without words
Quickly make a cross on your mouth
Measure your breathing

Politeness

Greet people in the street, even if they are strangers
Respect grown-ups
Say thank you
Don't be greedy

Truth

Always tell the truth
Or be silent

Work

Don't be idle
There is always something to start doing, to finish, to correct
Work
Learn your lessons
Clean the house
And sit down, deserving, having earned your bread

Man Ya's Five Ministries

Entertainment

Wash
Sew
Iron
Scour
Sweep
Work
Work
Work
Take a breath
Rest

Man Ya does not want to leave me in peace even for a minute. While I would like to spend endless time joking, making up stories twiddling my thumbs, wasting time chasing Élie or Rémi to give them "last lick," frittering away my time lying down wearing out my eyes reading a book, Man Ya bores me to death with her dreadful taste for work. She would like me to work myself to death as she does, from morning till night, on ungrateful household tasks, whereas I have my whole future to prepare for, mountains of lessons, thousands of homework assignments, and most of all Mickey's magazine or a copy of *Hi Pals* hidden under my notebooks. She calls me three times. I am getting weary of it. Four times. Five times. So, I finally shout the unanswerable reply, always ready, which puts an end to her commands: "I AM-LEARNING-MY-LESSONS!!!"

Man Ya is not an exemplar of learning: sometimes she sees it clearly on our faces, at those tense moments when we are trying to make her write her name. In the world in which we live, Reading, Writing, Arithmetic, represent the holy trinity in the Pantheon of Knowledge. We experience glory when we walk in these labyrinths. We discover that we are learned, erudite, philosophers, great scholars. And we are grateful to heaven for having put us on this earth long after Schoelcher had delivered the blacks from slavery. 1848.

Training

1848. Date of the abolition of slavery. Man Ya's grandmother had been alive at a time when she knew slavery. But that word was not to be spoken out loud or too often. Who knows if it would not come back again . . .

Slavery! It is a word banished by grown-ups. Just the mere fact of pronouncing it hurls them into a tub where the bones of the past lie bleaching. Slavery: the savagery of flesh sold, ships with holds packed with blacks chained to each other, dogs tearing at calves, the fire of the branding iron, stakes, birch rods, the whip. To ask questions is to put them on the spot. To question is to lose your footing in the deep waters of the History of the world, now raging wild, now deceptively sleepy. They ask us only to live in the present day, to let the dregs of the past lie, and not to cut open the dingy bags where they have shut up the shame and humiliation of being descendants of black African slaves.

Man Ya alone dares to tell us about it. She excels in this area. When she says the Word, shores where there is no sun open before our eyes. Shivers. Slavery! . . . Once already, she says, they gave freedom to blacks and took it back. Man Ya had heard old people tell the story. They had taken off their chains, thrown away the keys, and then cried out to them: "Go!" which meant landless poverty, drifting into the hills. They had begun to guillotine the white masters one after the other. For nearly a decade the blacks had believed in it and taken this breath of freedom as cash to spend. Ladies and gentlemen, they had gone off, had run off, men, women, and children, before getting caught up in this fine freedom. They were being told that they had French law on their side. Signed and sealed. Damned fine freedom! So, they had drunk and danced during that first abolition, calling out everywhere: "We are free people! We are free people!"

Some time passed, a time of jubilation and madness. When they heard the cry: "The canes are awaiting your labor, good people. From now on you will be free workers!" they filled the roadways and fled in disarray. There were some among them who paused, who began to expound glowing theories, hoping through the mystery of French law to get back onto the path from before the great voyage. Wordlessly, staring intensely at the horizon, others began to map out the country Guadeloupe. You saw them walking the length of the beaches and along the edge of the cliffs, intensely scanning the remote little islets and eyeing the far-flung unknown lands on the other side of the waters. A band of blacks explored the forests all the way up into the clouds; they never found any trace. Canoes, christened *Hope* and filled with people, were launched out on the immense sea, which swallowed them up with a single flick of the oars. Africa was already too far away. Lost behind the veils of time. Buried in the recesses of memory. "No use going back" said the most blasé. Where would you go? In what village, in which family would you set down your body? Your relatives' name? The language that they speak over there? Say one or two words that you have kept for the day of homecoming! Alas, all those seas crossed had drowned the traces, the marks, and the scents. There were some who never got over it, and who would set off, in a dream, their nose to the wind, their wings unfurled. They would journey at night and return in the cool trade winds, in the morning, their heads covered with the blossoms of the baobab. They were perfectly recognizable because they were loaded down with charms and smelled of wild beasts. From their travels, they brought back stories in which they were the heroes. They had supposedly braved and conquered lions, tigers, and colonies of grasshoppers. They had held discussions with African chiefs, signed pacts and accords that promised to send to the Sugar Islands gods stronger than Jesus Christ and the Holy Spirit in one.

And then, there were those who, joining hands, wanted to build themselves a country on this same Guadeloupe. Alas, by the time they counted hands, slavery was already being reestablished. The law came from France; it was written, signed, sealed. It was said that the Martinican Josephine herself, from her couch, had dictated it to Bonaparte. So, it was no use printing paper words to denounce the law, you would have had to take up arms in the name of freedom and die under the bullets. Dogs at their heels, the hunted blacks once again took the path

Training

to the plantations and the purgatory of the cane fields. Maroons, rebel blacks who rejected the chains, opened up the mountains. There they built villages where anger, hatred, and hope battled each other every day. They could not understand how they had been given a taste of freedom and then had it taken back from them, just so as not to ruin the landowners, the Guadeloupean whites, who wept over the good old slavery days. How many slaves cursed these lands where they had been brought to lose their African souls . . .

Slavery! Man Ya sighs deeply, shakes invisible chains, and speaks of the abolition of 1848. Schoelcher, the white savior . . . Even if you have never been to school, you know his name, you know the date of the liberation.

1848. The blacks in Guadeloupe entered abolition without believing it. They had already gotten burned with a first wind of false abolition. So, they waited to see, they did not want to get used to the rites of this new freedom. They remained paralyzed in a sort of mistrust, always expecting the return of the hard times of slavery. And then, little by little, they built houses, of wood, with no foundation, which they set down just on four big rocks and moved from one piece of land to another. They put women in the houses, dared to have families, made children on the bodies of other women. They only half believed in this liberation, abused it to the point of intoxication, for fear of seeing it disappear in the middle of the night, when they were leaving the bed of one woman to run to another. 1848, that's not so long ago, says Man Ya; you don't have to go back as far as Satan's milk teeth, just the night before last, just the other day. Who knows if one day soon, some law won't put the blacks back in chains? The law on paper, stamped, makes all men bend, pretty writing and violet ink.

We shudder.

The idea of slavery occupied my nights. I saw the land of Africa. A village in the bush. Men returning from the hunt. Women, their lips stretched with disks, pounding millet. Chil-

Man Ya's Five Ministries

dren running after monkeys and gazelles. Such a peaceful village. And then the slave ships. I could see the hold of the ship, the bodies piled one on the other, the crossing, the infernal pitching and tossing, the terror. Which of my ancestors had experienced those chains? Where exactly did he come from? What was his name? His language? Everything had been erased . . . Questioning Man Ya told me hardly anything. Even when white people shouted at her to go back to her country in Africa, she did not go back beyond that crossing. She left that to those who could not be consoled for having lost their family of kings and queens in Ethiopia or in Guinea.

Slavery! . . . Accursed slavery that had caused blacks to be cursed! Against this heritage of damnation, Man Ya used to say, how many of them were there back home, who were stumbling about in rum, becoming mad, walking hand in hand with Beelzebub's brethren. Generation after generation, with great patience, black people had tried to save their descendants by mingling their blood with light-skinned people. There were so many, even more, who rejected their race just because they thought they came from bad stock, the world's outcasts. We refused to believe in this fatalism.

Man Ya had not set out to lighten her descendants. It was Monsieur Asdrubal who had chosen her, a black woman with a big nose and nappy hair. He said he was descended from a family in Charentes. In France, in the course of his military campaigns, some white people had shown him on a map the exact spot where his name originated. His name came directly from France. It was neither a name made up on the day of the abolition nor a remnant from Africa. He was proud of it. That is why he had not gone to war like a mad dog. Just to follow others. He had gone to help the Motherland, to defend the land of his ancestors.

For Manman, the past is dead and buried. "No, don't scratch your young souls on the thorns of that long ago time, when the devil wore short pants!" she exclaims, to keep us from the burden of knowing. But her words, a tangle of dry sticks, catch fire all by themselves in the wind of the whys that collide within us.

Training

Man Ya's stories fringe other visions gleaned from *Tales and Legends from the Caribbean* by Thérèse Georgel and put together from fragments and gibes from television: colorful old American movies, with explorers and docile blacks, documentaries of Africa; television newscasts showing a street in Los Angeles, in the midst of the struggle for desegregation and civil rights.

. . . *"Suddenly, before his horrified eyes, a slave village appeared, with its streets made of earth and its straw huts, and the drum of the days when the moon shines. And from the huts, from each hut, came slaves . . . On their backs they bore the marks of leather straps. And Malvan—the wickedest of the Caribbean planters—recognized them. They were speaking:*

"I am the one you buried one Christmas night, beside your treasure."

"I am the one you buried alive, leaving out only my woolly head. Red ants devoured my eyes."

"And I, I am Domingue, Domingue whom you flogged. My body was one big wound. I was saved by being rubbed with salted peppers. So, I ran away a second time, this time with my wife and children. We took refuge in a hole near the riverbank. Remember: you set fire to it after you had barricaded the two openings and you burned us, alive."

"Look at me, I am Akollo. You tracked me in the woods and you put me in irons, my hands and feet chained, under the white-hot oven in the bakery, in the hot sun."

"I wept with weariness, after singing to forget and my bones ached. And they were all shouting curses. They were horrible to see, horrible in death. And the old man died without closing his eyes."

I remember the hand that held out the book, but I have forgotten the face. Who was it who came one day to give me these *Tales and Legends from the Caribbean*? An aunt, a godmother, one Christmas night, some Holy Communion Sunday?

As for me, I found neither tales nor legends in that book, only truthful stories that made real Man Ya's words about the curse on the black man and the life of the spirits. These stories drive the world of the Caribbean, where the living and the dead speak to each other naturally to settle each individual's affairs. The Devil breathes on destinies and fights with the Good Lord's angels and archangels. Josephine Tascher de La Pagerie and Bonaparte fall in love to the misfortune of blacks, who, by force of circumstances, use cunning and always emerge victorious over death, unfolding their wings for the journey to escape the chains. Ti Pocame, Vanousse, Chrisopompe de Pompinasse, Féfène, Cécenne, the most beautiful, at the bottom of the wooden tub, struggle with life and its tricks. And so many others, loquacious animals, and humans who change into beasts with hooves or big beaks, Br'er Tiger and Br'er Rabbit, Ti Jean l'Horizon, come to me as soon as I call their names . . . They have over fifty inexhaustible lives, and no matter how often I read and reread, plunder the pages, the Caribbean never stops filling the empty bags of my quest. There, nothing and nobody, not even time, ever quite dies. There is always the possibility of a resurrection, the probability of flight, the recurrence of a narrow escape. Then I understand Man Ya's melancholy better, her fear of dying here, in a silent land where the trees don't have ears, where the sky and the clouds block the breath of the angels, where time marches on, a conqueror, without ever looking behind him, trampling on all things.

She says: "I don't know if Asdrubal would have made me bear so much and so much more if I had been a mulatress. I can't tell. When he came back from his war in France, I just thought that you cannot cross your destiny, you have to bear the pain of the iron without crying out. He beat me harder than before. As if he needed relief. To forget the blood. And the arms torn off. The hearts of the blacks from the colonies stilled in the mud of the trenches. Eyes open in death. Hitting out always makes you feel better. It's like when I am pulling out Guinea grass in the garden. I don't think about anything else except pulling. I don't think of the sun that is splitting my head, nor of the ancestors' journey, nor of tomorrow, which will come,

God willing. Asdrubal was trying to feel better. He was afraid of stifling in the thought of the dead he had seen in the war in France. Dying without closing their eyelids . . ."

She says: "My God! Make me go back! Those children are big already. They don't need me as much as Monsieur Asdrubal. I have laid down the path for them . . . And even if they speak with RRR in their mouths, they understand my language. And even if they answer in nothing but French, they are flesh of my flesh. And if one day they should come along to Routhiers, they will not be lost. I have laid down the path."

The morning when Man Ya opens Élie's notebook under the tap, nobody is surprised. Élie is asking for a new one. Man Ya takes the situation in hand. One after the other, she holds the pages open to the cold water and calmly watches the writing coming undone and flowing down the hole in the sink. She doesn't need to rub or brush. Just to let the water carry away the purple ink of the words lying there, in order to make a clean new notebook. Accustomed to her dazzlingly simple ideas, we watch her washing all the pages, with great patience. Just turning the leaves of the notebook under the trickle of chlorinated water, which untangles the letters of the alphabet. Contenting herself with watching the words pass by, just as after a hurricane she used to watch the huge uprooted trees and the high, big rocks go by, in the river at the bottom of the ravine, behind her house. Just to feel flowing between her fingers rambling words and grammatical rules, adjectives, proper nouns and writing errors. Man Ya is already shaking the faded notebook which she puts on a radiator beside her pocket handkerchief to dry. The next day, the pages are hard, frightfully crinkled. Élie uses them all the same, for his most beautiful drawings: suns and houses in Guadeloupe that he has seen in Man Ya's eyes.

She says: "Asdrubal liked that about me. I have never wasted nor thrown away anything. Always economized. Him, he was the man who had airs and graces. Aristocratic manners and elo-

quent words, with poses and silences. Authority and discipline. I
have never discussed anything with Asdrubal. He would bark at
me. Or else he would grunt. Or he would whistle or tap his foot
or his cane. Or again, he would toss away food not to his taste,
or clothing that was not properly ironed. I would pick it up. I
bent my back. I said in my heart: "Torturer! One day you will
see the Good Lord's eyes and you will have to answer for all
your actions." But perhaps they won't let him get to the other
side . . . Who says they will give him two wings to let him reach
heaven? There are some who inherit hooves to gallop *ad vitam
eternam* on this earth. If that is his destiny, glory to God! It's not
wickedness that put him here, to thrash me. Perhaps it is the
eyes of others. All that was in the glance of other people. And
he must have asked himself what he was doing with an ignorant
creature like me. He loved black women. All the women who
bore his fruit were of my color. He would take those with slim
waists and round mouths. Some of them used to pass in front of
my house, and they would say: "A very good evening, Man
Asdrubal." I never tried to find out about their family. The
young women that he would run after! They fell for the glory
that he had brought back with his War Veteran's pension. They
only saw the bunch of decorations hanging like charms on his
starched white jacket. They remained caught in his French and
the way he had of walking stiffly and of taking off his cap to
greet ordinary girls. They have never heard him, with his teeth
chattering, in the night."

Medicine

The longing for home manifests itself everywhere and all the time. It appears in the absence of colors in the sky of the traveling spirit, which lives on nostalgia. Enduring this emptiness, wallowing in it or brooding over it, means sure suffering and sighs. It means living Over-There, preoccupied by Home.

Nourishing this longing means buying freshwater fish in France, soaking it in imitation brine—there are neither limes nor bird peppers here. Fry tomatoes and onions gently in an ounce of Masclet red butter out of a package from the Antilles. Put in the fish, let it cook, then eat it. Take note of the offense. Then, think about Home. In your memory, go in search of odors and the joys of tasting. Reinvent a Caribbean sea. Put yourself on a strip of beach. Wait for the return of the fishermen. Haul in the canoes with the regulars, as if you had never left Home. Look at the fish dancing their deaths in the bottom of the nets. And go off, with your booty: two goatfish, a sunfish, three sea bass, and a grunt in the shade of a basket. Later, close your eyes, suck a fish head from a red snapper, crush a thick slice of breadfruit in the *court-bouillon* sauce, sweat from the heat of a pepper. Relive all those tastes. Breathe in and belch.

For Man Ya, warding off this emptiness means dressing the wounds of her nostalgia with recollections raked up from the bottom of her memory. Dreaming and living the return journey. Everlastingly, until she is worn out. The magnified vision of her home place—with its estates, its talk, its folktales with a hundred thousand *soucougnans,* its meager favors, and its deep-rooted wickedness—haunts her, soothing or sharpening her pain by turns. Neither can she escape from the thought of Asdrubal. She remains sitting in the same place for hours, her eyes covered by a veil. Deep down inside, she pulls apart bits of stale news from long ago, turns them over to see the other side, picks them apart, and then sews them back together again any old way. She can never resign herself to throwing them out, even when all these visions are nothing but rags flapping in the wind of her memory. Sometimes she thinks of the people in Guadeloupe who have the power to step across the sea by passing their foot over a basin of water. Who knows the spot where people like that end up? . . .

A fellow from Routhiers, practicing black and white magic mixed together, said that he had touched the coast of Guinea one day when there was a strong trade wind. He made a great song and dance about the mask made of seashells that he had brought back—so he said—from his landing on that other shore. Another one, a *câpresse,* a sorceress from Cacoville, had landed, and even broken a bone in her big toe, in a region of coffee-colored blacks who screwed birds like women; it was a land to conquer, to fence in. An iniquitous man who dreamed of producing a colonial administrator from among his descendants, at the very least a governor, succeeded in putting one foot in France and the other in Africa simultaneously. He remained with his balls torn apart and, until his death, continued to waver between the two lands. No one could ever tell which place his spirit returned to.

If Man Ya had held a single strand of this power, she too would have stepped over the basin of magic water, to go back to Routhiers. Just to see whether anything had changed, whether the termites hadn't eaten her house to the ground, whether Asdrubal was no longer tormented by his ghosts, whether the river still brought the same cool water. Just time enough to pull up two or three clumps of greedy old weeds, to reap coffee and fertilize vanilla, to watch the sun come out from behind the woods . . .

Imagine the life that is being lived on the other side of the sea. Untether her spirit from here to there, change into a flying spirit.

Medicine

Leave her France-skin on the bed.
And fly away, wings open to the wind.

For some time now Man Ya has refused to leave her bed. A kind of melancholy has laid her low. She lies on the sheets, like the blue dolphins that come to die, beached on the shore in Four-à-Chaux or Roseau. She is there, without being there. Her mind can go back but her body does not follow. And so she utters very deep sighs. It is as if she is trying to blow wind into the sails of an invisible engine, reluctant to take off. Alas, the wings do not even unfold. Her breath does not unleash either a whirlwind or a storm. Her feet never raise anything but the dust from the sheets. Only her spirit wanders, spans long periods of time, tumbles down the hillsides of the *mornes*, steps across seas. It escapes at will and goes off.

In this time long ago, Man Ya no longer speaks, keeps her tales to herself. Her genius is waning, and her ideas about education (work, work, work . . .) no longer come to pester our ears. Anxious, like newborn puppies mewling plaintively around their sick mother, we watch over her night and day. Of course, each of us knows the origin of her trouble. But the remedy seems worse than the disease. To send her back to Guadeloupe, under the Torturer's boot, to us was like sending her straight to the gallows, with the blessing of Satan and our remorse in a ringside seat. Faced with this dilemma, we call a doctor—a general expert. The man, very, very, gentle, blames Homesickness and promptly prescribes a whole page of remedies.

The illness lasts.

Drags on.

Sees three seasons come and go.

Wears out two young doctors.

And swallows up hundreds of tablets.

It seems that Julia has lost the gift she used to have of taking each day as it comes, hauling it in until evening. She is neither hungry nor thirsty. She wants to go back. She wants to see Asdrubal. He needs her. Daisy explains to her that life in France is easy and healthy for her body, to no avail. Paris, the Eiffel

Man Ya's Five Ministries

Tower! France, country of freedom! So many blacks dream of the Champs Élysées, the Arc de Triomphe. So she ought to thank her good fortune and understand that she was right to leave poverty and savagery. Here in France, she can rest, sleep late, eat meat all the days that God makes. But Julia does not appreciate all these benefits of being in France. The Eiffel Tower can stay standing on its stiletto heels, Josephine Baker can continue to sing of her two loves, the General can liberate France a second time. Man Ya doesn't care. She wants only one thing, one single remedy: her return ticket, her old house in Routhiers, her garden, and Monsieur Asdrubal . . .

We had to give her the hope of an imminent return to hold on to, to get her to come out of her gloom at last. She leaves her bed and agrees to take her place among us again. Unable to prevent her heart from pining, she waits. Patience. The medication exhausts her. A bit of her strength has been left entwined in her bed. Desolation broods under her eyelids. New lines have appeared between her eyebrows, little Vs that look like wings poised for flight. She is entirely preoccupied by the idea of seeing Routhiers again. She is waiting for the hour to strike.

She made an X on her French I.D. card.

She signed up for how much time?

For what purpose?

Just an X that has enslaved her.

The year the *Torrey Canyon* runs aground, spilling its oil all along the coasts of Brittany, Man Ya appears to me in a dream. Changed into a seagull, she defies the black tide, exhausting her last breaths in an enormous effort, repeated endlessly, over and over again.

In this period, the cold, which she tolerated at the beginning of her life in France, suddenly attacks her. She begins to have pains all the time no matter what the season. The doctor identifies them: rheumatism, arthritis, bronchitis, old age, old bones. But Man Ya laughs in derision. In her eyes, the doctor is a great ignoramus. She has already made her own diagnosis and stubbornly believes it: the pain she is suffering from is the result of certain practices, sorcery, intended to torment her until she goes back to her husband. The description of these sufferings strikes us with terror. Imagine needles driven into her bones, volleys of blows with sticks breaking over her back. Fires lit to burn her insides. Imagine her head split in two by a blow from a saber, her heart pierced in her chest, bad blood, clotted, dripping in her veins instead of flowing freely. Imagine her back broken, her legs bruised, her tree of life completely stripped of leaves . . .

She says: "You are taking care of my body. You ought to have made infernal powers cry out. I sense them all around. For sure. They will not let go of me as long as I have not gone back. France is Tribulation and Trial . . . Lord, I am begging for relief, but Your will be done. You are in charge of my life. You know my thoughts, my actions. My body is in pain. I do not give You commands. I am Your servant . . . Only I can tell You that all these quantities of seas between Asdrubal and me, that's not good. That does not turn back those who are in the habit of dismembering the unfortunate. They want me to go back. They have the right to do everything to make me go back. And I too ask You to make me go back, Lord. I can feel that ordinary medicines have no power over the diseases that befall my bones. They are sowing evil to reap good. How many years have I been living in sin, separated from my husband before God? I am the one to whom Asdrubal gave his name. If Asdrubal does stupid things it is just to feel that he is alive, that the dead who torment him have not buried him with them in the ditch, where death leads the dance."

Treating her pains in a France where everything is lacking is heresy. Back Home, Man Ya never went to the doctor. Her garden gave her plants in profusion. To get rid of gas, there was shell ginger, broad-leaved thyme, lemon grass. If she happened to have a pain, a plaster of leaves from the castor oil plant, or a rubdown or two with male papaya flowers would give her relief. Each ache had its remedy. *Pomme-coolie*, stinking bush, Bahama grass, bilimbi, purslane, candle bush, trumpet tree, carpenter's grass . . . The Good Lord did not leave humans at the mercy of attacks, fevers, worms, chills, diarrhea, inflammations. Over here, in France, she had to be content to watch the children scratching their posterior, having stomach aches and heavy coughs. Not a single root of wormgrass anywhere nearby . . . At times, they really needed to have a bath, a rubdown, an enema, a purge, some herb tea. But over here, you see only the path to the pharmacy, money paid out and genuflection before white pills manufactured in a factory. Back Home, she had natural remedies available . . . The cure-for-all shell ginger, comfrey, periwinkle, silver bush, water grass . . . Each leaf, flower, seed, or root had its use, its actions, its allies and enemies. Man Ya would name the plants that were beneficial and those others that were used for evil spells or poisonings. Those, secret and rare, which had not yet been named but which demanded respect. You had to wait for their time, because, assuredly, the Good Lord had not created them without a reason.

Once, just once, she found what to do to stop a child's diarrhea. Put a handful of rice and a hunk of toast to boil together. Act as if the missing guava bud does not do any harm, doesn't hamper its effectiveness in any way. Thanks be to God, the patient is saved. For one or two days, Man Ya seems reinvigorated and waves her standard and her doctrine once more: work, work, work.

When she falls back into her melancholy state, the housing estate appears to her like a land deprived of basic knowledge. She sees all the ignorance of the human race growing there. One day will these children be able to identify the leaves of the breadfruit tree, those of the soursop? There are so many species to count on earth, in the heavens, and in the sea. The children who are growing up there, in the prison of these concrete houses, are surely losing the way to good sense, wandering about so far from the essences of life, as they are, she says to herself. Already, they are dulling feeling, taste, and touch. Their eyes see only the surface of things. Their ears no longer hear the world breathing, only words, the confused voices of the TV, coarse noises. And she fears for all the abandoned knowledge that, at present, lies dormant in her, like water that has no powers. Her knowledge of plants, beneficial or poisonous, seems to her at times to be dissipating in a memory dried out and blown apart by the wind of the winters. How many winters already? Three, four, five . . . She has forgotten. Time and its comedies over here make her stagnate in a feeling of uselessness. The bulk of the time is desolation. She watches the days go by. The laws that rule here have nothing to do with her knowledge. She is an encumbrance in France. The French tell her so: "Go back to where you come from! Go back . . ." She wants to go. Patience. To fill her days, distract her thoughts, she sits in front of the TV and watches white people prattling and moving their bodies. Occasionally, she smiles gently at the screen. But, more often, her eyes are seeing other sights passing before them, interior and intimate, other films that show her life with Asdrubal, the half-century that she has already spent on earth in hope and submission.

Sometimes she is stifling. She has to rush outside. She wants to breathe fresh air, feel the earth under her feet, touch branches, leaves, flowers. And too bad if there isn't the smallest plantation nearby. She closes her eyes and walks back and forth on the big forbidden lawn. There are only stunted trees, imprisoned in the concrete sidewalks. In the spring their buds sprout like yaws. Seeing them like that, half-dead, struggling to revive, to put out flowers and leaves, she understands why over here they don't bury the cord of newborn babies at their foot . . . How long has it been since she touched the earth to plant a branch or a root? On these days, even Aubigné-Racan is a courtyard of Paradise that they will get to some future July.

At times Man Ya founders in the face of her inability to dominate the course of things. Waiting is a trial also. To ease her aches, which defy ordinary medicine, we have so little to offer her: bay rum to rub her terrible pains. Cupping glasses applied to her back to dislodge the old tree, rooted in the middle of her stomach, on which her bronchioles shiver like birds after a hurricane. American Saint Bernard plasters stuck onto her back . . . Alas, all these practices are shipwrecked one after the other in the face of the evidence and the power and the unleashing of the forces at work. France has to let her go, she says, thinking of Asdrubal. And she endures all her sufferings without ever thinking that her ruminations are perhaps only inventions, suppositions, sets of unresolved questions, the infirmity of exile.

During her last days in France, she allows herself to see her skin crack in the hard water and her complexion grow gray from lack of sun. When her castor oil is used up, she subjects her hair to Bioliss whale oil from a tube. She goes to bed without having her herb tea, like people here who don't care for their bodies and who no longer know how to clean out their insides. She puts herself in the hands of God since there's nothing to be done about it; she has been reduced to living in the ignorance of the modern era. They tell her over and over that the old days are finished, that she must not look back. So, she waits every day for the tomorrow that will bring her return ticket.

At times her manman's words come back to her: "A black woman must show the whiteness of her soul and do good to merit Christ's peace." And she wonders how long she will have to endure life in France, what torments, what sacrifices are still left to come . . .

She lies down on her foam mattress and dreams of her old straw mattress in Routhiers. Above her head, the rusty metal roof warding off the rain. Asdrubal's snores in the adjoining room. The moon's frolics. She closes her eyes to experience once again the good sensations from long ago. Alas, she has hardly yielded when *Monsieur l'abbé* rises before her, brandishing Bible, cross, and rosary. The mayor follows, the marriage register under his arm. Holding each other by the hand, the black robe and the tricolor sash call out . . . "Julia! Julia! Julia! Go back to your house to your lawful husband! He is waiting for you! You must give him one last chance!"

Sometimes the homesickness in her seems to fade. She no longer talks about going back. Her bed sees her only when night comes. She watches television very late, with a passionate desire to see the other faces of the world that she puts together in a calabash gourd. A dark gourd where all the deprived peoples huddle together. She surmises the vastness of the world; she pictures it.

Medicine

She considers the desolation and the disorientation that those who, like her, have been kidnapped from their land must have lived through, and be living through. She sees the state of the world, its wars, devastation, hunger, violent death. She re-lives her crossing and embarks for other crossings, final ones. Miles and miles of sea between the lost country and the new world. Miles and miles of suffering . . .

Colors

Deliverance

When Man Ya leaves us, I think I will never see her again . . .

A cousin passing through France is taking her back to Guadeloupe. Her proposed departure is carried out in a sort of contained haste. She holds back her joy, as if to ward off the demons who pick apart plans drawn on hope. She is unwilling to rejoice fully, one never knows . . . She grits her teeth, thanks Christ, telling us that—God willing!—deliverance is coming soon. Deliverance, the word has found its lawful place. Liberation from the Old World. Last circle in the wan light of purgatory. "Thank You Lord, Eternal One. In Your greatness, You have answered my prayers! Glory to you, Virgin Mary, Mother of the gentle Lamb!" she says over and over in her evening prayers. During those days, her face shines. At the idea of the journey, her eyes, up until then dulled by the thought of never gazing at her garden again, see life flowing once more, like the eyes of a blind person miraculously healed. At nightfall, the promises of the morrow make her body shake with coarse laughter. And then, in a soft voice she starts singing old songs in which *belles matadors,* beautiful lion-hearted women, strut about. She even wants to dance, but she can only spin around awkwardly, sing couplets from an old Bertrand and Léogane song . . .

Dépí mwen kontré vou	Since I met you
Dépí ou rann mwen fou	Since you drove me mad
Dépí sé vou tou sèl	Since you are the only one
Mwen ka touvé ki bèl . . .	Who I think is beautiful

In her young days, she never went to dances. To tell the truth, she had scarcely had the time to want to look like the made-up young misses with grand tight-fitting dresses and lace and silk who know how to entrap males. A black woman from the fields, that is what she was when Asdrubal had met her.

Dépí sé vou tou sèl	Since you are the only one
Mwen ka touvé ki bèl	Who I think is beautiful
Dépí ou enmé mwen	Since you love me
Mwen pa konnèt ayen . . .	I know nothing any more . . .

A black woman without airs and graces. Always planting all kinds of roots, fertilizing vanilla, climbing trees, and setting her shrimp nets in the river. The Good Lord had given her ten good fingers, a sturdy body, a quick mind. She could make a meal from nothing, did not waste a penny. Neither was she the kind to have an outstretched hand, expecting something from the war veteran pension. She sold her spices and vegetables to the shops in the village, and as a result she always had cash. She loved the feeling of being in the middle of her field, surrounded by all her trees: the trees she had planted and the ancestors she had found there. Each one had its place, and she did not cherish any less those that bore neither fruit nor seeds but gave shade to her Creole kitchen garden. She had known them when they were young plants, offering only the promises of their sap. They had grown up, and she considered them her flesh and blood as much as her children. She herself sometimes adopted the posture of a plant, not moving until she was numb, imagining herself to be a mother-tree, with dark bark, toes mottled with earth, arms reaching out to the sky.

At last she is going back, after this long detour in France. She wants only one thing, to go back to her land in Guadeloupe . . . even if it is true that this wretched land casts a spell and ties up destinies. She does not ponder or question the why and the how of the attachment to her land. Reason gives way before the movements of the heart. There are no words, only the emptiness that blinds and stuns. There are no great theories, only naive recollections that memory embellishes, irritating trifles, an ecstatic mime. The earth, like a mother who gives birth, nourishes, and reaps.

Deliverance

Julia is going away.
A white steamer is waiting for her.
Adieu foulards
Adieu madras . . .
She leaves.
She leaves us to ourselves.
She leaves us in sadness and snow.
She abandons us to France.

Soon her absence is weighing over all of us. All of a sudden, there is Before and After Man Ya. Before and After . . . Time is gauged differently, for me it now becomes measured in segments of hours, drafty days, and hurried days of counting. It is as if Man Ya had left taking with her the measure of time. The room where we sleep on our beds, one on top of the other, seems empty, deprived of her essence.

Julia leaves us to ourselves.

The metal hangers that held her dresses swing to and fro in the wardrobe. The place for her things remains empty for a long time. We take turns sleeping in her bed, just to breathe the memory of her smell in the folds of the mattress. "When Man Ya was here!" we tell each other. When Man Ya was here . . . She forgot her slippers, and no one touches them for that whole long winter. Even the broom sweeps around them, respectfully. We find a foot of a khaki sock in a corner of the chest of drawers. No one dares to throw it away. A tin of American dressings lies there for three centuries gathering dust on a shelf. Overcome by idleness, the graters, files, tweezers, and nail scissors suddenly rust.

Life in the room adjusts to a new freedom, imposed, exciting. A scintillating freedom, embroidered with fake pearls, which encumbers us like a fancy ball gown with flounces stolen from a princess. Gone was the curfew, gone were the commanding looks and listening ears! No more complaints and fiendish tales! No sooner was the door of our room closed than we spread our wings wide. We sat up late, finally! We went back and forth in long intimate conversations dissecting our feelings one after the other. We sighed over the injustice of being born girls, the stupidity of boys, Paul's secrets and our parents' rigidity. Alas, we discover that if Man Ya is no longer here in the flesh, her thoughts pursue us, her voice comes back to us as if coming from within ourselves. A breeze brings the whiff of a lotion. Sighs rise from her bed, which creaks strangely and censors all our actions. Man Ya has gone, but her absence is a presence as tenacious as the homesickness that took her away from us.

The strong smell of bay rum.

The pulling off of American Saint Bernard dressings.

French apples.

The stories of *diablesses* and *vieux-volants*.

Routhiers-Cacoville-Capesterre-de-Guadeloupe.

Cupping glasses.

Sacré-Coeur.

Votive candles to the Holy Virgin.

The snores, the rubs, the "*Pa pléré ti moun*—don't cry little one."

Br'er Rabbit and our friend Mr. Elephant.

The curse of black people . . .

Julia leaves us in sadness and in tears. We could tell she was happier than a saint in heaven at her departure. She is going back to her garden, which gives her food, herbs for healing, her road to Routhiers, her big woods at the foot of Soufrière, her house at the foot of the Carbet Falls . . . Her house, open on four sides, open to the four cardinal points. Without asking, without knocking, life comes in. We hear the chatter from Louise's shop, the rustling from the garden, the noisy river, the gurgling of the spring, the grunting of the animals. And all the smells from round about, all the sounds, gathered by the winds, come and go, take from some to take to others, and so on, all day and all night long.

She abandons us to France.

Go back to your country, *Bamboulas*!

Go home! To Africa!

I would really like to go back to my country. But which country? Which Africa? The Africa of the time when Papa was in the army only comes back to my memory in unreal shreds. I want

Deliverance

to appropriate clear and definite visions, for the remainder of my life. I close my eyes, tight. I call on Saint Anthony of Padua, who brings back all things lost or misplaced. A series of cardboard boxes is given to me. I open them one after the other. So much straw and tissue paper for such minute treasures: old dried-out insects, spider webs, flashes of sunlight, murmur of dry winds, shadows crumbled into dust, warrior masks, ivory trinkets ... Africa! Huge, motionless almond trees. Columns as big as elephants' feet guarding the front of the house. Distant talk from the mouths of grown-ups ... the story of a lion devouring a family. The tale of Br'er Tiger massacring a village. Zembla, Akim, Tarzan. Old picture books where Africa's big cats smile through their whiskers drawn in Indian ink. Ostrich eggs, brightly colored wraps, trifles, trifles ...

Go back to your own country!

Freedom holds us in its embrace. Man Ya where are you? What are you doing? ... If the wolf were here, he would eat us! For a while, I lie down like Man Ya, on her bed. I breathe hard, to fill the sails and go away, to cross the seas, and like the Apolline in *Tales and Legends*, to fly, fly, to the West Indies. They have to shake me to get me out of the apathy that is overcoming me. But for all that I don't give up. I want to leave this land that rejects me. So I become someone who writes in the afternoons, a midnight scribbler, a scribe in the wee hours. Write to invent existences for yourself. Migratory pen, magic ink, wizard letters, which take you back every day to your dream country. "Over here, you are at home!" you hear the murmur. Balm for the heart. Write the burned bottom of a saucepan of chocolate custard, memories of kites, children dancing in the rain across from a blue savannah. Write to quicken memories: Papa Bouboule under the verandah, a lamp that smokes, the skin of a flying woman hanging on the nail behind a door, curses by the armful, the straddling of seas, waves searching the shore. Write to freeze the surroundings, and to melt the snow of winters that make you weep from cold.

I open the window. I smell, I breathe in. And, head filled with the world's odors drifting about outside, I believe I can pick over the perfumes from the winds like rice grains or peas. I tell myself that, perhaps, a trade wind will bring me the smells from Man Ya's garden. Vanilla, cinnamon, cocoa, roasted coffee, nutmeg, curry powder. I bury my nose in the tin that holds sticks of this, cloves of that, essences of bitter almond and dried orange peels. I take a deep breath. And, breathless, I run into my room where I release all these intoxicating fragrances.

Go back to your own country!

They believe that I am hiding my idleness behind my craze for useless writing. I am writing Julia's tales and legends . . . I see her back in her Routhiers in a new glory. Asdrubal prostrates himself at her feet. But Julia has no time for his fawning, she is delivering lost souls pledged to the devil, undoing Br'er Rabbit's tricks, restoring riches and confidence to the black man, the power of speech to dogs. Sometimes she lunches with the Holy Virgin, Kubila from Africa, the angel Gabriel, and one or two spirits. Julia is walking in the air. Reaches the heavens. Goes back to the old slavery days. Scales centuries and stirs up the mystery of unknown countries. She goes up rivers and drinks from the stream that relates its journeys, from the days of yore when the devil was an innocent boy, when the earth bore men and not wild beasts. Sometimes, the dreams delude me into believing that I am part of all her wanderings, riding on her back, my feet encircling her waist. Then time and space are conjugated on the same tables.

A year passes.

Then two.

And three.

Her absence weighs less heavily in the empty space in the rest of us. You might say that the recollection, by dint of shining memory's pewter too brightly, ends up mirrored in oblivion. Clinging to the remains that she has left us, our stomachs full, we nevertheless feel like the Ethiopian children, who, pulling at their emaciated mothers' withered breasts, stand planted like dry trees, with shining eyes, so wide open, in front of the camera of "Headline News."

In the beginning, we write to Man Ya, who gets a literate

neighbor to read her the letters. But not receiving a great flood of replies, we fear for her life, imagining Asdrubal to be angry. Just thinking about it unleashes apparitions of hell that pierce us through and through. Brief letters, insignificant, tell us that she arrived safely, fell into the arms of her deserted love. Supposedly, she would no longer be beaten by the Torturer. He had, it seems, become sweet-honey-syrup and proud of his Julia, who had known France and her greatness. It would seem that she went to mass with her beautiful nylon dresses from France and her scarves with the Eiffel Tower and the Arc de Triomphe. She no longer had pains in her bones and would have started to work in her garden again. So far from her, separated by miles and miles of seas, we just have to hope. We want to believe all these rumors that make our hearts happy and soothe our souls. The period of the letters does not last very long.

Letters from France

Dear Man Ya,

On Sunday, Manman and Papa went to Les Halles. They brought back blood and tripe to make blood pudding and also a big pig head for pâté. It snowed this morning. Soon it will be Christmas. We hung balls on the pine tree. As she does every year, the neighbor invited us to come and admire her paper crib. Baby Jesus was sleeping under the eyes of the other figures. They won't move from her drawing room till the middle of January.

The avocado seed that you put in water did germinate, it is beginning to sprout leaves. Outside, the trees are bare.

I hope that your pains won't come back. You left your dressings. If you need them, let me know, I will tell Manman to send them to you. Well, what did you think of your house? Is your spring that came out of a rock still in the same place? Yesterday I cried, over nonsense . . . And I heard you telling me: "*Pa pléré ti moun!* Don't cry little one." Lots of love and kisses.

Dear Man Ya,

I hope you are well. Even if I sometimes have thoughts that make me tremble, in general, I think of you as happy. I see you singing in your garden, picking mangoes, golden apples, and oranges. I tell myself that already you must have fertilized your vanilla, reaped your coffee, and made your chocolate sticks. Is Grandfather Asdrubal well? If you could ask somebody to write the replies for you, I would be very happy. Well, I don't have much news to give you. Perhaps you only want to know how we are, one or other of us. Papa was a bit sick—a chill. Manman put on cupping glasses but she didn't know exactly how much heat to use. So Papa snapped at her. He shouted: "*Ou pa té ka gadé lè Man Ya té ka pozé sé vantouz-la!* Didn't you look when Man Ya was putting on the cupping glasses!" It was awful . . . Paul is becoming more and more of a guitarist; he has friends who are musicians and singers. Perhaps one day he really will become as famous as Claude François. Lisa is going to be a secretary. She is going to school at the École Pigier. She writes with bizarre symbols. I wanted to start too so that we could have our own private code that nobody in the family would understand, but it's too complicated.

Rémi and Élie are learning to do woodwork with Papa. Papa bought a woodwork saw. It is in the cellar. When he turns it on to make our furniture, the whole building shakes. Manman sighs. Since Papa became a carpenter, the people from upstairs give us funny looks. Suzy is growing nicely, but since she was always in your lap, we can tell that she is a bit sad and dreamy. As for me, I have started to write the story of your return to Guadeloupe. I am tired of winter, and I am waiting for the holidays and summer so that we can go to Aubigné-Racan. Lots of love. And I am hoping to see you soon.

Dear Man Ya,
I thought of you last night. Edith Piaf, the *Compagnons de la Chanson,* Georgette Plana and Leny Escudero were on TV. They sang: *"Mon Dieu," "La vie en rose," "Les trois cloches,"* and *"Mon légionnaire."* I wonder if you wouldn't like to see TV now and then, over there in Routhiers . . . Manman told me that you don't have either running water or electricity. Have you been able to get used to going to bed with the sun again? I often think about the spring water that comes out of the rock. To tell you the truth, I didn't really believe it at first. But I see it now. I know that it exists. And I hope that one day I'll be able to bathe in it with you. Man Ya, my lessons are waiting. Love.

Dear Man Ya,
Whenever I eat lentils, I think about the Antilles. Lentils, Antilles. Can you say that Guadeloupe is one island among so many others that make up the Antilles? Each grain is an island

in my plate. I know that there are heaps of islands in the vicinity of Guadeloupe. Manman cooked lentils yesterday. And in the evening, as usual, she added water and put the rest in the blender to make soup. Guadeloupe, I have forgotten the few short moments that I spent there. Each lentil is a land floating on a brown Caribbean Sea. Sometimes I pick over the lentils. I secretly keep all the little stones that I find, like the beginning of a collection of precious stones. Where do these stones come from? I already have a whole boxful in a Rising Sun matchbox. To those who tell me to go back to my own country, I can reply that I do go back from time to time. And that one day I will stay there. And that I even brought back earth and rocks from my Country the last time that I went there.

I did not look at it enough when I was there. I was too little. I remember when Man Bouboule made creamy chocolate, when our bodies were bathed in the warm water from basins with bush baths. And smells of vanilla, morning coffee, smells of cow-foot soup come back to me. I can see the flowers in front of the verandah, but I have forgotten their smell. I remember stories about demons, devils, and guardian saints. Arrows to pierce the powerful Satan. Pa Bouboule's round face, Man Bouboule's tanned one.

Do you go down to the village of Capesterre these days? Are there changes? If you could dictate a letter to a neighbor who can write, that would be good. Love.

Dear Man Ya,

I hope that you are keeping well, and Grandfather Asdrubal as well. Papa and Manman are well. We have just come back from Aubigné-Racan. It was hot this year. Manman took us to the river almost every day. We even went to the sea. We begged Manman so much that she finally gave in. It was a real expedition in the Renault 4L. Five hundred kilometers both ways! Manman was very tired and at the same time very proud of herself. The sea was freezing cold. We couldn't even dip a toe. There was no sandy beach. Only pebbles. It was hard to walk on it.

Letters from France

We have no nutmeg or cinnamon left. Can you take some to Man Bouboule? She will send us a package. Thanks in advance and love.

Dear Man Ya,

At last, I am getting breasts! I was beginning to give up hope. In the dressing room, after gym, I had already noticed that some girls in my class were wearing bras. I was embarrassed with my baby vests. I asked Manman to buy me a bra. She told me I still had to wait a little. I was so angry, I kept sulking for a week. Yesterday I took one of Lisa's bras. Too big, of course. I stuffed it with cotton. During gym class, I felt like everybody was interested in my false breasts. I climbed the rope, very quickly. I was already quite far up when I heard: "That's normal; they climb trees in their country!" When I got to the top I didn't have the strength left to climb back down. I could have let go of my rope so as not to hear them snickering. I would have fallen on my head. And there would have been no more skin color, only a mighty death with no tributes or fuss. After a minute, the gym teacher blew the whistle, and I came down. My thighs were all stiff and my calves were knotted. I did not get undressed in front of them.

Every week, I measure my bust. My breasts are growing really slowly. When Élie and Rémi get on my nerves, I tell Manman that they hit me on my breast. Manman can hear everything, except that. She is afraid that I will get a malformation. So, she starts to run after them around the table with the strap. While we wait for the time for bras to come, Manman bought me a panty girdle with lace and ribbons (it's the latest fashion!). Well, enough of these stories about breasts. I don't even know if I am going to send this letter.

Dear Man Ya,

Are you always punished for your wrongdoing? Manman blamed the boys because of me and the breast malformation thing. That made me laugh. And now something terrible is happening to me. I am not pretending to cry any more. Please pray for me in order to save me from this situation. I can't write it on paper. It's very, very, very serious. And no one can help me. Apart from the Virgin Mary, and all the saints who you know much better than I do, I don't know who I can turn to. In my evening prayers, I am promising the Good Lord not to get my brothers punished on purpose any more. Love.

Dear Man Ya,

We got the cinnamon, the curry powder, and also the cassava flour. The very same day, Manman made a chicken curry with rice. In the afternoon, I lay down on your bed and I closed my eyes. When night comes, I fall into dark holes in my dreams and, during the day, I manage to fly away far, far, from here, in my mind. Lisa tells me that, around midnight, I talk and walk around in the room. So, after the curry, I did not brush my teeth, to keep a little of the taste in my mouth. I closed my eyes, and I saw you in your garden, in the middle of all your tall trees. I sat on a rock and looked at you, without saying a word. I think you couldn't see me. Night was beginning to fall. I said: "Man Ya! Don't forget me!" You looked at me and you said: "*Pa pé a yen! Ou ké sové* . . . Don't be afraid! You will be safe!" Then I opened my eyes, and I went to do my writing. And I felt full of energy thanks to your words. Man Ya, love to you.

Dear Man Ya,

I don't know if you have radio in Routhiers. Do you remember Martin Luther King? Well, he was assassinated in his country. You remember, you used to say that even if we did not understand his language, we could clearly see, in his eyes, that he was bringing words of peace. He just wanted blacks in America to have the same rights as whites. Whites always think they are superior to all the races on earth. In their minds, they are more intelligent. They think they have the right to go and conquer all the lands in the world, but no one must come to their country. They alone have the right to say: "Go back to your own country!" Say a little prayer for Martin Luther King.

PS: I have twenty-five stones from the lentils in my box of matches.

Dear Man Ya,

I am writing you this letter, but you will never receive it. I know that you already have to fight against Grandfather Asdrubal's ghosts. No one will read you this letter. Sometimes, I think about you a lot, and I try to communicate with you through my mind. I don't know if my thoughts come to you like letters in the mail.

At school, things are not going well at all. I have a teacher whose name is Madame Baron. She can't see me. I had already noticed it at the beginning of the year. When I raised my hand, she would never call on me. She marked me harder than the others. Things got worse after the Christmas holidays. She told me that I smiled ironically when she was speaking. So, she punished me by forcing me to go under her desk. Now, I go there in almost all her classes. Like a dog in a kennel. I obey. I breathe in the odor of her feet. I can see the hairs of her fat legs squashed under her stockings. I clench my teeth so as not to cry. I can hear the pupils' voices. I am ashamed. I am afraid. Squatting under the desk. Nobody protests. Nobody comes to my defense. I wait for the end of the lesson. Everybody accepts that I spend my time under the desk. Why? Because Madame Baron is mad to all appearances; the children are terrorized. I am her scapegoat. She does not like to see my black woman's face, my black skin.

I don't say anything either to Papa or to Manman. It has been going on for too long. I am waiting for the end of the school year. Now, as soon as I am locked up in a room, I feel like I am stifling. Manman says that I am suffering from oppression. I haven't told Lisa any thing either. At night in my bed, I cry. I wait for sleep, which makes me fall into dark holes and carries me far, far away. That is the awful thing that is happening to me. I pretend to laugh and to be insolent, but all the time my heart is tight.

Colors

Dear Man Ya,

The Easter holidays are coming soon. I won't see Madame Baron for two weeks. I am going to try to write the story of my life, like Anne Frank. Manman gave me the book. She lived in Holland with her family. As they were Jews, during the war they stayed hidden in a tiny room until Hitler's Nazis found them and arrested them in 1944. They were taken to a death camp. Her story gave me a lot to think about. I think after the holidays I will put up with having to go under the desk better. I will think of Anne Frank who stayed cramped up in darkness for two years of war and then died without being able to realize her dream: becoming an actress in Hollywood. How do you live in a country that rejects you because of race, religion, or skin color? Locked up, always locked up! Wearing a yellow star on her coat. Wearing your black skin, morning, noon, and night under the eyes of whites. So, when I hear the words coming from far off, "Go away, in spirit!" I feel like hanging up my skin on an old rusty nail, behind the door. Getting out into the skies. Following the great winds that sweep my Country.

Dear Man Ya,

The Good Lord saved me. School is over already, at the height of the month of May. Because of the Events. I won't go under the desk like a dog in a kennel any more. I won't see Madame Baron's pointed shoes, her long twisted hairs under her stockings with runs, the fat overflowing between her thighs. I won't smell her odor, like a dirty woman's, when she spreads her legs to read a poem from Verlaine . . .

Les sanglots longs	The long sobs
Des violons	Of the violins
De l'automne	Of autumn
Blessent mon coeur	Wound my heart
D'une langueur	With monotonous
Monotone.	Languor.

This month of May is really extraordinary. This is the situation: the students are taking the streets apart, they put up bar-

ricades, throw cobblestones at the police, and burn cars. Manman forbids us to go out. She is afraid of the demonstrators. She
has found packets of Mousseline soup and ravioli. That's what
we eat everyday. But most of the shops are empty. At one fell
swoop, we can't get almost everything. Since I read the *Diary of
Anne Frank,* I see life differently, and I say to myself that in
other places in the world, at this very moment, there must be
children who are still living like Anne Frank. Invisible threads
link us together so that we can stay on our feet on earth. Anne
Frank will never die. What she wrote keeps her alive for eternity. Lots of love.

Dear Man Ya,

What is it that persuades people to leave the everyday mo-
notony, take to the streets, and want all of a sudden to change
the world? No one saw the Events coming. No one was expecting it. One day, you told me that in Guadeloupe the birds, the
dogs, and even the insects feel and give notice of the upheavals
of nature. Earthquakes, heavy rains, or hurricanes. The leaves
play a different tune. The wind brings smells of destruction. The
river begins to bring down little leaves from the forests in the
mountains. The sky takes on the colors of the Apocalypse,
sketches the seven trumpets of the End Times. You used to say
that many humans had lost that sense. Perhaps if you had been
here, you would have been able to warn us about the Events.
Manman would have done the shopping, and we wouldn't be
sitting down to ravioli, fish sticks, soup from a packet, and all
these kinds of tasteless factory-prepared foods.

Dear Man Ya,

They are always telling me that I have too much imagination
and that all the problems I encounter come from that. I don't
call the thoughts, but they come before me. I don't want to reject them. I read somewhere that thoughts can become reality
by themselves. And I wonder if the Events of May '68 aren't the
realization of one of my thoughts. You never know. Perhaps I
have a gift . . . I asked the Good Lord so many times to find a

solution to prevent Madame Baron from putting me under her desk . . .

Dear Man Ya,

I am writing you again about the Events. Still no school. Still no Madame Baron on the horizon. Still canned food. The farmers, the workers, and the students are in the streets, and people are now looking for the beach under the cobblestones in Paris.

Papa can't get over the fact that General de Gaulle could be so disrespected. He discusses it with his army friends. The ingratitude of the French is a constant refrain. How can they act like that with a Savior of the Nation? Has France forgotten the horrors of the war? The era of Hitler, of Nazi Germany? Don't these people owe eternal gratitude to the great man who took them out from under the boot of the great dictator? Papa is so disgusted that he threatens to leave French soil forever if the General is forced to abandon the country to the Communists. Decidedly Mankind has no memory and feeds on forgetfulness, he says.

Dear Man Ya,

It has been decided. I heard it from Papa's very own mouth: if the General resigns, we will leave for the West Indies. Papa will immediately ask for a Transfer. France will become for him like a lost country fallen into the hands of a demon. If the General stays at the helm, Papa and all of us will stay too. You see, our fate depends on General de Gaulle.

Dear Man Ya,

On TV I saw children dying of hunger in Biafra, in Africa. I was sad. There is a war over there. I was ashamed of myself. I felt like a privileged child crying for one last Scooby-doo. After all, we lack nothing. We have new shoes, and even if they are forced on us and have crepe soles like they wore in the fifties, we ought to be happy. We are not suffering from cold. We take our licks, but it is for our good, for our education. We even go on holiday. We have a house in the country. Papa has a car, Manman too.

We are not dying of hunger. What else do I need? Manman says that we are never content and that there are lots of children who would envy our lot.

Dear Man Ya,

At last, I realize that I am not sending you any more mail at all. I am a copycat. I am imitating Anne Frank and am writing to a diary. You are replacing Kitty, except that you really exist. One day, when I come back to Guadeloupe, I will read you these pages. Today, I would like to tell you that I really have compassion for children who are dying of hunger, who live in countries at war. But I can put all the suffering in the world end to end, force my mind to imagine the horror in all its dimensions, and that still does not prevent me from feeling very unhappy, here in France.

PS: I have thirty-nine little stones. Almost a country!

Dear Man Ya,

It's summer, the long vacation. School never reopened its doors, but Madame Baron has followed me all the way to Aubigné-Racan. I told Lisa about the time I spent under Madame Baron's desk. That made me feel better. The nightmares were going to kill me one of these nights. Last night, Madame Baron was showing me the desk with her ruler. I went down on all fours. But this time she did not sit down. From under her skirts she took out planks of wood, nails and a hammer. And the desk turned into a crate that she threw into the sea. I woke up in tears, and Lisa put her arm around my shoulders. That's when I told her everything. The next morning Manman knew already. She told me that she did not understand me . . . "You spend your time making up stories, writing useless novels, and you hide real things instead of bringing them out into the open. What do you have inside your head, my girl? Life is not a novel. You cannot carry a secret as heavy as that, not while you have a manman." I started to cry. "But why did she do that to you? Why, my God? Nobody in your class said anything? But why? They left you all that time without saying anything? That's not possible! But you yourself, what were you waiting for before telling me? Stop your writing; it won't get you anywhere. Is all that true, are you sure that it's true? . . ."

Dear Man Ya,
Madame Baron has not reappeared for several nights. Just one time, I dreamed that you were beating her in a fight between women. But I don't want to speak about this diabolical woman any more. For as long as my eyes have seen Aubigné-Racan, nothing ever changes. Still the same cobblestones that go from the church to the town hall square. Still the same bread from the baker, the same slices of bread with potted meat from Le Mans, the same geraniums on Madame Bourasseau's balcony.

Dear Man Ya,
Lisa and I have sorted through all the rubbish piled up in the attic a bit. At the beginning it was a real chore. But then I found the bound books that I used to go through long ago. I turned the little key, opened the door of the rusted case. Lisa cried: "What are you doing? You aren't allowed!" The books covered in red cloth were eaten at the corners. The pages, full of tiny holes made with great patience, were even more yellowed and were coming apart. I stroked them all the same, with a little bit of pity for the Marquise de Merteuil, who surely wanted to appear in her same old splendor. Beautiful and proud. She was still writing to her friend Valmont. But her letters will soon fall to pieces; the words will be eaten up by time, vermin, and neglect.

Dear Man Ya,
The Events have been over for a long time. Going back to school went well. I am in grade eight. Madame Baron has disappeared. The teachers don't trouble me. I don't work too hard. I am no good at math, and I don't try to understand. For the other subjects, it's OK. In French, I amaze them all. We do compositions . . . Describe this, write a letter to your best friend, imagine you are in such and such a situation . . . Well, in that, I get the best marks. Manman says that at last I am using my

crazy imagination for something worthwhile and that where there's life, there's hope. When I am busy with my writing, which no one has the right to read, they leave me alone. The students in my class suddenly find me interesting. They can't get over the fact that the only black *Bamboula* from Africa in the class is better than they are in their beautiful French language. They come to talk to me. I let them come, I give them explanations, and then we talk about other things. They have all forgotten that Madame Baron used to put me under the desk. I pretend that I, too, have forgotten.

Dear Man Ya,

Right now I am following the television news very closely. When your life depends on it in a crucial and vital way, politics becomes a very fascinating thing. General de Gaulle has appointed a new prime minister. But everybody thinks that the old one, Pompidou, will in a short time be the next president of the French Republic. Is de Gaulle going to go? That is the question that keeps coming back in all the discussions that Papa has with his friends in the drawing room. Will Papa be true to his word and go back home to the West Indies, if his role model is no longer in charge of the country? The other day I was watching Suzy putting her blocks one on top of the other. Papa, too, is putting blocks one on top of the other. Since he spoke about leaving for good, he has been keeping us in suspense. Now we are waiting for all the new government's blocks.

Dear Man Ya,

My letters are not very long these days. I have heaps of lessons, exercises, and homework. I have lists of irregular verbs to learn in English. But it will soon be Christmas holidays. Today I am going to try to write you a long letter. Here is the present situation: Papa does not understand France any longer. Manman is waiting. And the rest of us are growing up. We continued to grow after you left. We are no longer the same people. Time commands us to grow up. We are growing up. We are obeying time. People say . . . Those children are growing nicely.

I who wanted so much to grow up so I could have breasts, I am beginning to miss the time when I was younger. Now, I would like time to forget me. Yesterday, I realized that I was growing too fast. I'm growing and growing. While I am writing to you, I keep on growing. My feet and my fingers are getting longer. And also since I went back to school I've been wearing a bra. Manman still plaits my hair but I feel that the time for that is past. All that is teeming in my head does not go with these squares and these plaits that have the look of a *diablesse*'s horns. On the way to school, I undo all the plaits and I twist my hair into a bun. Aren't I going to arrive in the West Indies too grown up? Will I see Guadeloupe in what is left of my youth or in my old age? I am growing up. I want jewelry. I open Manman's jewelry box and I go to school with her thick gold bracelets, her rings, and her necklaces. I am growing up against my will. And while Élie and Rémi are complaining because their friends went to see Walt Disney's *Jungle Book,* while Paul is practicing the Beatles' "A Hard Day's Night" and Simon and Garfunkel's "Mrs. Robinson" on the guitar, while Lisa is trying to dress in the latest France Gall fashion, and while Suzy is starting to learn the alphabet singing Julien Clerc's "Cavalry," men have already walked on the moon, and General de Gaulle is not making up his mind to give up power, even when he sees Henri Tisot imitating him on television. Can time forget someone on its way? I don't want to get to the West Indies all grown.

Dear Man Ya,

In future times, they will write about General de Gaulle's fate. They will say that he announced a great referendum in the month of February 1969. Historians will put down the dates and the proper names of places and people. But, I am sure, no one will be able to pull the thread of the story that leads to our family. Who can say that our destinies are not linked to that of the General? He is there at the beginning of Papa's life in the army. He is the one who gives honor and congratulations, promotions and war medals. If Papa had not broken away to join him, where would we be at this time? If Papa had not worn the uniform of the French army, would my manman Daisy have said yes to him for life? That is how West Indians come to be born in France.

Dear Man Ya,
Papa is down. Imagine Cassius Clay beaten by a knockout. Throughout the whole campaign, Papa believed in it. De Gaulle is, for him, the man who has never lost face, the Savior of France. We had to put pamphlets in all the mail boxes in the project . . . Do you remember the Appeal of June 18 . . . It was just yesterday . . . France in danger . . . France outraged . . . Today once again France needs the same man: General de Gaulle . . . No future without de Gaulle! . . . France must say YES to him massively! Vote de Gaulle! . . . I went again today with Élie. He enjoys doing it. I don't really. For a short while I pretended to and then I stuffed everything into a garbage dumpster. In the evening there was a documentary on the '39–'40 war on TV. Papa still believed that the French would vote YES. They said NO.
So the General himself placed the block of the referendum on top of our block of Christmas in the snow. And then the people of France put down the "NO" block. Everything fell down. And the General resigned.

Dear Man Ya,
The house is quieter than a tomb. (I read that expression in a novel.) Papa does not go to work in the mornings. Since the General's resignation, he walks around the apartment in his undershirt and pajamas. He has brought up his old army trunks from the basement. He is sorting and rereading his old papers. He does not talk. Nobody talks. At the table, you only hear the noise of the cutlery and of the water being poured into the glasses. Papa is here all day long. In undershirt and pajamas. When he isn't digging in a trunk, he holds his head in his hand, sighs deeply, and watches us passing beside him as if we were prisoners on death row. Or else he stays in his room the whole

day. We don't see him, but his presence weighs even more heavily on us.

Dear Man Ya,
France is no longer quite the same without the General. Papa isn't the same either. A part of him has lost faith in the army, in France, in life, in honor. The other day, he shook his head and declared that all values have been lost with this sacrilegious vote. He has started to go back to the barracks, but he goes half-heartedly. He tells his friends that he has nothing more to do here. France has dishonored herself. He cannot remain in a country without honor. He is ashamed for France. He thinks aloud of the General, alone with Yvonne at Colombey-les-Deux-Églises. And he aches for him. The ingratitude of the French is beyond him. No, undoubtedly, he cannot stay. He is preparing for his departure.

Far from everyone's eyes, in his house in Colombey-les-Deux-Églises, I imagine the General. He walks with long strides, writes his memoirs, and glances out the window. He does not know that a Man Ya from Routhiers-Capesterre exists, his glance does not reach that far. He won't speak about her in his memoirs. Before her departure, Man Ya had told us: "*An ké prié ba zot!* I am praying for you!" Her prayers worked. Perhaps one day, in another world, they will tell the General that there once were old black women in the country parts of Guadeloupe, simple women who could neither write nor put two words of good French together, women who turned the times in France upside down and shrunk miles and miles of oceans.

Dear Man Ya,
We are leaving soon, soon.

Dear Man Ya,
It's summer, perhaps the last here. We are in Aubigné-Racan. I strain my ears to hear every conversation the grown ups have. Transfer, that's a word that says a lot about leaving. Leaving. Home. Martinique. Guadeloupe. Waiting. Waiting. The signs are

good, Papa decidedly does not accept the idea of his General de Gaulle not doing anything anymore besides writing his memoirs.

Dear Man Ya,
I am back at school. For how long? We are going to leave. But when? Patience . . . Be patient for a little longer. My feet have gotten bigger again. I am afraid of getting there all grown up. My God, make me be a little girl without my period again. Sometimes I close my eyes, I clasp my hands. I ask the Good Lord to take the world back to when I was ten. You are leaning on the kitchen window, and you are looking at Sacré-Coeur in Montmartre.

Dear Man Ya,
I cry for nothing. Everybody gets on my nerves. The grownups don't speak to us. We have to be listening constantly to catch any fresh news. Manman is waiting like the rest of us. Is this transfer going to come soon?

Dear Man Ya,
Paul will not come with us. His life is here now. He has a fiancée who he is going to marry. He has his work, his friends. He is too big. He grew up here. He no longer dreams about the West Indies. The days are going by. We are getting used to living with Papa's silence. He doesn't talk about leaving. But we all know that it will be soon. We have taken out our coats from last year again. Too small, of course. But there is no question of buying bigger ones; it's the last winter . . . I am standing at the kitchen window. You know, I don't need to climb on a stool anymore to lean on it. I am looking for Sacré-Coeur through the grayness. If I strain my eyes a little, I can see beyond thick layers of cold. I fly over the ocean. And I reach Guadeloupe. I don't feel the cold anymore until Manman shouts to me to close the window.

Dear Man Ya,
We are leaving on January 10. For MARTINIQUE. The date fell from Papa's lips like a death sentence. He is leaving like a

conquered warrior. Instead of showing our joy, we kept our tense appearance all day long. While we packed our things in army trunks, we spoke in undertones about our future life. We had to give away or throw out a lot of things. We gave up our toys. Too bad! We are leaving, we are going to cross the ocean, to go back to the West Indies! Thank you, God! The big move is coming soon.

Dear Man Ya,

All the numerous little windows in the project did not shed a tear seeing us leaving for good. It was snowing this morning in Paris. We got to Aubigné-Racan in the afternoon. The rain was waiting for us. Papa and Manman do not laugh. Everybody is on edge. I am writing in secret. We spend our days working, putting things away, cleaning, making packages. We stop at night to begin again the next morning before sunrise. Our joy is tempered in an atmosphere of shouts and madness. I can't tell you whether Papa is happy or unhappy to leave France to go back to the West Indies. He is not selling the house in Aubigné. Everything that we can't take is staying there. Last night, the 31st of December 1969, Papa woke us up suddenly . . . "Get up in there! You are not going to begin the year in your filth, your bad thoughts, your idleness! Go and have a bath! And pray to God! We are going back home soon. You must get started! Ask God to take away all your sins, your lies and your vices!" We obeyed, of course. One after the other we went under the ice cold shower. We soaped our bodies, praying to God to cleanse us of all our sins, to take us back Home clean and pure.

Farewell, Bamboula

Bamboula
Négresse à plateau
Y'a bon Banania
Snow-White
Farewell
Farewell . . .

All those names followed us as far as Orly. They made a sort
of untidy guard of honor, then remained at the foot of the plane
steps, arrogant and pitiful, half torn. While we were going up
the big staircase, I could feel their stares in my back, ready to
pounce. But their feet remained caught in the snow.

I was saying to myself: where we are going, blacks are at
home. Never again will I let anyone call me *Bamboula* . . .
Never. Never again will I go and hide the blackness of my skin
under a desk . . . I will not be the fly in the bowl of milk any
more, nor little black riding hood, nor the only black that they
love among all the other blacks that they hate . . . Never again
will sleep hurl me headlong into the void. And I will be myself
in my people's country. Where I am going, people of color—as
whites put it—have the right to speak out, to appear on television, to be angry too, and to be proud, just as whites are proud
of themselves . . .

I was saying to myself: over there I am going to find books
that tell stories about the lives of black men and women, love
stories, tales of adventure where all the heroes are blacks. Black
Tom Thumbs, Sleeping Beauties, Puss-in-Boots.

I was putting out promises like a climbing vine stretches out
its tendrils: Here I am! I am bringing my arms to build this country with you! Tell me the true story; I will write it for those who

are to come. Tell me over and over again about the intertwined lives of the living and the dead; I will give life to the words and put old fears to death. I will make myself paper, ink, and pen to enter into the flesh of the Country.

I was repeating silently: At last! Thank you, Lord! Thank you, Lord! Let this not be a dream! Let me really be experiencing reality!

I saw Manman and Papa Bouboule in the center of their house. Figures from long ago came to meet me. The portrait of archangel Gabriel striking down the devil, beside a big mirror with a gold frame. Children dancing in the rain. Man Ya in her garden. Grandfather Asdrubal, turned into a gentleman, on his old horse, doffing his helmet and bending low to greet me . . .

I saw ancient black men, mulatto women with long hair, Indian women, blue and thin, carried by a little evening breeze.

I saw a frilly train of land emerging on the surface of the sea: the Antilles.

I was thirteen.

How can you block images from your mind?

How can you subvert the thoughts that assail you?

Sleep. Settle comfortably in your plane seat. Close your eyes.

Say: Have mercy! My head is full!

Alas, dreams come along like conquerors. Without asking permission, they capture sleep. They sweep along a little of everything, destroy myths, burn yesterday's idols, dismast invented islands where childhood frolics. Fears encounter *gens-gagés* who come tumbling in, their great wings unfolded in the whirlwind of folktales. Fears, aroused by the memory of a cane field, call out to the arc of the rainbow.

How to disentangle dreams from reality? Invention from truth? The real from the folktale? Put some order in your brain. Judge, separate, sort through words, surround yourself with reason and logic. Fear that these islands shaped at a distance are nothing but papier-mâché constructions, CinemaScope décor, *mornes* painted with poster paint to color exile. Fear and imagine that everything was invented by Man Ya. Imagine that slavery, Schoelcher, the Maroons, were only actors put on stage by

Farewell, Bamboula

Man Ya, just to give us pride, a history, an existence, a country to love.

Suddenly, see yourself standing, torn apart, like the black man torn between two lands, one foot in France, the other in Africa. All at once, put off the imminent arrival in the real Country because it will never be the one you have constructed, day after day, with scraps of memory plucked from nostalgic talk, from tales and stories of curses, of *diablesses* and of visions of extraordinary gardens, of rivers, of springs gushing from rocks, of houses with doors open to the four points of the compass . . . The warm sea, cassava, snowballs, coconut sorbet, savannahs scorched in the dry season . . . Laugh at your naïveté.

Won't we be strangers in our Homeland? That Homeland that beats and leaps like a heart, over there. Will it recognize us as its children? Snuggle up in certainties. Then fall flat on your face in doubt. All of a sudden, surprise yourself by chasing a fly buzzing around in your head. Curse. Realize that it is all about an insignificant question. It goes around in your head, flies, alights, and buzzes, annoyingly: what did Man Bouboule put in her creamy chocolate tea that made Manman's never have this exact taste that we have on our tongues, that we are forever seeking, that opens up countries of vanilla and nutmeg? . . . Gather together all the gestures of the ancestor. Close your eyes. Chase essences. A zest of lime. A cinnamon stick . . . An insignificant question goes around in your head, fills up all the spaces. And fragrances from yesterday go back through the course of time to sidetrack, confuse, scatter the thoughts that are trying to put themselves in order. Perhaps Man Boule used to roll the lime peel inside out . . . Maybe the vanilla came from an island, Anguilla . . .

Thoughts wound, sometimes . . .

Bamboula!

Négresse à plateau!

Y'a bon Banania!

Snow-White!

White hands throwing words as rough as rocks.

White looks, so white, staring at the density of blacknesses.

Light white touches on the woolly-black-sheep hair.

Have mercy! My head is full!

And what if the Homeland watches us pass by without shivers or sighs, as if we were strange bodies, just like the uprooted tree trunks after a hurricane that come down the flooded river, in the midst of rocks and dead animals, behind Man Ya's house? That come down the river to go and lose themselves in the sea and live forever tossed about, driftwood. That come down to go and batter themselves on the shores of continents. To go ashore in dreams. To drift without reefs or moorings. Never to turn back. And to end up one day marooned inside of yourself.

Sleep.

I see a procession. The Torturer is walking alone behind a cart that is taking a coffin to the cemetery in Capesterre. And what if Man Ya had had time to lose her life before I get back? Will the plane go faster than the cart? Will I get there on time to see Man Ya's face one last time?

Think about something else!

The din of the rain on the corrugated iron roofs.

Bush baths in enameled basins.

The sun pouring all her molten red gold into the sea.

Picture the blessed tree that, on a day of great scarcity, gave Man Boule three green mangoes.

Think of the lamp in the evenings. Its yellow light in Man Ya's house. The votive candle.

The eyes of the Holy Virgin in her golden frame.

The voice of Pa Boule who is no longer, his eyes that looked you up and down. His cane that hooked children.

Creamy chocolate tea . . .

A fly buzzes around the saucepan to be scrubbed. Alights on the cinnamon stick.

Coming back with so little baggage.

The plane will go faster than the cart, that's logical. Man Ya will be alive. You will have the chance to see her again up and about.

Think of your cousins. Those who were born at Home. It won't be too late to take part in their games. You grew up in France, but you will have a little time yet. You don't want a bun anymore, only the wild plaits of a little girl, plaits like horns that keep time from coming near you, that push it back.

Run in the savannahs.

Lose your eyes in the wind of the sky that is carrying away a thousand kites.

Build a house in the deep woods.

Park your shoes and go off barefooted.

Suck a mango right down to the seed.

Sit down to listen to a story and shout: *"Listikrak!"*

Believe in devils that come to catch children.

Believe that Back Home has remained exactly the same as when Man Ya was there.

That it doesn't go anywhere; that it is waiting for you.

That it was expecting you all these years.

Man Ya is waiting for you too, standing in her garden. Go, go! She will teach you the herbs for healing, the medicine-roots, the blessed barks. She will show you the secrets of bushes, teach you to recognize the jagged edges, the lacy shapes and the scents, the feel and the right use. Don't look her straight in the eye! Open your ears! Listen! Breathe in! Untwine the branches of the tree growing in you. Its sap will nourish you.

Take care not to walk about like a crazy woman! Careful. Right here: four-o'clocks, purslane, chicory. On your right: basil, ginger, fever grass, silver bush. You don't walk without looking, at the risk of crushing and bruising everything that I planted! Respect!

Think of the long, long time you are going to spend Back Home, God willing . . . Throw away snows and icy stares, shame and scorn, like useless ballast. Release yourself! Let France wallow in her grandeur. Burn your overcoat, your hood, and your stockings. Unravel all the canvases of the years Over There. Loosen up your body. Hold up your new breasts, your rebellious plaits. Tear down jails. Dare to laugh out loud because the *Bamboula* time is coming to an end.

No, Man Ya is not dead. You will have time . . .

Call on the holy apostles, the angels and archangels, the Good Lord, the Virgin Mary . . . May they protect the plane.

Colors

Spell the names of the souls in distress, people of the night, spirits who roam the earth, the air and the seas, the powers of darkness. But don't let them intertwine their wings with the two wings of the plane!

Think of that world that you have never seen, living and dead, humans and animals . . . devils and *diablesses,* dogs that speak, three-footed horse, Josephine Tascher de la Pagerie, Maroons, Epiphanie and Apolline, Christopher Columbus, Schoelcher, and the toothless, one-legged slave, Ti Pocame, Kubila from Africa, His Majesty the King, Sonson, Br'er Rabbit . . . Think of Guadeloupe altogether . . .

Guadeloupe. In the process of moving, I mislaid the Rising Sun matchbox and, with it, all the little stones picked out of the lentils. Precious stones, without veins of gold or diamond glints. Rocks that add and subtract . . . Eight years in France. Four seasons and company. Three years since Man Ya traveled. Thirteen, I am thirteen years old. I have lost the little stones from my Homeland, but I am going back. Man Ya has marked the way. I am like Tom Thumb. His parents took him to get lost in the deep woods. There are always people who don't have anything to feed their children. Not even a crust of stale bread. Tom Thumb preferred all the same to have nothing to eat rather than to end his days far from his own. Worthless stones took him back home to his manman . . .

We are almost there. The island is approaching. Quickly gather up all the bits of your memory. Make an inventory. Scattered pieces, wonderful stories, vague memories, creamy chocolate, image of a big savannah with yellowed grass spread out in front of Man Ya's house, seeds of nostalgia, the warmth of the water from the bush bath, manchineel trees, seaside almonds. Sorry visions, rehearsed over and over again, hackneyed, worn out.

So many lost images would drift about in the everlasting recurrence of the four seasons Over There. And memory gave me back only these fanciful gardens. I had invented a Guadeloupe for myself alone. This 10th of January 1970, an Air France Boe-

Farewell, Bamboula

ing was carrying me toward this land that I had desired more than anything else, to escape from all the Madame Barons, all the distrustful looks, all the cries of "Go back home, black girl!" . . .

Sleep.

Fort Desaix,
Plateau Fofo, Martinique

It isn't really a fort like the ones we used to see in movies about cowboys and Indians. More like one of those American bases that we saw in films from after the war. Buildings rapidly put up to store machines, armaments, military and household supplies. Plenty of everything, protected, jealously guarded. A constant coming and going of French army uniforms, jeeps, camouflaged, khaki brown, and dark green vans that give you the feeling of being at war. In a perpetual state of siege. In a Country conquered, but not really subjugated.

Fort Desaix, that's where they took us as soon as we got off the plane.

Becoming aware that at last we have reached our destination, understanding that indeed our feet are treading this soil, dreamed of for so long, is a painful and violent mental exercise. We are really in the West Indies. In Martinique. Guadeloupe is very near. The recollections that memory imprinted in us resemble the landscape of this neighboring land. The faces express the same suffering and the same dreams. The Creole that Man Ya spoke to us is here, in the streets, in the market, in school, in freedom. It expresses moods and the weather, business, love and its games, the everyday, anger and excess. It is in the songs. It gives change, it insults, and sizes up, and woos.

In Martinique! How to acknowledge this marvel?

Joy, shivers, ecstasy mix. Yes, it's really about the rest of us, it reaches us in our flesh. Indeed it is about our very lives. We have come back, even if no one was asking after us, even if our absence did not weigh heavily on anyone's heart. Man Ya, Man Bouboule, the families in Capesterre, Trois-Rivières, and Goyave, we missed them so much, even those we have not met. All we will have to do is take one last breath, make one big leap, to straddle the sea that separates us. So little sea. But time is less pressing now. This interval can last a bit. The greater part of the journey is over. I imagine the soldier from the colonies coming home from war. Exhausted by the echo of gunfire, he brings back with him the gasps of the wounded and the heat of the battles. He is returning home, rich with nothing but his poor life, happy, insolently whole.

The day after our arrival, Rémi, Élie, and I chatter away for a long time before leaving the house, without permission, to see the sea in its true splendor. Our parents are dealing with some army matter elsewhere. The sea is there, so near. The window promises it to us. Yes, we will have the time to go and to come back. We have the right to go just to dip our feet in it. That morning awakened us as different people, enterprising, rash, freed from the shackles of discipline that ordinarily restrict all our actions. Something in the air encourages us to leave the precinct of the fort, gives us the right to defy prohibitions, to remain deaf to the voices of prudence and threat that went up, singing the lament: "Don't do this! Don't do that!" A breeze, stronger than the fear of spankings, draws us, while the sea, at the window, unfurls its breakers. To wait for our father's consent suddenly seems to us unspeakable. We survived in France. We endured all those years of life spent Over There. After this period of penitence, a minute lost is equal to ten centuries, an hour to eternity.

We set off, without a care, clothed only in our rights. We walk along without ever losing sight of the sea. The places are not strange. Everything here is unknown and yet recognized. Zinc roofs, houses made of gray board, verandahs with doors opening on a bed, with a flowered coverlet, a rickety rocking chair, curtains chatting with the wind. Everything here is friend and foe. Tall green bushes and red flowers. What are the names of these varieties? We don't know anymore. Perhaps we have never known. Yet there were some in front of Man Bouboule's house. Memories of poisonous flowers, careful! Don't touch! Flowers with big prickles. Red, yellow, pink, orange flowers. And the road climbs and urges us on behind Élie, who is leading the procession, reciting to us the best parts of his crossing of Paris, holding Man Ya's hand. Let's go on! Until we reach our destination, we too, like Man Ya, who did not know the streets of Paris and yet got there.

Everything here causes amazement, because poverty and splendor, beauty and ugliness are so intertwined, so interlocked, so overlapping. Houses just started or being completed, perched on piles. Unfinished walls made of blocks, overgrown with weeds. Chipped fibrocement slabs screening a dark kitchen and saucepans hanging on the walls, saucepans sparkling like magic stars in a black sky. Sand from the seaside, decorated with shells, spread under the cool of a venerable old tree that watches over people and imposes its rhythm. Piles of gravel waiting for a helping hand. Innumerable, perilous steps that descend between zinc roofs rusted like the devil.

And then there are the people: men and women in conversation on the side of the road, striking poses, relating a piece of news in Creole. Straw hats. Handkerchiefs that dry sweat. Arms akimbo, hips swaying, to express contempt. Broad laughter to defy poverty, patched clothing, toothless mouths. Stops to gird one's loins. Probing looks that wordlessly find their mark. Signs of the cross. Jaws clenched from straining. Colored ribbons in girls' hair. Polished dress shoes. Shoes with the toes cut out to last a little longer and to give space to growing toes. Dresses of white lace and silk side by side with rags . . .

Our eyes see too much for one day. Each step takes us back deep inside ourselves. All the poverty of the surroundings speaks to us and consoles us, tells us: "You are from here!"

Suddenly, roosters with feathers trimmed into a point leap in narrow wire cages. We run. Farther on, a black pig covered with dried mud grunts and stares at us as if he were asking for something. A tree with round, green fruit tells him in reply that we are looking for the sea. We run. We run the whole length of the road, on a narrow strip that descends sharply between tall weeds and a gutter carrying along dirty water from the *mornes*. We run toward the sea. The sun is giving such a strong light that we have to lower our eyes. And then we are looking into the darkness of houses, where poverty hides its oracles: votive candles, horseshoes, blessed crosses, scissors in the form of a cross, holy icons. There an old lady nods her head to the sound of memories crowding in under a faded madras head-tie. Outside plates and cans recycled as tin cups are drying in the open air, on a twisted board. Washing adorns stacks of red bricks. On lines strung between the houses, trousers spread apart beat, flap, and struggle in the wind. And white blouses, caught on the branches of a pea bush, call out for help.

We are going to ask our way. An old man is coming up the hill, cane in hand, small tie shiny like a smoked herring, white shirt jacket over gray trousers, shiny, squeaky shoes . . . Please, sir, is the sea still far away? . . . He laughs. His entire body shakes with laughter that rolls out, a bag of marbles thrown on purpose at our feet. Let's go on! We have to believe that it is really there, the sea, since we can see it beyond the roofs. Let's go on for a little longer, exclaims Élie, in spite of the laughter, which makes him falter. We are not very far away from it now . . . Remember Man Ya, who walked through Paris until nightfall to see Sacré-Coeur.

Alas, the sea, unfurling its waves out there, seems to get neither closer nor farther away. It simply seems inaccessible. We would have to cross this bustling town that has risen up between us. High buildings, new, white, in view after the houses. Electric poles intertwining their wires in the sky. Fort-de-France. Bold structures sprout up on one side of the *morne*. Zinc and wood, any old way, stakes, rickety beams holding up unfinished houses, gaping holes for doors, and missing windows that promise to come one day, God willing. Narrow roofs. One-room structures. Shelters erected in one night. Fort-de-France. A hive of lives. Shouts. People in a hurry who conduct business and go about their affairs in a determined way. Jet-black women walking like men. One, carrying a tray on her head and calling out to the customer: "*Doudou-chéri,* darling, come and buy from me!" And in her voice, in her cries, you understand that there is urgency. She must sell all her wares, cakes and sweets, coconut

Colors

cakes and lollipops, peanut brittle and roasted peanuts in paper cones. You understand that she must go back home with money for there are mouths to feed . . . How many? Four, five . . . She laughs and sweats beneath the tray that she sometimes holds with one hand. No one can sing the praises of her sweets better than she can. Her words flow thick and serious in the smile that she gives the customer. And then, all of a sudden, all the hardships of existence crease her face, and her features harden for a moment with an ugly thought.

Suddenly, fear takes hold of us. We have gone too far. We don't know how to tell the time by the sky. We did not take note of our route. Terrified, we retrace our steps in haste. Too many expressions on the faces. We are not used to it. Eyes that speak. Mouths that twist with raw suffering. Bodies that move about as if they are running to some battle. Bodies in no hurry that hang about and go back and forth. Faces on which are written all the strong emotions that you find in novels: love, hate, anger, scorn, jealousy, adoration . . . Words that sum up the world in three words: parables, maxims, reprimands. Words that tear down: insults and rolling tongues, hissing, "Ah-hah now" . . . And crazy colors put together as if to disturb and defy the palettes of good taste manufactured day after day according to the canon from Over There. No, we are not acclimatized to these excesses, to these eloquent faces, to this fever that inhabits the street. And then, there are all these blacks around us. So many black people, more or less black . . . *chabins* like Rémi, black women with straightened hair, others with afros wearing African *boubous,* mulatto women with long hair, touching their bottoms, *capresses* with light eyes, red-skinned blacks, pink albinos with yellow hair, indefinable mixtures, *métis* with Arab faces, replicas of the Surfs, Nancy Holloway or Tom Jones doubles, whites with red shoulders, freckled hands, whites with peppercorn hair, pale Chinese in the shadow of a counter, dark Malabar Indians, shadows of East Indians, sharp noses, shiny straight black hair, brushing against shop windows that offer: cloth from the Orient, Limoges china, American goods . . . And then there is also this deafening music that carries words about love, abandoned and torn, about impassioned declarations. And people walk along, buy and sell, and cut their prices, to the insistent music of these tunes that deafen our ears with a new sound and awaken all our senses. Neither Sheila, nor Claude François, nor Henri Salvador, nor the Compagnons de la Chanson . . .

Two feet in the town, we are reeling. A kind of intoxication comes over us, as if we were on the edge of an abyss, as if we had to decide whether or not to throw ourselves into the lava of a volcano.

Fear grips us. No, we did not want to go running to meet death. A force possessed us. A mischievous spirit must have led us to leave the security of the fort. What do we know? We don't know anything about this place.

Fear grows and then bursts like gall deep down inside us. Perhaps the old man was a *soucougnan*. The houses, the flowers, the curtains, the glitter of the saucepans, were no doubt just the décor of a great diabolical theater. All these people, minor players in a bad play, a caricature of the world. And the temptation of the sea that kept growing more and more distant was surely a lure to entrap us. Weren't we going to become lunch for some Beelzebub from a neighboring region? Thanks be to God we escaped from this bewitchment alive. From now on we know that we must proceed with caution. You don't get in without permission. Fort-de-France is seething. Hot! You risk getting burned at each turn in the road. You have to give warning of your arrival, wait to be invited. Don't get caught up in a voracious desire for images, sounds, sensations. Fort-de-France is alive. She has a body and a spirit.

Approach the town patiently.

Wait until she opens the door to you.

You will receive her favors when your time comes.

Behind the windows, the horizon drawing her lines is not deceptive . . . You see what you want to see: the sea two and a half steps away, a Sacré-Coeur as the Kingdom of Heaven, the Holy Virgin's smile in the rounded clouds, an entire world wedged, like an orange, in the palm of a hand . . . Sometimes the windows break the rain's blues and reflect rainbows invented by your eyes. The images that they frame sometimes ease the heart and tell sentimental tales of love. You need to know that the seashore is always far away for those who believe in nothing.

Man Ya is no longer very far away. We will see her in the long vacation, Papa has promised us. An army Fokker aircraft will take us to Guadeloupe. We don't stop dreaming about this reunion.

For the time being, we leave Fort Desaix for a vast concrete house perched on Plateau Fofo in the heights of Fort-de-France.

We would like to begin a new life in these surroundings. Gather together bodies and minds to start over again with vigor on this side of the seas. Forget all the winters. Forget the searing stares. Forget all the *Bamboulas*! We would like to build our nest in that forest tree, that gum tree, on the trunk of which is carved: Take flight, my heart . . .

What essences perfume life here in this place? Patchouli, ylang-ylang, cheap lotion. Eau de cologne, incense, leaves for bush baths. Gather the smells. Recognize the balms. Unfurl your wings.

On what forest tree does life here in this place depend? Balsa wood of hope. Silk cotton tree with great branches where *soucougnans* argue endlessly while ginning cotton. Daily breadfruit. Trumpet tree. What color are words here in this place? Tell me! What is the weight of silences, gestures and looks, shade, breath, laughter—the laughter of this old body climbing back up the *morne*? Tell me the thickness of barks, cocoa pods, conchs . . .

What are the gods of this place, those who slash and who sever, those who bring morning, those who undo destinies, these others who rule and those whom you implore for health, love, money?

Don't harass your soul. Don't rush. Answers will come with the obstinacy of years. Like wrinkles or white hair, they will settle on you, imprint themselves silently. And you will surprise yourself one day, filled, you too, by the very spirit of the new world.

Go down to town. Station yourself by the side of the road. Raise your hand to stop the local taxi that comes speeding by. Intoxication. Take your place in the vehicle, packed in tight, one against the other, one shoulder up under the chin of a light-skinned man with a smile behind his moustache, one elbow in the stomach of an Indian woman whose eyes travel beyond the present. Walk at ease among people of color. All of a sudden, on the sidewalk, remain planted there, stupidly, a cry in your gut. Painful ecstasy. Understand that this Country, like Guadeloupe, has always haunted your heart, even if it was lost far from your sight.

Walk. Go along the buildings of the Brasserie Lorraine. Stride across the Levassor Canal. Feel life pulsing. Capture the smell of the fish market. Run your fingers along the white wall of the Lériche cemetery. Listen to the Creole speech that never ceases to fill the streets. Try to catch bits of words. Walk in the middle of fruits and local vegetables set out on the ground on jute bags. Find Man Ya in each old black woman. See her again in the housing project, sitting in the drawing room in front of the TV, hands crossed in uselessness. Remember her, in the middle of the night, waking one or another of us, deprived of dessert, just to slip a French apple between the sheets. Picture her in the middle of the market women. See her once again, stretched out on the bed, blowing hard as if to raise the sails of our return to the Homeland. Touch her in her joy on the day of the great departure. Understand her melancholy. Walk. Buy cloth at Meyer's because you have to sew and dress in bright colors here. Boys look at you and call you. Learn to walk in heels swinging your hips, like Martinican girls. Straighten your hair with a hot iron. Wear your hair in a bun. Learn to dance, to tell the different types of music: biguine, mazurka, quadrille, soca, cadence-rampa, bolero . . . Assess your ignorance. Open both your hands to gather one or two crumbs of this knowledge. Admit your hunger.

I don't seek them out, yet the boys notice me. I walk on the tightrope of their gaze. I pretend as if I don't hear their Pssstt! *Chabine!* Pssstt! . . . I learn to look them up and down. Because you must not smile at strange young men with your lips. Just walk past the thoughts of desire that they spread out like spider's webs. Only smile with your eyes. Don't answer their good evenings. You need to know, they take that as ready money and consider you ripe for the picking. Then they will follow you

through the streets of Fort-de-France thinking that you are taking them to some bacchanal. They laugh, and if your laughter
mingles with theirs, they will sing you songs and talk-talk-talk
trying to find your secret weaknesses. If you flinch, they will cut
you down and make mincemeat of you. It seems they have
sharpened swords that bring fire and life at the first alleluia!
They promise you the hell of a belly on credit. You don't understand. They wave in front of you the threat of scandal and
its trail of tribulations. You see the specter of a curse, but you
don't know its name or its generation. You become frightened.
At the same time your heart is happy. You are living. You are
walking on the tightrope of the male gaze.

The private school run by the sisters of Saint Joseph of Cluny
opens its doors to us. The daughters of army officers must not
go to public high schools. I am thirteen. In my class there are
pupils who are up to seventeen years old. They interest me intensely. They are already big women. Powdered, heavily made
up, hair straightened, curled, on stiletto heels. Some—especially
those who have long red nails—really come just to pass time between yawns and then amuse themselves by making eyes at the
young white VATs, technical aid volunteers, who are our teachers. Powerful cars with tinted windows drop off their majesties
in front of the school. Among themselves, they chatter away in
undertones under the noses of the nuns. Stories about adultery,
periods that are late, virginity lost or recovered a hundred times
by the magic of some infallible recipe. Stories, gossip, about es-
capades parked at the seaside or in the La Medaille woods. They
also go to nightclubs, and day breaks to find them with rumpled
hair and panties put back on inside out. They show off presents:
shoes, gold beads, gold watches . . . In closed circles they reveal
the names of girls who are pregnant, feel sorry for them, and
then laugh at their misfortune, before putting them in the hands
of God. At recreation I find out that some of them have already
had fights with lawful wives. In passing I catch the names of
generous married men, uttered in secret. I pass bits of paper,
notes . . .

"Meet me at eight o'clock this evening by the Croix-Mission."

Fort Desaix

"I will wait for you until three o'clock this afternoon on Madiana beach."

"My heart has been captured by two men at the same time . . ."

"The pain of love is healed by the medicine of another love . . ."

"Jealousy today, deception tomorrow morning . . ."

Grown-up black women sitting on school benches, these young ladies fill me with amazement. They belong to another world that is beyond me, that goes way ahead of all that I had imagined. They practice the art of love with derision and facility and take great pride in it. My innocence disconcerts them.

"What did you learn Over There?"

"My dear, you have never been with a man!"

"It's very good! Yes, it's good!"

"That's what life is all about . . ."

"It's not a sin to take a man."

"The Good Lord didn't give you a rounded mandolin to hide it. You must play it, girl!"

In the schoolyard, white girls from Martinique, called *Bekées,* meet among themselves, a minority. They don't mix with the other races, not even with white girls from France, the *zorèy* (daughters of soldiers and technical assistants mainly.) They count among their ancestors former masters from the time of slavery. At recreation, they speak the same Creole as the black girls, the Indian girls, the mulattoes, the *chabines,* and the girls of mixed race from here. They sport the same uniform, white blouse and red plaid pleated skirt. They have the same gestures, the same gait, the same accent. But they have to carry the burdensome legacy of their forefathers. So they maintain their rank and keep their distance, and above all they don't mix with the black girls. They keep their noses in the air. They look right through you without seeing you. The circles that they form open only to one of their own, who comes to put down her load right in the midst of the others, just long enough to do the rounds, to relieve a shoulder. They gaze at one another and seem to see a light in the blue of their eyes.

Colors

I have friends . . . black girls and *chabines* my own age who came ahead of me. They laugh at my Creole, sprinkled with RRRs, at all the French words that fill in the gaps of my lack of knowledge. They laugh at my ignorance about things basic to my survival here.

"Don't lend out either books or notebooks, pens or pencils!"

You want to be kind, noble. Alas . . . without knowing it, you have just abandoned yourself and your fate to demons with pretty faces. Be careful! These creatures visit cemeteries at the farthest corner, where dogs yelp through their tails. They bury your textbooks and your future at the foot of a nameless tomb. The very next day, you don't understand your lessons anymore, you forget tables, theorems, the exceptions that make the rule. Your head is of no use, you don't know how to write anymore. In no time you end up illiterate, whereas you had been destined for a future crowned with laurels and rolls of honor from your earliest childhood . . . Your parents can go back and forth to consult the *gadézafè,* run up and down from Miquelon to La Pointe-Simon. They will need a lot, a lot of money to undo the evil and to find the page on which the jealous person exults. They can take you to the narrow path where your book is lying, already scarcely recognizable, eaten up by worms. If luck is with you, you can save a little of the lost knowledge, the dust of learning, ashes amid the bones. But at that point there are other recipes that they don't reveal to novices. So, always find a pretext not to lend anything.

"Don't let anyone lay hands on your shoulders or your head!

There is a very evil spell in that gesture. What do you know about the prayers they are mumbling at that very moment to ruin your parents' hopes? What do you know of the weight of ignorance that they are putting into this parody of friendship? How many papas and manmans implore God without being able to identify the root of the evil that is whittling away the fate of their future high school graduate, fallen into stupor or dementia in the space of one night . . ."

"Don't laugh, don't smile so easily."

"Don't be too quick to smile back! Devils too have teeth to feign friendship."

"Recite the novena to Saint Expeditus, the patron saint of scholars. Copy it out to ward off all the impediments that they are throwing at your feet to keep you from studying. Say these prayers with faith in order to succeed in your exams. Don't be afraid to talk to the Good Lord, who is listening to you at every moment."

"Oh Saint Expeditus, I come to you, imploring your prompt assistance, so that your powerful intercession may obtain for me from the Lord's infinite bounty the help that I humbly ask of the divine mercy."

"Oh Christ, protect us tomorrow and always, but especially today."

Thanks to these invocations, you can slip between the drops of the rain of jealousy that beats down on those who shine too much at school. So my friends put me on my guard, initiate me constantly. In confidence they tell me fifty true stories, extraordinary and magical, peopled with spirits and supernatural lights.

Nicole: "Every evening a flame used to come and settle on my wardrobe while I was studying. Instead of going in, the lessons would go out of my head. Every evening a little more knowledge went away. After a while, when the light began to pull out things I had learned in elementary classes, I became afraid. I held up the cross that I have around my neck and I cried: 'Go away, Satan.' The next day I began a novena to Saint Expeditus, and the light never came back to my room again."

Eloise: "Wickedness is a nation, and its color is black . . . You have lived in France, you don't know the first thing about bad-mindedness. Listen! I repeated grade nine not because I wasn't willing to work . . . Not at all! Jealous people had put evil spells on my family. They were like vines that kept us tied up in bad luck. Like glue. Like shit that stuck to our feet. My manman became distressed. She thought every woman was my father's mistress. One day my Papa raised his cutlass to chop my mother in two. It was the Good Lord who held his hand. He fell on his knees. It was the first time that I saw water come from his eyes. He begged my manman's pardon. And they went all the way to Diamant to consult a certain Mr. So and So. That's what saved them."

Marie-Anise: "Every day a neighbor would come to ask my manman for something: black or white thread, salt, bunches of local onions, lemon grass, scissors, an envelope, the last page of Saturday's *France-Antilles,* pepper, pumpkin. My manman, who is a schoolteacher, would give her things out of friendship or generosity. You can't understand those things. How can I tell you . . ."

"Yes, yes! I will understand!"

"Well, everything that my manman's hand touched would end up spoiled. If she was making a dress, she ruined the cloth; if she was making a cake, it wouldn't rise; if she was cooking fish, the sauce would spoil. And it was the same with everything . . . in her class things stopped going well: she explained lessons the wrong way round, hit the good students, and congratulated the idlers. One morning she got up with her hands swollen. All she did was soak them in salt and water. Do you believe me?"

"Yes, yes! Go on!"

"The next day there was pus under her nails. She saw forty doctors! She went all the way to France to listen to the tales of the most eminent professors. And then, one day, they spoke of amputating her two hands. Her nails had become black. There was a threat of gangrene. Everyday she was talking about the cemetery and her burial. My papa was already consoling himself with another woman. Can you understand all these things?"

"Yes, yes . . ."

"Then, one of her old aunts, who came from Saint-Pierre, came to Fort-de-France. She immediately understood that it was witchcraft. You can imagine, my manman laughed in her agony. 'Witchcraft! Ha! Ha! Ha!' But the old aunt insisted and told the story that long ago, in 1902, a beautiful society woman had been through similar suffering, just before the eruption of Mont Pelée. 'Jealousy! That's the odious cause. And the remedy can fit in a pocket handkerchief: two prayers to be recited for thirty days from six in the morning to six in the evening, and tea made of three types of bush to be taken in the morning before sunrise, at noon before lunch, and in the evening exactly at nightfall.' The treatment went on for nine days after the swelling had gone down completely and the pus had disappeared from under the nails."

"Oh!"

"And that's how my manman was cured."

"Really?"

"Yes!"

"That's all?"

"Yes, that's how it was."

"And did she find out the name of the person who was jealous?"

"I don't know."

"That's a pity! And what happened with the neighbor?"

"She died."

"Oh!"

The Five Plagues of the Return to the Native Land

. . . There came great swarms of flies into the house of Pharaoh and into his servants' houses and in all the land of Egypt the land was ruined by reason of the flies . . .

Cockroaches and flies . . . The evening we arrived at Fort Desaix, enormous cockroaches—that we came to call beetles later on—covered the walls of the housing that we had been assigned. They ran about. Flew. Fell in our hair. Landed on our faces. I began to scream. Soldiers came rushing in, pursued them, crushed them. A shovelful of roaches succumbed to this massacre.

To see and hear for the first time their bodies crack under boots, dismembered, wings broken, with a disgusting yellowish fluid coming out of their skinny entrails, is awful. They hover, then settle on the walls before being assassinated as easily as in the movies. Sometimes a foolhardy roach dares to put his legs on my hand or on my foot or my mouth while I am asleep, a nightmare! I wash myself fifty times with soap; it's useless, at the spot where the creature landed the memory remains, making me shudder and itch for a long, long time afterward. They are shiny, they glitter like counterfeit money. But we have to get used to them. They hide their colony in the cracks in the floor. A whole world, in fact, that we envisage with repulsion. They multiply. They are there, with us. Everywhere. In the doorways, in the bowls, the cups, the soup tureens, in the sheets folded in the cupboards, in record jackets and the bound covers of the Larousses. We hear them going about their business. We imagine their bacchanal. We surmise that they are there. We have to live with them. Everybody lives peacefully with them here. Roaches. They go about alone or in swarms. And lay their eggs where eyes don't go, where brooms venture only once a month.

The Five Plagues

Roaches that visit drawers and tell drinking stories to their young ones, young ones that never stop being born and appearing and escaping being struck by Fly-Tox bombs. Feeling nauseated, wash every plate, every glass, every knife and fork all over again. Smell their odor in napkins that have been washed, bleached, ironed. Wash stained linen over again. Surprise a colony plundering the food safe, deployed on the bread, drawn up behind the rows of onions, besieging the plates. Intellectual roaches interested in reading, leaving their empty eggs stuck to the pages of books that we don't open often enough.

Little by little, we get used to them. Élie bombards them coldly with a chemical spray that brings down the whole mob at one fell swoop. Lisa crushes them. Sweeps them up. Manman sets glue traps. Puts out poison. Fights against them every day like an age-old enemy. I don't scream any more when they fly onto the walls; they are a sign of rain. I know that now. Sometimes we let one run away, out of pity, one day, because we see that it is nothing more than a hunted creature, a heart beating wildly, in a shield of ugliness.

Flies have their season. The dry time with its heat brings them. They put down their dirty legs on everything. Where do they come from? From some filthy place, of course. You have to cover food and not stand there gawking like some big idiot. Blue flies with shiny-shiny satin wings buzz around over there in the savannah near the big pats of cow dung. We know them; they lie in it, gorge themselves, then come and wipe their legs on the best pieces of our lunch. Learn to cover everything. Mechanically, as if that is what you had always done. Eat surrounded by flies. "You have to eat to live, even at the height of the fly season," says Manman. Sometimes a greedy, rash fly, especially in a bad luck wind, half hovers above a fish stew. It lands on a mooring made of onions, struggles until it drowns. It floats, legs in the air. But, no problem, all you have to do is catch it and throw it out the window. Force yourself to imagine that it did not have time to lose its fluids and its antennae in the sauce. Eat fanning yourself constantly to chase them away. They love the syrup at the mouth of the barley water bottle. They settle by the hundred on bread spread with guava jelly, on the glass of juice, on sugar at the corner of your mouth. Thanks be to God, this season is over, and the rainy season sends them back to their manmans' land.

. . . And it shall become fine dust over all the land of Egypt; and become boils breaking out in sores on man and beast throughout all the land of Egypt . . .

Mosquitoes and sand flies . . . The mosquitoes attack me constantly. In the euphoria of our return I don't notice that they are making a collection of my legs: Marks and Bites. I am patient. People say that the blood of children born Over There is sweet, to the mosquitoes' liking. But be patient, their attraction will only last for a while. Little by little—with the sun, the air that gives your skin its fragrance, good Creole food, fish, root vegetables—your blood will become like that of people from here, apparently. One day, the mosquitoes will get tired and go away, supposedly, to hunt in other new places, on other unexplored lands. Alas, after a year, the creatures are still after me. The skin on my legs looks like a country torn apart by bombings. A war that goes on and on and is becoming bogged down. Enemies, practically invisible, who toil day after day, *in an old silence bursting with tepid pustules . . . And it scratches, like an old poverty rotting under the sun, silently. And it scratches and it itches.* And the skin that is healing over is scratched a hundred times. Anger at having succumbed to the temptation of scabs that take too long to come, that open up to a drop of blood and rend the heart. The drunkards bite and draw blood. Night and day, day and night, insatiable. How can one little mosquito bite provoke such devastation? There are some wounds that one would have said were incurable. Memories of large infected wounds treated with penicillin. Holes left by relentless sessions of pulling off scabs. I pray that my legs covered with cuts might become like before. I hate them. Will the marks go away later on when I am a big woman?

Little by little, they heal, thanks to remedies, balms and bush baths, and especially thanks to the effort of will to control my hand that claws and scratches the mosquito bites. Use cunning to thwart their sense of smell. Plaster my legs with citronella oil. Rub the rebellious marks—every day, morning and evening— with cocoa butter. Be patient while standing in shorts that expose the shame and the unsightliness of your messed up, newcomer's skin.

. . . The river shall swarm with frogs; they shall come up into your house and into your bedchamber and in your bed, and into the houses of your servants and of your people, and into your ovens and your kneading bowls . . .

Frogs, green lizards, snakes, and mabouyas . . . They tell crazy stories about mabouyas.

Roaches repulse us. Mosquitoes eat us alive. But mabouyas terrorize us.

We feel a certain affection for the little frogs that spend their lives on the stovetop in the kitchen. They bathe in the sink at any hour and jump about on the dishes that are drying next to it. It never occurs to us to kill them. Among all the new species that we now live with, we consider them the most friendly. A chance encounter with one of them never elicits screams, even from the most easily outraged among us.

. . . I don't want to believe all the stories that they tell about mabouyas.

The green lizards avoid human company. They like to trail their cold bodies over the warm walls of concrete houses, but they like to be left to their own devices, to feed on flies and mosquitoes. The boys try to put lassos made of grass around the necks of green lizards. Not very skillful, they still keep trying all the same, to get to the level of the children from Plateau Fofo who came to us without being called. They allowed us to go into Zouèles-serrés and Délivrance as if we had always lived there. I think I am a little too old, of course, to be running about with them on the private property that serves as a playground for the neighborhood children. But I enjoy it, even if I think I am big and ridiculous to be running about and sweating, while the girls in my class are already women with rounded mandolins. Too bad, I play hide-and-seek. And when Josy exclaims: *"An nou pétey!"* my heart beats a little faster. A sharp point goes right through it, and I remember Man Boule's creamy chocolate tea. Same happiness, same awareness of a little something that gratifies and fills you until you are overflowing. We repeat: *"An nou pété!"* because we don't really know what *pétey* means. We don't pronounce it correctly. The accent from Over There has not left us. We only understand that *pété* starts us off. We don't ask for an explanation. We just repeat it to feel the Creole words sliding off our tongues. *"An nou pété!"* To bring back to life the language that Man Ya put in us. *"An nou pété!"* To fill with life the sap of the tree that holds our hearts in its branches. Sometimes I want to make myself see reason . . . Playing hide-and-seek is not for someone your age, girl! Leave that to Suzy. You want to wear a bun, straighten your hair, polish your nails, wear the latest style dresses. And at the same time you are running after those younger than you! Running after childhood kites that are now no more than little black dots in the great blue of the sky.

There are nations of lizards on the property. There are green ones with yellow throats, brown ones mottled with black, red ones with multicolored heads. Livio hunts them for his manman, who suffers from asthma. Apparently, she puts the lizard to soak for so many days in a bowl of milk covered with a napkin. Then, she drinks the milk with her eyes closed. Soon afterward she is sure to get relief. This type of recipe given confidentially amazes us and then gives us the shivers. Visions of lizard legs soaking and bloated with milk; nightmares of sessions where we have to swallow milk with lizard sauce, the hell of a lizard resurrection in the middle of your stomach.

. . . But all that is still nothing compared to the crazy stories they tell about mabouyas.

The long creatures from Martinique feature in all the conversations. We have never come across any. We must make them run away. Our warlike cries open up paths, and the sticks that go ahead of us make the tops of the high grass bend low. Plateau

The Five Plagues

Fofo remembers snake bites, hunts, and having caught some. They swear that serpents live in the field where we go to look for rabbit grass and Job's tears seeds . . . We go there all the same, following the neighborhood kids. They know. They have always lived here. They run about without shoes and laugh at our tender feet that bleed and protest at the first prickle. When it is the season for Job's tears, thoughts of snakes, disturbing them, death and the funeral that they are sure to bring in their wake because of their ancestral curse do not move us. We are there to reap what no one has ever planted. Each Job's tear is a pearl, and we are already calculating the length of the necklaces.

. . . However, there is something even more terrifying still . . . mabouyas.

The name alone makes us sweat, *mabouya*. The first time we see one we are speechless. We believe a piece of a nightmare has remained stuck to the ceiling. Then we scream Aaahhhh! These creatures come straight from the deep woods where there is no sun. Their skin is transparent and pale. Why hasn't Man Ya ever told us about mabouyas? She told us about *sikriyé, foufou*, blackbirds. She told us about Elephant, Tiger, Monkey, and Rabbit. But she forgot about mabouyas! Worse than rats. Worse than cockroaches and mosquitoes put together. Mabouya. You are sleeping. Mabouya is walking on your sheets, plakety-plak, plakety-plak. Your open mouth is dribbling in a dead sleep. Mabouya goes in as if to his own home. Your mouth closes, your life is over. Its padded, sucking-feet cling to the deepest part of your throat. You struggle. You are stifling. Mabouya drinks your breath little-little until it is no longer thirsty . . .

. . . *And not a green thing remained, neither tree nor plant of the field . . .*

Zeb-à-lapin, rabbit grass. . . In the project, the grass was forbidden lawn. The trees would stretch out their branches to implore heaven and to ask the Lord to bear one or two fruits for a season. The sky came out white in fine weather, blue in summer. Otherwise, it put on its gray and black masks alternately.

The trees in question had no name. They were planted as full-grown trees; then they were rooted up to add more buildings to the project.

Plateau Fofo, although the houses there were taking up more and more of the land, nurtured in each yard trees on which hung all sorts of fruit. Our preference is for mango, gooseberry, June plum, coconut, and soursop, among a quantity of others that cram the colorful stalls of the market women in Fort-de-France. They are new tastes that irritate out palates like all the new Creole words that we are given. We have to learn everything . . . How to put the coconut to your mouth to drink the coconut water out of it, without spilling half. To always ask to have it split in half so as not to lose your life through negligence. You never know, a friend of sorcerers can be watching for an opportunity, steal the coconut, fill it with an evil preparation that casts your fate forever into despair ad vitam aeternam fatalitas! Learn to eat the coconut jelly with a spoon cut from the coconut shell with a cutlass. Learn to soften the flesh of the hairy-mango, then to suck out all the juice, just as we learn to round the angles of the RRRs that give away all our incongruousness. Not to stain your clothes with the yellow-orange Julie mangoes. Not to say *"Mangue-là-ça"* but *"Mango-lasa!"*

When they are not bearing, the trees in Martinique whisper to the wind the mystery of their names. Recognizing the leaves to point out the different trees is a difficult task for anyone who has not grown up in their branches, who has not known the stain of *chenette,* the scratches from sour orange trees, and the rain under the leaves.

Papa has decided to raise rabbits. He has built hutches all along the fence. Going to look for *rabbit feed* becomes our cross. Recognizing the bush that brings life and not death, the one the rabbits love and that you have to root up from fences, pull out from behind wire fencing. Note down in your memory the places where it grows more lush than elsewhere. Rémi and Élie learn to use a sickle. A raffia bag on their back, they go into the field where the snakes live and cut grass for the rabbits. We, the girls, who are treasuring our long nails, are most often spared. Nevertheless, at times, I have to go for *rabbit feed*. Those animals eat every day, even when the boys aren't there. Are those leaves climbing up over there a good kind? Certain bushes are violently poisonous. I hate rabbits; they are always hungry. I loathe seeing myself, a bag on my back, carting around my load of *rabbit feed*. I detest these chores.

... *On all your cattle, which are in the fields, the horses, the asses, the camels, the herds and the flocks, there will be a very great pestilence* ...

Geese, hens, ducks, pigs ... The rabbits are no longer enough. Papa discovers he has a calling to be a great breeder of all species of animals ...

The house is a permanent structure, with a wide verandah in front. Three big rooms look onto the yard, planted with fruit trees that bear generously. A beautiful big white villa, with shutters painted green. On the walls, there is no wallpaper, only paint. Pink, mauve, blue, yellow, green, a pale pastel color for each room. Around it, an expanse of lawn leads us to believe that hard times are over. The hutches for the most part are the boys' business; thank you, Lord, for having created us female! ... Maybe we will be able to strut and pose waving our hands to dry our nail polish ... Maybe we can spend our whole vacation sewing dresses in the latest fashion to be on par with Martinican girls. With a piece of inexpensive cloth, we can make a dress to go to a dance. Art is in the finish. It took us a while to be daring enough to use the strong warm colors that hurt your eyes but attract glances. We learn to do it. Our hearts get used to it with time, develop a taste for it. Lisa abandons her navy blue fetish and discovers flowers and birds, seashores, checks and shades of colors. We give up the severity of pleated skirts, the formality of blouses with Claudine collars. We fall into mixtures of polka dots and stripes, ensembles in matching shades, cuts and cutouts, flaps and frills. We learn to match dresses and shoes. Standing in front of the counter at the MEYER shops, holding a sample of cloth, eyes lost picturing the outfit to be made, we dream of glamour and beauty. We want to be beautiful, big women. Puffed sleeves, skirts with flounces and lace, combinations of cloth, materials, and shades. Here it is not enough to cover your nakedness, just to wear clothes for the sake of wearing clothes. Clothing becomes adornment and plumage.

While we philosophize, pulling the cloth of our dream dresses under the needle of the sewing machine, Papa envisages a farm in the grassy yard, which sleeps tranquilly under the fruit trees. He counts how many hands his children have. Since it isn't good to encourage laziness and idleness (grandmother of all vices, cousin to jealousy and witchcraft), he calls his sons and daughters. Right away, in one day, the chicken house and the pigpen for Plateau Fofo farm are built. The following day, a pipe attached to a tap in the garage gives water. The evening of the third day, feeding troughs, drinking troughs, and roosts appear. The fourth day brings chicks to feed on the grain. The fifth day, geese, ducks, hens, guinea fowl and gamecocks. The sixth day, the pig, its emissions, its grunts, come on the scene. And its life, the promise of black pudding, legs, and chops, mortgaged until Christmas.

If girls have the right not to be able to use a sickle to cut grass, they have the ability to feed the pig before going to school and the capacity to clean the pen, full of excrement and dirty water, and of stale, rotten feeding, of swollen old bread, of green bananas that soak in the mud, and of peelings in the midst of excrement, that the pig eats and eats, grunting contentedly. Impossible to escape. Papa has no regard for how much patience it takes to get nails of the same length. Neither does he have pity on our feet with polished nails that we have to put in boots always a little muddy. He does not understand that we are not used to these smells and this mud, to all these animals that we have to feed every day. Through force of circumstances Manman has become a farmer too, so I yield, deeply embittered, so great is the hurt.

When Christmas comes, Papa slaughters the pig, then buys another that dies from an unnamed disease. The pen stays clean for a long time.

The Five Plagues

We ate hens, geese, guinea fowl, and rabbits, lots and lots. It was the period of grace, feasting, and hearty laughter. Then there was a sort of parenthesis. Time seemed to be suspended, nursing what was left of an old resentment. This moratorium did not last long. Warning signs came from the four corners of the globe. Fate attacked the farm fiercely and unrelentingly. Epidemics, decimation, stillborn chicks, yaws, slaughter, mutiny by the gamecocks, eggs rotten from jealousy, invasions of rats, havoc from mongooses . . . And then the time of Apocalypse descended on us.

. . . The sun became black as sackcloth, and the whole moon became as blood, and the stars of the sky fell to the earth, as when a fig tree shaken by a violent wind sheds its green figs. The sky vanished like a scroll that is rolled up; and every mountain and island was removed from its place . . .

Hurricane Dorothy, her black horsemen of the satanic troops led by the great dragon, came charging down, smashing and derailing the Plateau Fofo farm. Chicken house, hutches, feeding troughs, and everything else went flying. The paving and the walls of the pigpen were all that remained.

Facing the great wind. Alone, in the midst of dead creatures, stripped of feathers, wings broken off, heads cut off. The pigpen standing like the ruins of a city struck down by the wrath of God. Standing, to tell us that we could start living again. Once the hurricane had passed, all that was needed was a sheet of zinc, even one with holes in it, to shelter a young pig and on its head to build dreams of Christmas fare. Let us thank heaven for having spared our lives.

In town, the shops opened their shutters on a sight of desolation. The floodwaters rose everywhere, drowning animals, soaking goods. You walk in the streets of Fort-de-France with dirty water up to your thighs. Syrians, standing on crates, are already auctioning off bargains that Dorothy has put on sale: dresses with lace that has run, shoes with soles coming unstuck, out-of-shape hats, shirts that have faded and shrunk, suits with frayed linings. People go into gutted stores that wait for a proprietor who has no doubt drowned. They help themselves. They pick up everything lying around; resourcefulness saves you from hopelessness. Armed with long poles, they fish and haul in what the waters have swept away. Old schoolbags made of pasteboard float away in shreds, spilling from their ripped pockets remnants of notebooks and discolored books. A battered package little by little belches black nylon panties that float away on a wave, reaching the sea like schools of big jacks. A victory cup won by a cyclist, caught in the branch of a mango tree, is grasped just in time. A radio is saved likewise. A man with a round head inherits the windfall of several big straw baskets that came in his direction as if by special delivery. A patent leather shoe with a stiletto heel finds a buyer who watches in vain for the other foot. Thinking he sees patent leather in each flash, he wears his eyes out trying for the impossible. But night is falling. So, he goes off, holding in his fingertips the single surviving foot, which he eventually throws into the Levassor Canal.

Fort-de-France lives in the aftermath of Dorothy for days and days. And then the town looks like business is good once again. The Syrians' shop windows no longer display signs with discounts or extraordinary bargains. The women, traveling street vendors, have come back with marvels of linen embroidered in Tobago or Saint Thomas, lotions from Puerto Rico, miracle hair-relaxing products that make black hair smoother than European hair. New brands of lightening creams appear amid false braids and the latest style wigs from Miami. The town gets back its novelties, its hawkers, its crowd, its lively bargaining, and its sweltering heat. Sometimes your eyes look through a doorway and hit upon a tray resting on a three-legged stool, which still offers, for want of anything better, a jumble of goods from Hurricane Dorothy. But no one wants them any more. The colored cottons that you find on the counters of the cloth merchants have an originality that defies the imagination. Shoes cry out: "Please buy me!" The piles of chinaware with counts and countesses dancing on them say: "Let me waltz in your home!"

The Five Plagues

Life goes on again. The Lebanese still cajole the customer, flatter women, putting a hand around the kids' necks. They unfold their bodies in the same way. Hasten to take down silks and sequined shiny-shiny fabrics. Their eyes shine with the vision of the gold promised once again by Fort-de-France.

Guadeloupe

The desire for Guadeloupe overtakes Plateau Fofo. Daisy's thoughts have gone on ahead of her. She doesn't see us anymore; in her imagination she turns the pages of a book that goes back a long way, caresses old photos. She thinks of Man Bouboule in her widowhood, of Man Ya and her Asdrubal, laughs at the idea of returning to the country of her birth, then sees herself again at the time of her youth, on the verandah in Goyave, inventing tomorrow. She is going back home in the body of a mature woman. She has lived through France and Africa. She has tasted both. Over There, she has had to wipe away so many children's tears, tell stories, explain, calm . . . She cannot forget what they endured.

Go back to Africa!

Bamboula!

Dirty niggers!

Go and eat bananas in your straw hut!

A strange thing, her children want to be like the children here. They force themselves to speak Creole. But their Parisian accent does not go away. In their mouth, the words get stuck and mangled. Daisy did not teach them Creole. What would they do with it? It only escaped her when she was angry, to tell them to be quiet, to put a stop to insolence, or to command patience.

Speaking French is a sign of a good education and refined manners.

A man who speaks to you in French is a civilized gentleman . . .

A fellow who shouts at you in Creole is an old no good from a race with no upbringing, a *boloko* of the first order, a slovenly fellow with fleas, a rascal with a loose tongue, a thief with fifty-four machetes, a womanizer, king of the henhouse, a coward with long legs, Judas Iscariot, Beelzebub in short pants, spirits of hatred . . .

Ah! But a gentleman who talks in good French French is a spotless masterpiece, a prophet in a hallowed tie, the hope of a good marriage.

Shun the fellow with no prospects who addresses you in Creole. In the speech of a doomed black, there are cartfuls of scorn, caravels of wickedness, despair by the armfuls . . .

Nowadays, those kinds of statements, which young ladies of former times exchanged in the blindness of youth, come back to Daisy like a ridiculous refrain on a scratched record. See how everything changes!, Daisy thinks, talking to herself; times come to settle, one on another, like seaweed on the beach. Look at how nowadays the *pale à vyé nèg*, the old people's language, interests these children who were born in France. They put Creole high up there, make it a thing of honor and respect. They stumble over words that start off bravely and then end up tripping. Lost in the mystery of words—that easily carry fifty meanings, scales, sharps, and flats—the children struggle. They ask for translations in an undertone when everybody is laughing, and they remain there stupidly, mouths open, waiting in suspense for an explanation, always one laugh behind. They are from here without really being from here, but they have a go at it, every day, passionately, with the determination of city dwellers who are going back to the land.

Leave Martinique. Just for the long vacation.

Cut a little into the roots from here.

See Guadeloupe, Man Ya, Man Boule, again at last.

At each departure, you leave a little of yourself behind, even just the dust of dreams. They leave empty spaces in your heart, like those light-colored spots that are left on walls when pictures are taken down.

While Lisa and I were learning to sew, to walk like Martinicans, to dance to the rhythms of Rico Jazz and La Perfecta, to loosen up our hips in the cadence-rampa. While we were sitting in front of the stove straightening our hair with a hot comb. Polishing our nails. While we were dreaming of one day possessing the easy style of girls from Fort-de-France, what was Man Ya doing? What had become of Grandfather Asdrubal, his horse, his gun, his colonial helmet, and the nightmares that took away his nights? At the very time that we were busy growing up, struggling to chase away the RRRs that rolled off our tongues, what was Man Ya thinking about? For how many children was she still stirring her spoon in the saucepan of creamy chocolate? Where had the children who used to dance in the rain gone?

Lisa and I had left behind our baby fat. Awkward and self-conscious, as if in dresses with ill-fitting armholes, we had become young ladies embarrassed by our new bodies. And even if I often wavered between playing the Deliverance in the yard and striking poses of a grown-up woman with my grazed knees that did not fit well with my female aspirations . . . Even if I wanted to recover childhood years, like my due, I did not stop growing and maturing. This time seemed to me then like the light of a beacon on the horizon, my eyes constantly seeing and then losing sight of it. The mangoes that hung from the trees had their season to grow and to mature. I was beginning to understand that the time had also come for me to give up the regrets that weighed down my shoulders. Each time that a boy's eyes met mine, I knew that I was no longer a little girl. When one of the beauties from the sisters' school spoke about her nights in the love of a man, my body showed signs of other games to come.

Leave Martinique.

I thought I had kept the memory of Capesterre faithfully. I saw the road to Man Boule's old-fashioned house as bigger. I remembered a huge savannah. Long ago, legendary bulls guarded the outskirts. One of them had even chased me one day when I wore a red dress. I had pictured a long wide veranda, with flowers, beaten by the sun. What! A narrow gallery squeezed its rough-hewn benches behind two or three old hibiscus bushes. Man Ya's house had fallen to ordinary dimensions. And the drawing room where we used to sleep, how many of us . . . ten, fifteen, was reduced to a narrow little room where, at present, we constantly got in each other's way. The prints of saints were still there, the Last Supper, Jesus Christ in the middle, the heavenly angels, Saint Michael striking down Satan. But these naive images, crinkled under their glass, had lost their fascinating power of protection. The spell was broken. And everything now seemed vulnerable and fragile, in a state of neglect, subject to the elements, and even—more terrifying still—once again in the power of malevolent beings and all those travelers of the night who straddled the sea and turned the heavens upside down in a moment. A white building, housing for the schoolmasters, had sprung up in the middle of the savannah. Its four stories looking haughtily down on Man Ya's house said to her: "*Ka ou konpwann! ka ou konpwann! ou sé dé fey tòl et twa planch! Nou sé fè évè béton! Ou pa lan mòd ankò!* You must understand! Three boards, two sheets of zinc, your time is past, finished, over and gone!"

Man Boule still had her plaits, which reached—contrary to the yard-long braids of memory—only to the small of her back. She herself had lost her height, and her authority had gone away in the same wind. Recently her eyes had become covered with a whitish film. The tears shed in all her bereavements had left pain all scrolled up. In order to give them light to see, she washed them every fine morning with the last juice from the filtered coffee. In the first few hours, her voice seemed subdued, then chattered lightly until evening, without booming through the house. She kept herself busy looking after food and drink but scarcely went out anymore. Only to visit her doctor or to go down to mass in Goyave. Some children went to get water from the fountain for her. A boy whom she paid took care of emptying the chamber pots in the canal. She spent the afternoon curled up on herself, sitting on a bench thinking of the beach at Boule, her hands between her thighs, or else shelling a few peas, combing a child's hair, leafing through *Images and Opinion,* which showed her the kings and queens of the world and their grand marriages, legacies, testimonies, scandals. Elizabeth, Fabiola, Grace, Margaret, and the others paraded there in carriages, displaying their gold necklaces set with huge stones, their ceremonial clothing. Evening brought Man Boule back in to her rocking chair, a kerchief on her head so as not to catch the evening dew. Other hands now prepared the chocolate. A new gas stove had made its entrance into the kitchen. And even if zinc and boards were so black that they seemed to have escaped from some fire, fire was no longer the dreaded bane of former times. The creamy chocolate put to soak had also lost its charms, its essences, and its flavors. The rest of us had grown up, and we left to the little ones the concern of fighting over getting the bottom of the saucepans. We awaited more eagerly the Creole midday meal. The idea, the smell of a courtbouillon fish stew made our mouths water. Biting a pepper no longer frightened us. And with lips on fire, we were in heaven, eyes watering, sniffling and sweating.

Man Ya!
Man Ya!
Here we are!
Man Ya!
No one had told her we were coming. So, when she saw us, Julia started to dance, sing, and shout in the middle of the narrow path in front of her house. Her tears expressed her joy, and her eyes shone differently in that eye water. How many? . . . Scarcely four years since she left us. It is silly to cry. *Pa pléré sé ti moun-la! Pa pléré!* Don't cry, children! Don't cry! Wipe her face to see and look, measure how much taller we had grown during the absence. Have we got fatter? She laughs. We must go in! Can't stay in the street! There are so many cars in Routhiers now. Route taxis that come and go all day . . . It would be idiotic to come this far and to die by being run over right in front of my door . . . Come in, come in!

No one remembered Man Ya's house. Perhaps we had never been there. We had invented it in our dreams. In front of the door, quantities of coffee beans were drying in the sun on jute bags that we had to step over. Speckled bananas, eaten in places, hung on cords from joists overrun by wood ants. The house was not an ordinary house; it was a house with fifty doors, in front, behind, on the sides. Two or three steps came from nameless

rooms where round straw baskets, old cardboard boxes, empty
bottles, newspapers, and raffia bags were piled up waiting for
some future use. Under the sheets of zinc, which came close to
your head, the kitchen sheltered an old lamp on a wobbly old
table. It was the house that Asdrubal had put up. With scraps
from his pension, three bags of cement, ten blocks, three dis-
carded boards, he had added room after room, and he could say
that he owned a house, on top of the *morne* in Routhiers. Each
one now had a room. Thanks be to God, the trial of being alone
had made the man lose his mania for beating and kicking. On
her return, Man Ya had made him know that she had come back
a mad woman and that he was no longer to touch her. If he ventured to commit some outrage, she would not answer for what
would happen.

She wanted to give us everything, to see, to touch, to taste . . .
A piece of meat browning in a pot. A stick of sweet chocolate
made that very morning. A curry paste. Three breadfruits getting bigger on the branches. The room of the sad gentleman
with, in the middle, an ancient tin trunk, receptacle for all his
war things: helmet, gun, uniforms, puttees. On the wall, cita-
tions and congratulations that assured him of his courage and
of the recognition for which France was indebted. Her room
had a bed on four legs. Her dresses from France, that she had
preserved as they were, hung on a loose cord. The yard with its
hard-packed surface. And then the far end of the property: huge
trees that had seen a stream of nations long before slavery, forest trees hung with innumerable vines to make Tarzan happy,
plants, a thousand intertwined bushes, a thousand different
greens, and tall flowers, so red, so yellow that you would have
said they were the work of a mad painter. Behind the henhouse,
the river flowed rapidly down. Julia listed to us all that she had
already seen passing there, in the days when it was churned up.
Finally she showed us the spring flowing out of the rock, shining and sparkling, gurgling in the sun.

We want to go and touch that rock. At last!

Swim.

Go under the spring.

Right underneath.

Feel the water beating on your head.

Man Ya showed us all her woods, the surroundings, the yard, the love of her garden. Her prolific vanilla vine. Her *chenette* tree, her bell-apples. The giant nutmeg tree . . . Her eyes said: You showed me the face of France, now look at my country, as it really is, with its peaks and its valleys. Elsewhere there are certainly other lands that men and women don't want to leave. There are certainly other lands more beautiful, less ungrateful, without hurricanes and earthquakes and tidal waves. Interesting lands with friendly people that merit a visit. Lands that have never known blood, nor ever borne terror. But no one can prevent me from wanting to live and to die here, since you have to die somewhere even if you have circled the earth a hundred times in one single life . . .

Suddenly she clasped the trunk of a tree and disappeared into its branches. She left us on the ground, heads thrown back, in a daze, peering into the mystery of the foliage. There was no question of being worried about her breaking bones. In France she had told us over and over that she climbed trees; those words had not taken root in us. And now, she was up there, in the light, and we were down here in the shadow, quite incapable of following her. And the insolence of her old age, her plain knowledge, and the richness of her garden obliged us to humility. When she started to throw down bunches of *prunes-Cythère*, each of us knelt down to pick them up, or started to run, frantically, after those that were rolling down the steep sloping land. We ran, without being ordered or threatened, chased by the images from France that we had kept of Man Ya. We pulled them out like cards from the deck of memory . . . Man Ya in Aubigné-Racan, Man Ya back from Sacré-Coeur, Man Ya and the gendarmes. But none of these memories could be superimposed on this Man Ya who was laughing, way up there, in the branches of her tree. All at once, as always in these moments of confusion, time began to bounce along, like great wheels of a cart that bumps and bounces on a rocky road. While the sky held back the course of the clouds, a wind sprang up.

Then we truly understood what Man Ya had done for us . . . Cleared the paths of her Creole language. Layered feelings in the rest of us, pale, drooping young forests. Revealed perfumes. She had given us: words, visions, rays of sunlight, and patience in life. She had pointed out to us the three sentinels, past, present, future, that hold the threads of time, had twisted them together to weave for us, day after day, a solid rope bridge between Over There and Back Home. During all those years of snow and cold, she had kept alight the torch that showed the way. Her hand had never let go of us. At the time, of course, what she was offering us seemed uninteresting: useless rooms in a house that was too big, tasteless marinades of an outmoded past, an old woman's funny ways, a black country woman's Creole sayings, whims and wanderings, bilge from centuries of slavery. Educated, we wanted, at all costs, to teach her to read and write, to take her out of the darkness where we felt she was stuck. To our mind, to be able to put down statements on paper, to trace letters in ink, was the entire definition of knowledge, and a sign of progress. And here, several years later, at the foot of this tree, our certitude was in jeopardy. All our fine learning was rolling away behind the apples that Man Ya tossed down. And suddenly we were prepared to hear everything, to listen and to stack up for the future.

We did not have enough of an afternoon to survey her property, to go through her woods. The river saw us another day that I am not going to talk about, too much water has already flowed since then . . . While Manman stayed in town, with Man Bouboule, we went up to Man Ya's. In the course of these holidays she taught us to parch coffee. To see to the preparation of castor oil from the palma christi. To split cocoa pods. To pound on a *masala* grinding stone: turmeric, rice, coriander, cloves, *calchidron, coton mili,* to make the curry paste that Indians from here—who came from far off India, from Calcutta— had brought to Guadeloupe at the same time as their gods Maldevilin, Maliemin, and Kali. She showed us leaves and flowers and told us their names. To teach us, she made holes in the earth with her own hands and planted seeds, buried young stalks. We were at her school. And the little letters, so easy, that she could not write, the infernal alphabet, begged her pardon for having called her "Ignorant!" "Imbecile!" "Illiterate!" so many times.

I have never mourned Man Ya's death. She has never gone away, never left my heart. She can come and go at any moment in my spirit. Jump from a branch. Climb up the endless steps of the Sacré-Coeur. Her garden in Routhiers is filled with her presence. And the days to be hauled along until evening comes are not as heavy at her side. She is there, right now, today, living. At times she wears military dress. She writes Julia on a slate with a facility that you can't comprehend. She no longer bends her back for her Torturer's whip. She is sitting on a cloud. She is laughing and eating rose mangoes.

Glossary

Adieu foulards Literally "Farewell kerchiefs"—an old traditional song of farewell; *madras* is plaid cloth used to make head ties and dresses and typical of creole women's costumes.

An nou pétey A formula for starting off "Hide and Seek" or similar games; literally, "Let us burst."

Bamboula Frivolous, pleasure-seeking person; a racial insult, from a Bantu word for drum and the dance accompanied by this drum.

Béké(e)s (Fr. *blancs/blanches créoles*) A Creole term designating white people born in the Caribbean.

boubous Loose flowing garments worn in West Africa by men and women.

boloko A stupid, ignorant person.

câpresse A woman of a certain racial type, of mixed, mainly African, descent, often with dark skin and long wavy hair.

calchidron; coton mili Spices used in the preparation of curry powder.

chabin(e) A person of mixed African and European descent who has a light skin, light brown, blond, or reddish hair, often kinky, and sometimes freckles or light eyes.

chenette (Fr. *quenette*): guinep/genip/kenep: A small Caribbean fruit.

chocolate sticks (Fr. *bâtons-caco*) Used for making "chocolate tea"—sticks rolled by hand from a mixture of finely ground or pounded cocoa beans and hot water.

clafoutis Fruits, especially cherries, cooked in batter.

Dissidents In Martinique, members of the Resistance.

diablesse Also written: djabesse/jablesses/djablesses—literally "devil women /she-devils"—evil spirits who take the form of a beautiful woman and wander about at night to entrap travelers.

doukunnu (Fr. creole: *doukoun*): A small pudding, typically made of corn meal, with sugar, raisins, and spices, wrapped in a banana leaf and steamed. Sometimes spelt *dokunu, dukuna,* or *doucouna.*

femme/belle matador Literally "matador woman"—a strong, lion-hearted woman.

foufou The Antillean crested hummingbird, a variety of small hummingbird.

gadézafè Literally "one who takes care of things"; obeah-man, *quimboiseur*—person who practices obeah or *quimbois,* a form of dispensing remedies, healing, or casting certain spells, sometimes considered witchcraft and illegal in many Caribbean territories. The term *quimbois* comes from the French instruction: "Tiens, bois," "Here, drink."

gens-gagé People who are bound by a contract with evil spirits.

mabouya A small harmless reptile, resembling a gecko, with the ability to climb walls; some species have a dismal, hoarse cry. There are many superstitions about these creatures all over the Caribbean.

Maliémin A Hindu deity.

manman, man Mother, mama, ma in creole.

Marianne Symbol of the French republic.

métis(se) A person of mixed race.

morne Eastern Caribbean word for *hill* used in both French and English-speaking islands; a small round hill.

négresse à plateau Referring to women of an African people whose lips are stretched by means of disks; a racial slur, with no equivalent in English.

pommes-Cythère/prunes-Cythère Green or yellow fruit known by various names in different Caribbean territories: e.g., golden apples (Barbados); Jew/June plums (Jamaica); pommes-sitay (Trinidad).

poulbwa Wood ants.

Glossary

sikriyé (Fr. *sucrier,* literally "sugar bowl"): A small bird known as a sugar bird (Barbados, U.S. Virgin Islands) or as bananaquit, banana bird, or yellow-breast because of its coloring.

soucougnan/soukounan/soucouyant An evil spirit, a sort of vampire in the form of an old woman, who hides by day, but by night sheds her skin, which she hangs on a nail, to go in search of sleeping victims, especially babies, whose blood she sucks.

Soufrière A volcano in Guadeloupe.

soursop (Fr. *corossol*) coros(s)ol/kowosol: a Caribbean fruit.

Ti moun Child, children.

vieux-volant An evil spirit, like a *soucougnan.*

Y'a bon Banania Advertisement for a chocolate-flavored cereal in France which used a stereotypical caricatured image of a West African riflemen in native dress, smiling broadly.

Afterword

As a result of its colonial history, France hosts a large immigrant non-European population composed of a multiplicity of ethnic groups with overt racial markers. These people come from the former French colonies of Vietnam, North Africa (Morocco, Algeria, and Tunisia), Western Africa (countries such as Senegal, Cameroon, Benin, and Gabon), and the Antilles (mainly Martinique and Guadeloupe). Ethnically and culturally different, relegated to the lower social strata of society, these populations are often subjected to the contempt of the vast majority of the French. Various policies of *adaptation, assimilation, insertion,* and the latest watchword, *intégration,* by successive governments from the mid-1960s to the present have not resulted in the social, economic, and political incorporation of these immigrants. The concept of integration is the dominant concept today in France's political discourse. As Alec Hargreaves writes, it is "closely connected with a renewed emphasis on the 'universal' values of French republicanism, said to be exemplified in the integration of individuals—but not of communities—of immigrant origins."[1] France's identification with the ideology of "universalism" has functioned for several centuries as a powerful force of national cohesion. Thus, integration, interpreted by many as a new word for assimilation that seeks to acculturate immigrant minorities, has not translated into their right to cultural differences nor into their social and economic insertion. Even though cultural hybridity has become increasingly evident, and a large portion of young white French people embrace diverse ethnic cultural forms, the politics of assimilation continues, with the effect of ostracizing non-European groups from France's majority population and nurturing prejudice and racial tensions.

Afterword

It is in this context of alienation that Gisèle Pineau was born in Paris, in 1956, and was raised during the first fourteen years of her life. Her parents, who originated on the island of Guadeloupe, were part of the massive post–World War II transplantation of Antilleans to the *métropole*.[2] They had left their homeland to better their material conditions and their children's prospects. Geographically and culturally displaced, they were migrants but not immigrants, as they were born with French nationality and enjoyed complete equality of rights in a territory considered, since the departmental law of 1946, as within the boundaries of *la mère patrie* (the motherland). After all, had not General de Gaulle declared during a presidential visit that Guadeloupe was "a bit of France palpitating under the tropical sun"?[3] Indeed, the island is one of several Overseas Departments, known as DOM (*Départements d'Outre-Mer*). These administrative divisions, together with the Overseas Territories known as TOM (*Territoires d'Outre-Mer),* are the last remnants of the colonial empire, still administered and, one should add, still colonized by France. Along with other minorities from the former colonies, Antillean migrants generally live on the margins of French society and at the periphery of their cultural space of origin. As the daughter of a military man, Pineau grew up in the gloomy, mostly white-populated Paris suburb of Kremlin-Bicêtre, where state-owned housing was assigned to subordinate civil servants. There, the young girl felt outcast in an overtly racist environment. "Dirty negress! Return to your country!" she was often told by her classmates. "[I was] the only black girl in my class at the beginning of the 1960s. The only black to walk on the streets under the scornful gaze of the whites," she recalls in her essay "Ecrire en tant que noire" (Writing as a black woman).[4] Her dark skin made her legal status as a French citizen invisible to her peers and to the people in the street, who belonged to the majority ethnic population. Perceived as an immigrant, she was a victim of racism in the form of violent discourse, contempt, intolerance, and humiliation. She felt isolated and lived in psychological exile in the country of her birth. She yearned for acceptance and belonging. Where did she come from? Would she ever be able to claim a homeland? Would the color of her skin always stigmatize her? The Guadeloupe of Gisèle's ancestors had become a distant memory for her parents, who had silenced their Creole heritage to the point of denying it, trying to conform to the French way of life in the hope of being "assimilated."[5] Consequently, the young girl did not have a reservoir of traditional knowledge to fall back on for strength, support, and guidance. When the family visited the island for a vacation, young Gisèle, by now aged five, discovered a foreign country whose language and customs she did not understand. In the derogatory jargon of the local population, she and her family had become *négropolitains* or *neg'zagonals*.[6] They were disconnected from Guadeloupe's cultural milieu, and the children did not speak a word of Creole. Fortunately, her grandmother, Man Ya, returned with them to live in France: her presence suddenly opened a new world. Man Ya's stories and formidable personality nurtured the girl's imagination and gave her a sense of belonging that would transform her life. This is the story that Pineau unfolds in *Exile according to Julia*. She explains: "In [the novel] I tell the story of my grandmother, the six years she spent in France. [. . .] I lived in France an exile by proxy, at my grandmother's side because it was she who really was an exile. She had not chosen to come to France. She came because my father wanted to save her from the brutality of her husband who beat her [. . .] . So I was at her side, and I was searching for a hospitable country, and I recognized this country in my grandmother's stories. I longed to belong to this country, to say to myself: 'Yes, I am from Guadeloupe, me too.'"[7]

Pineau's quest for her grandmother's country is a metaphor for the exploration of her identity through her writing. Her feeling of exclusion reveals the double cultural displacement she experienced. She was not integrated into the dominant metropolitan French culture, and she possessed only tenuous links with her parents' homeland. Neither totally French nor Antillean, she was a "curiously vacuous hybrid," to borrow Adlai Murdoch's definition of Jérémie in Suzanne Dracius's novel *L'Autre qui danse*.[8] She felt that only by belonging to Guadeloupe could she give expression to a buried history that resonated deep within her. Only by belonging to Guadeloupe would she be able to recover her identity as a black Creole woman, bringing her voice to the voices of other minorities, particularly those of women. Through her own painful experience in the hostile milieu of Kremlin-Bicêtre, Pineau identified with her grandmother's traumatic displacement. Man Ya could not speak or understand a word of French, and she was illiterate. During the six years she spent in France, she remained totally alienated from her environment. But she nevertheless possessed an immense knowledge that she passed on to young Gisèle. She told many gripping stories rooted in the history of her island, going back to the time of slavery: stories about the Middle Passage, Schoelcher,[9] the Maroons, and so on. She told about nature's magic power and described the delicious aromas associated with its rites, medicinal herbs, curses, and evil spirits. She symbolized the island mother, a repository of the history of the people from whom she came, a history that became a source of comfort and pride for the girl. Man Ya's storytelling, exemplary of the island's oral tradition, was a defensive need for both grandmother and granddaughter. By reinventing the country, Man Ya found an antidote to her disarray and confusion in a foreign culture. And young Gisèle found an escape from the emptiness of her lonely life. Her grandmother's stories provided an anchor to counteract the erosion caused by the loathsome humiliations she experienced at school.

Thus Man Ya's oral stories acted as the catalyst for Pineau's writing. In her essay "Ecrire en tant que noire," she writes that as long as she can remember she wanted to invent stories, create characters, real and imaginary, just as her grandmother did. Writing became a necessity nourished by her "fascination for another world, powerful, visible, or invisible, so vibrant with life in Man Ya's stories."[10] Inspired by those oral stories, she would re-create them in writing.

Moreover, Man Ya's personality added another dimension in young Gisèle's development as an observer of the mysteries of life. She was bewildered by her grandmother's submissive nature as if she still labored under the yoke of slavery. Man Ya longed to return to her miserable life as the docile and cowed servant of her tyrant husband. Soon after she arrived in France, she fell into deep grief for her home, seemingly oblivious of the beatings and vituperations she had endured for years. For a long time, Man Ya's attitude remained incomprehensible for the young girl. But when she returned to Guadeloupe, she recognized the reality of servility, abnegation of self, and acceptance of suffering that is characteristic of the condition of many Antillean women. This reality prompted her to search out their stories and tell about their lives. She found that these women are abused by their men; they are raped and abandoned, and they are exploited economically. Nevertheless, they stand up for their men, forgive their outrageous behavior, duck under their blows and insults, and respond to their caprices. [11] These women are very real; they lived in the past, and they are our contemporaries. They have been silenced historically as Man Ya was. The urgency to relate the condition of Antillean women marks all of Pineau's novels and short stories and is particularly reflected in her 1998 book *Femmes des Antilles: Traces et voix* (Women of the Antilles: Memories and voices), co-authored with Marie Abraham. Through a series of historical reconstructions and autobiographical narratives, the authors give voice to black women's early plight as slaves and to silenced contemporary women. In the introduction, Pineau writes: "One hundred years after the abolition [of slavery], I listened to the heartbeats behind the long words and silences of today's Antillean women. Their past as slaves overwhelms them by its ugly light, at times blinding them, and at times illuminating them in a shattering way." [12] *Femmes des Antilles* is a text that combines recorded oral history with literary invention. It presents some significant similarities to Dany Bébel-Gisler's *Leonora*, a *roman-témoignage* (testimonial novel) that attempts to recover the buried history of Guadeloupe through the voice of Leonora, "a woman, a peasant, [who] speaks out to proclaim her differences and her contradictions, those of an entire people." [13] Pineau's approach in her fiction and testimonies parallels Bébel-Gisler's reappropriation of "anonymous" history. Through her rendition of personal experience and links to collective memory, she also joins an array of remarkable figures among Guadeloupe's women writers. There are Michèle Lacrosil, Suzanne Lacascade, Maryse Condé, Simone Schwarz-Bart, Gerty Dambury, Dany Bébel-Gisler, and Myriam Warner-Vieyra, to name a few. These authors speak for the oppressed who attempt to escape alienation and reconcile their present lives with their complex past. But they also reflect the specificity of their history and its evolution, and the changing paradigms that affect so many aspects of their present society and their own lives. Insightful and ingenuous, the author of *Exile* follows in the footsteps of her elders.

Published in French in 1996, *Exile according to Julia* is Gisèle Pineau's fourth book. It is an autobiographically based account of the author's upbringing in France and of her eventual "return" to Guadeloupe after a few years' stay in Martinique. The narrator, writing in the first person, begins by reconstructing the history of her parents and then focuses on her relationship with her grandmother, the Julia of the title, affectionately called Man Ya. Through this rather simple story, the narrator/author engages the complex issue of individual identity and expression in relation to her Antillean heritage. In her essay "Chercher nos vérités" (Searching for our truths), the Guadeloupean author Maryse Condé calls attention to the dramatic transformations that have occurred in Antillean society in the past fifty years. She deplores the fact that those changes, which demand "revised definitions of identity," are not reflected in the literature presently produced in the islands.[14] She subtly derides the rigidity of the literary rules advocated by the proponents of the Martinican-based movement of *créolité*.[15] She writes: "Antillean literature always wanted to be the expression of a community. Writing wants to be a collective act. When he says 'I,' the Antillean writer is supposed to think 'We.'"[16] In other words, the Antillean writer feels that he has a "mission" to accomplish. The author of *Exile* says and thinks "I" in her quest for her own cultural authenticity. But she also writes in the name of the Antillean people—"the 'I' as metonymic detachment from 'we.'"[17] Indeed, she raises issues related to collective history, societal forces, and cultural traits, but she also engages in linguistic creolization.

The Trope of Color

Pineau provocatively opens her novel with a series of racial slurs that she experienced during her childhood in France. She describes how these insults were acts of aggression on her body and mind, as well as on her siblings. "They splatter us with dirty water," "lost arrows, long and poisoned," "spitting on pride," "raining rocks on our heads," "our souls slip, crumble" (3).[18] Those lethal words aimed at "destroying" the identity of the children, whose visible features were inscribed on their bodies. Their skin color, a marker of their irreducible difference, erased their individual specificity. The degrading names hurled at them—nigger, coal black, snow-white, "Y'a bon Banania"[19]— had a dehumanizing effect: they remained nameless. As Jean-Luc Bonniol comments: "For Westerners or Western-acculturated minds, nothing could be more indicative of identity, in a visible and permanent way, than the *color of the skin*. In its wake, smell and presumed sexual characteristics constitute a rich reservoir of phantasmal differences. [. . .] Therefore, color in terms of difference is invested with a social meaning."[20] Certain biologic or genetic traits "naturally" determine exclusion.

The narrator's white classmates were conditioned by mental representations and a language molded by the ideology of their community. Their racial prejudice exposed a reductive apprehension of difference, resulting in the dissolution of individual identity into a collective entity. In the mind of the whites, the Guadeloupean girl did not exist as a distinct person but as the interchangeable incarnation of a collective type, classified in the category "black." Moreover, she had no chance to redeem herself, since according to racist thinking, intellectual and moral characteristics directly derive from physical and biological characteristics. In this environment, how could she escape the fatality of her physical appearance and remove the seal of her social marginalization? To build her self-esteem, she had to "find" her identity, that is, to experience her uniqueness as an individual and create a sense of belonging to a community.

Early in the novel, Pineau addresses another racial issue, which specifically pertains to Antillean society. It relates to the passage in which the narrator comments on the encounter of her parents, Maréchal and Daisy. When Maréchal, at the end of his tour of duty in Senegal, returned home for a visit, he met Daisy, his beautiful bride-to-be. Daisy was captivated by the perfect French of this handsome uniformed man and seduced by the dream of a Parisian life. Unfortunately, he was quite dark-skinned compared to Daisy's light complexion. But in spite of his blackness, she realized that she could not pass up such an opportunity. As the narrator says: "She could have looked him up and down contemptuously, squared her shoulders and given him her disdainful back, her corseted waist, and her outraged hips to gaze at. She could have smiled at him sidelong and said: 'You are a black man, sir! Go your way! My skin is too light for you!' *She had the right* to shower all those words on him, a man [. . .] bold enough to want to put a mulatress in his bed" (15–16, my emphasis). In this passage, Pineau touches on the ambiguous and complex issue of race in a society founded on the economy of plantation. From an original tabula rasa, these islands were settled by an imported population: planters born in Europe and a workforce imported from Africa. This organizing schema resulted in a phenotypic contrast linked to skin color. It legitimated, in part, the social order and hierarchical foundation of all plantation societies.[21] Consequently, Guadeloupe's human landscape—as in all Caribbean plantation societies—became permeated by what Bonniol has called a *functional* racism characteristic of colonial racism. Physical features and heredity justified social status and economic privileges based on domination and exploitation. When the plantation system ended, this racist ideology that had been internalized by all socio-racial categories served as the foundation of the "postcolonial" society. Racial stereotypes and myths reverberated from top to bottom of the social ladder. The white discriminated against the mulatto, who discriminated against the Negro, who discriminated against the Congo,[22] who discriminated against the Indian.[23] If in the Guadeloupe of today, the discourse of racial differences seems, on the surface, to have become irrelevant, the prejudice of color was still common in the 1950s of Pineau's parents. It induced social practices such as the choice of a spouse or a business partner. Daisy, as a fair-skinned *mulâtresse* (mulatto woman), the result of a mixture of black and white, "had the right," as the narrator says, to reject Maréchal, since her whiteness gave her superiority, regardless of her poor background. She was an ideal catch for any black man wanting to "whiten" his lineage in order to move up in the social hierarchy. From her side, she was willing to marry a black man for immediate economic benefit and social advancement. Indeed, Maréchal had strong assets in his secure army position and his mastery of the French language, an indispensable tool for accessing "the magic" of France and its "centuries of enlightenment" (15)!

When Maréchal was transferred to Martinique, a sister island to Guadeloupe, the narrator, now a teenager, discovered a world that was quite different from what she had experienced before. Although she encountered racial divisions at school, she realized that people were not strictly divided between black and white, as she thought back in Paris, but were composed of a bewildering array of colors: so many shades of blacks, so many variations of whites, infinite mixtures of African, Asian, European, and Indian. In this context, any notion of racial purity and singular origin seemed erroneous. She had discovered *métissage*, the reality that defines the complex structure of Antillean society. She too was the result of a *métissage*, the cultural emanation of two worlds: the metropolis and the Caribbean, France and Guadeloupe. She was ready to explore her newly found identity.

Creolized French and Grandmother's Stories

Similar to many works of fiction presently coming out of Martinique and Guadeloupe, the French text of *Exile* is replete with short sentences, expressions, or individual words in Creole and pulsates with rhythms that convey the orality of Antillean culture. Pineau's language can be characterized as creolized French. For most Antillean authors, such recourse to hybrid expression marks a conscious determination to protect and promote their threatened cultural heritage. It is also a mode of resistance to the linguistic control of the colonial power. "Language is a site of power: who names controls," Maryse Condé reminds us. "The politically and economically alienated colonized are first colonized linguistically."[24] Mandatory French schooling and the domination of French as the official language of administration, added to the massive economic and social transformations of the 1960s, have resulted in a general decreolization of everyday life.[25] This pervasive process was reflected for a time in the systematic deprecation of Creole by the colored middle class as well as the upwardly mobile blacks, who preferred the elevated status of French, synonymous with social and economic success. Moreover, it should be remembered that up to the 1960s, Antillean intellectuals themselves considered Creole as a nonlanguage, a language of nature reserved for familiar speech, absolutely unfit for literary production.

How should one define Creole? It is a language, not a dialect, "but it has no autonomous origin; unlike the 'primordial' languages in Africa, it was constructed out of the unequal, conflictual relation with the colonial language," writes Celia Britton.[26] It was born out of necessity as a means of communication between the European masters and the African slaves, and between slaves of different languages and cultures who had no common language to share, since indigenous peoples had been totally obliterated. Thus, diverse Creoles lexically based in French, English, Portuguese, and Dutch concurrently appeared in many Caribbean islands as well as in some nations of Central and South America. As for Guadeloupean Creole, it is composed of a preponderantly French-derived vocabulary and a syntax and morphology of African origin, and like all Creoles, it is fundamentally linked to the plantation system. As such it represents a distinctive marker of Creole culture. But with the disappearance of the plantation economy that was not replaced by any autonomous economic production, Creole has become a marginal means of communication in a country dependent on metropolitan subsidies and service industries such as tourism.[27] The Martinican theoretician, poet, and novelist Edouard Glissant writes: "Creole cannot become the language of shopping malls, nor of luxury hotels. Cane, bananas, pineapples are the last vestiges of the Creole world. With their phasing-out, this language will disappear if it does not become functional in some other way." For Glissant, who analyzes this situation in a Martinican context that is also applicable to Guadeloupe, the coexistence of the mother tongue, Creole, and the official language, French, provokes "an unsuspected source of anguish."[28] This anguish is, of course, most deeply felt by intellectuals, and writers in particular, who resent being linguistically colonized. On the contrary, Bébel-Gisler states that "despite all methods used (school, church, army, etc.), the majority of Guadeloupean peasants and workers think and speak in Creole, eat yam and breadfruit, dance and bury their dead to the sound of *gwoka*."[29] For them, the use of Creole versus French is obviously never discussed. For Pineau, whose mother tongue is "classic" French and whose second language is Creole, the problem of bilingual literary practice seems to be naturally resolved in her writing. Mastering all of the nuances of French and colloquial Antillean French, she resorts very effectively to the Creole language and a transformed syntax that translate the reality of Creole speech and the cultural environment of her island. In deconstructing the linguistic norms, Pineau "liberates" the French language from its lexical and semantic rigor, thus eliminating its alienating hegemony.

For the pre-1946 generations of unschooled Antilleans to which Pineau's grandmother belonged, the vernacular language was exclusively spoken. Man Ya never knew French and never learned to read and write. However, she was the depository of vast knowledge, passed on orally from generation to generation. Through her stories, tales, and riddles Man Ya fulfilled the traditional role of transmitter of her people's collective memory as it was practiced at the time of plantation life. During slavery and until the end of the agrarian economic system, grandmothers were responsible for the education of children. Their knowledge of history and nature's power and their wisdom and devotion to the group made them natural educators. With the politics of assimilation and the demands of a westernized lifestyle, oral tradition has almost disappeared in this part of the world. However, storytelling is being taken up by a written literature that integrates different forms of *oraliture* (oral expression) and gives a major role to the figure of the grandmother as creative power and transmitter of values. For example, novels by Maryse Condé, Daniel Maximin, Simone Schwarz-Bart, and Myriam Warner-Vieyra link grandmothers' storytelling with education, edification, or rebellion.[30] In *Exile,* Pineau conjures up Man Ya's stories, which she told like a living book whose page she would turn each night. When the narrator read the classic book by Thérèse Georgel, *Contes et légendes des Antilles* (Tales and legends from the Antilles), she had the feeling of having heard them before: "I found neither tales nor legends in that book, only truthful stories that made real Man Ya's words about the curse on the black man and the life of the spirits" (85–86). Thus, it was her turn to pass on her grandmother's knowledge. To recreate her world, she uses a "liberated French," transformed by Creole expressions and linguistic forms that convey the poetry, colors, ambiance, and rhythms of Man Ya's speech. This linguistic strategy that functions both as discourse and cultural sign succeeds in giving the narrative its Creole authenticity. When Pineau says that she aims "to make heard a different voice [*parole*] in the French language," she means that she creates her own creolized French.[31]

The Irony of History

Through the story of Maréchal, the narrator gives the reader a vision of world history from the perspective of the colonized. During World War II, Maréchal joined the Resistance movement, as did thousands of Antilleans and other men from

France's "et cetera of colonies," who fought for the freedom of the mother country (4). Urged by his mother, Maréchal joined the dissidents in hope of benefiting from France's prestige and establishing himself in society. Although his background and intentions were different, Maréchal found himself linked to the representatives of the mulatto class who enlisted en masse in the French army. On the one hand, they wanted to be assimilated into the white metropolis. On the other hand, if they admired France's institutions and values, they also wanted to counteract the power of the infamous *békés*, descendants of the former white plantation owners, who did not wish integration with France. As Burton writes: "Contrary to widespread anti-colonialist myth, it was French West Indians themselves, unprompted by governments in Paris or colonial governors on the spot, who desperately sought to pay the 'blood tax' (*l'impôt du sang*) by enlisting in the French army in 1914 and 1939. How better to prove one's total Frenchness than willingly to die for *La mère-patrie*?"[32] After World War II, Maréchal remained in the army and fought many campaigns for the Mother Country, learning to love her even more as he performed his epic duty. Inspired by the heroic paternalistic figure of Papa de Gaulle, he relentlessly served the *grandeur* of France with which he identified. "The army is [his] credo," he is led by "a spirit of almost mystical loyalty," comments the narrator (4). After the referendum of 1969 that forced de Gaulle to relinquish power, Maréchal, filled with indignation at the French people's "betrayal," requested to be transferred to the islands. He had chosen exile in his native land over a life of shame in the Mother Country!

Previously, at the end of World War II, Maréchal had been stationed in Senegal for a few years. This situation, as described in *Exile*, exemplifies another irony of history. Maréchal, whose slave ancestors were deported from Africa to Guadeloupe by the same imperialistic power that still controlled his native island, "returned" to the land of his origins as its military representative. Maréchal was proud to help France implement its civilizing mission in the African colony. But the family lived at a distance from the Senegalese "as if skin color alone was not enough to make family" (10). The narrator learned, then, that Antilleans are not Africans; they have been irremediably disconnected from their origins. More importantly, she has learned that the color of the skin does not define one's identity.

Conclusion: The Quest for Knowledge

In *Exile according to Julia,* Pineau constructs the story of a fictional heroine as a means of finding and defining her place in the world. By telling the story of her childhood through the voice of the narrator, she is able to confront the past and reflect on the feelings of exile and loss that she experienced while growing up in Paris. Her autobiographical fiction is an exploratory journey for self-knowledge that illuminates the consequences of France's failed policy of integration. The narrator and her grandmother must live the painful experience of social exclusion and racial hostility because the pressure to assimilate does not leave any room for difference, identity politics, or multiculturalism *à l'américaine.*

Pineau has been fashioned by two cultures, French and Guadeloupean, each one combining a multiplicity of voices, a plurality of identities and histories. But within a national ideology that links integration with assimilation, the author/narrator's desire to be French *and* Antillean is thwarted. As a black Creole woman educated in France, she exemplifies the reality of *métissage,* an aesthetic concept that "brings together biology and history, anthropology and philosophy, linguistics and literature."[33] Thus, in the process of articulating the complexity of her own métis heritage, Pineau also speaks for her own people: their condition as postcolonial subjects, their displacement, their various hybridizations resulting in extraordinary cultural diversity. She writes: "We never stopped mixing our races and our bloods with other people [. . .], Indians, Orientals, Europeans, Chinese, et cetera. . . . We are *bastards,* and maybe it is what saves us in today's intolerant world."[34] Through the derisive negative connotation of *bastard* as undesirable half-breed or undetermined racial category, Pineau expresses the transforming and unsettling nature of *métissage,* whose multiformed elements are changing our identities. Thus, *bastard* becomes the metaphor, to borrow Françoise Lionnet's expression, for our "heterogeneous postmodern condition."[35] The word also mirrors the hybridization of Pineau's writing, which impels her quest as seeker, as well as transmitter, of knowledge.

If on one level *Exile* is meant for a white readership, on another it specifically addresses the Antillean people, those who have immigrated into France and those who have stayed home. Moreover the novel's linguistic and narrative techniques weave together history, personal histories, portraits, stories, plus the combination of French and Creole languages. Taken together, these elements provide a multifaceted image of a reality usually ignored and sometimes silenced. In speaking loudly of this reality, Pineau criticizes the French "universal" values and advocates not only the recognition of the Other's difference but also the bastard elements in French identity. *Métissage* is inexorably transforming *Frenchness.*

Notes

1. Hargreaves, "Perception of Ethnic Difference," 18.
2. *Métropole* refers to continental France in relation to its overseas territories.
3. Quoted by Dany Bébel-Gisler in the afterword to *Leonora,* 234.
4. Pineau, "Ecrire en tant que noire," 290. My translation.
5. See Burton, introduction, in *French and West Indian,* ed. Burton and Reno, 2–4. Burton writes: "in a peculiar way, colored French West Indians have asserted their identity by denying it or, more precisely, they have asserted one identity (as French) by denying another (as West Indians). Social, political, economic and cultural advance were held to depend on a denial of difference: one became French to the precise extent that one abjured West Indian–ness or, to put it differently, the identification with the Other (France) required a prior negation of the (West Indian) self" (3).
6. *Négropolitain* is composed of the word *negro* and the contraction

of the word *métropolitain* (metropolitan). *Neg'zagonal* is composed of the contractions of the two words *negro* and *hexagonal*. The *hexagon* is a popular term for the topographic configuration of continental France. Burton writes: "the so-called *Négropolitain*(e) [is] the returning or visiting immigrant who brings back to the Caribbean Parisian attitudes, aspirations, values and lifestyles, who speaks Creole with a Parisian accent or cannot speak Creole at all and who is received by locals with a mixture of envy, amusement and contempt" (Burton, introduction, in *French and West Indian,* 12).

7. Makward and Githire, "Gisèle Pineau," 222, 223. My translation.

8. Murdoch, *Creole Identity,* 149.

9. Victor Schoelcher, a member of the French legislature from Alsace during France's Second Republic, was a famous abolitionist who labored intensely to "give" freedom to the slaves of the French Antilles. Abolition was granted in 1848.

10. Pineau, "Ecrire en tant que noire," 290. My translation.

11. Pineau, "Ecrire en tant que noire," 291–93.

12. Pineau and Abraham, *Femmes des Antilles,* 14. My translation.

13. Bébel-Gisler, *Leonora,* 235.

14. Condé, "Chercher nos vérités," in *Penser la créolité,* ed. Condé and Cottenet-Hage, 308. My translation.

15. The concept of *créolité* was developed by Jean Bernabé, Patrick Chamoiseau, and Raphaël Confiant, the Martinican authors of *Eloge de la créolité* (translated as *In Praise of Creoleness*). The term recognizes the multiple histories of miscegenation, slavery, colonialism, and migration that have shaped the identity of the Caribbean people. "Our history is a braid of histories. [. . .] Creoleness is the *world refracted but recomposed*, a maelstrom of signifieds in a single signifier: a Totality." According to the authors, this plurality that validates "original" authenticity, naturalness, and separation from what is "external" creates a cultural unity that is unique to the Caribbean (23–24).

16. Condé, "Chercher nos vérités," 309. My translation. Condé particularly refers here to male writers.

17. Jacques Coursil's interview quoted by Delphine Perret in *La creolité,* 227.

18. All parenthetic references are to the translated text unless otherwise indicated.

19. *Banania* is the name of a famous chocolate-flavored breakfast powder whose advertising campaign used for many years a caricature of a black man. In *Declining the Stereotype,* Mireille Rosello writes: "In France, anyone would be familiar with the yellow Banania box and its unavoidable 'L'ami Y'a bon.' [. . .] The smiling Senegalese Rifleman

enjoying a spoonful of Banania is an unforgettable cultural icon branded with the same intensity into the minds of white and black French and Francophone people" (5).

20. Bonniol, *La couleur comme maléfice,* 35–36. My translation.

21. In plantation societies, the social order was also determined by the legal barriers sanctioning the opposition between the free owners of the land and the slaves. Bonniol, *La couleur comme maléfice,* 13.

22. *Congo* is the name given to the migrant cane cutter in Creole.

23. Fallope, "Une société en mutation," 82–86.

24. Condé, "*Créolité* without the Creole language?" in *Caribbean Creolization,* ed. Balutansky and Sourieau, 102.

25. Burton, introduction, in *French and West Indians,* ed. Burton and Reno, 12–13.

26. Britton, *Edouard Glissant,* 26.

27. For a discussion of Martinican attitudes to Creole, see Britton, *Edouard Glissant,* 25–31.

28. Glissant, *Caribbean Discourse,* 127, 120.

29. Bébel-Gisler, *Leonora,* 234–35. *Gwoka* is a traditional drum of Guadeloupe.

30. See Rice-Maximin, *Karukéra,* especially the chapter devoted to "La Grand-mère," 14–16.

31. Pineau, "Ecrire en tant que noire," 295. My translation.

32. Burton, introduction, in *French and West Indian,* ed. Burton and Reno, 2–3.

33. Lionnet, *Autobiographical Voices,* 8.

34. Pineau, "Ecrire en tant que noire," 294. My emphasis and translation.

35. Lionnet, *Autobiographical Voices,* 17.

Bibliography

Writings by Gisèle Pineau

Fiction

La grande drive des esprits. Paris: Le Serpent à Plumes, 1993. Prizes: Grand Prix des lectrices d'*Elle*, 1994; Prix Carbet de la Caraïbe, 1994. *The Drifting of Spirits*. Trans. Michael Dash. London: Quartet, 1999.

L'espérance-macadam. Paris: Stock, 1995. Prize: Prix RFO, 1996. *Macadam Dreams*. Trans. C. Dickson. Lincoln: University of Nebraska Press, forthcoming.

L' exil selon Julia. Paris: Stock, 1996. Prizes: Prix Terre de France, 1996; Prix Rotary, 1997.

L'âme prêtée aux oiseaux. Paris: Stock, 1998. Prize: Prix Amerigo Vespucci, 1998.

Chair piment. Paris: Mercure de France, 2002.

Fiction for Young People

Un papillon dans la cité. Paris: Sépia, 1992.

Le cyclone Marilyn. Illus. Béatrice Favereau. Montréal: Hurtubise HMH, 1998; Paris: L'Élan Vert, 1998.

Caraïbe sur Seine. Paris: Dapper, 1999.

C'est la règle. Paris: Thierry Magnier, 2002.

Short Stories

"Paroles de terre en larmes," "Ombres créoles," and "Léna." In *Paroles de terre en larmes*, 5–20, 96–110, 112–28. Paris: Hatier, 1987.

"Une antique malédiction." *Le Serpent à plumes* 15 (spring 1992): 37–52.

Bibliography

"Aimée de Bois-Vanille." *Le Serpent à plumes* 28 (winter 1994): 45–61.
"Tourment d'amour." In *Écrire la "parole de nuit": La nouvelle littéraire antillaise*, ed. Ralph Ludwig, 79–87. Paris: Gallimard (folio), 1994.
"Piéça dévorée et pourrie." *Noir des Îles*. Paris: Gallimard, 1995, 159–203.
"Le ventre de Léocadie." *L'Express* (8 October 1998), 78.
"Amélie et les anolis." In *Nouvelles des Amériques*, ed. Maryse Condé and Lise Gauvin, 25–40. Montréal: L'Hexagone, 1998.
"Les enchaînés." *Tropiques, revue négro-africaine de littérature et de philosophie* 61 (2nd semester 1998).

Other Writing

"Écrire en tant que noire." In *Penser la créolité*, ed. M. Cottenet-Hage and M. Condé, 289–95. Paris: Karthala, 1995.
Guadeloupe découverte, with Jean-Marc Lecerf; foreword by Simone Schwarz-Bartz. Paris/Fort-de-France: Fabre Doumergue, 1997.
"Le sens de mon écriture." *LittéRéalité* 10, no. 1 (spring/summer 1998): 135–36.
"Sur un morne de Capesterre Belle-Eau." In *A peine plus d'un cyclone aux Antilles*, ed. Bernard Magnier, 25–30. Cognac: Le temps qu'il fait, 1998.
Femmes des Antilles: Traces et voix cent cinquante ans après l'abolition de l'esclavage (with Marie Abraham). Paris: Stock, 1998.

Studies on Gisèle Pineau

Bonnet, Véronique. "Gisèle Pineau: L'âme prêtée à "écriture." *Notre Librairie* no. 138–39 (September 1999–March 2000): 91–98.
Condé, Maryse. "Femme, terre natale." In *Parallèles: Anthologie de la nouvelle féminine de langue française*, ed. M. Cottenet-Hage and J.-Ph. Imbert, 253–60. Québec: L'Instant Même, 1996.
Dumontet, Danielle. "Gisèle Pineau ou une nouvelle voix féminine guadeloupéenne." In *Palabres, Femmes et Créations littéraires en Afrique et aux Antilles* 3, no. 1–2 (April 2000): 203–17.
Gyssels, Kathleen. "L'exil selon Pineau, récit de vie et autobiographie." In *Récits de vie de l'Afrique et des Antilles: Enracinement, errance, exil*, ed. Suzanne Crosta, 169–213. Sainte-Foy: GRELCA, 1998.
Hellerstein, Nina. "Violence, mythe et destin dans l'univers antillais de Gisèle Pineau." *LittéRéalité* 10, no. 1 (spring/summer 1998): 47–58.

Makward, Christiane. "Comme un siècle de différence amoureuse, sur Simone Schwarz-Bart (1972) et Gisèle Pineau (1996)." Nottingham French Studies 40, no. 1 (spring 2001): 41–51.

Mugnier, Françoise. "La France dans l'oeuvre de Gisèle Pineau." *Etudes Francophones* 15, no.1 (spring 2000): 61–73.

Murdoch, H. Adlai. "Negotiating the Metropole: Patterns of Exile and Cultural Survival in Gisèle Pineau and Suzanne Dracius-Pinalie." In *Immigrant Narratives in Contemporary France*, ed. Susan Ireland and Patrice J. Proulx, 129–139. Westport, Conn.: Greenwood Press, 2001.

Spear, Thomas C. "L'enfance créole: La nouvelle autobiographie antillaise." In *Récits de vie de l'Afrique et de la Caraïbe: Enracinement, errance, exil,* ed. Suzanne Crosta, 143–67. Sainte-Foy: GRELCA, 1998.

Suarez, Lucia M. "Gisèle Pineau: Writing the Dimensions of Migration." *World Literature Today* 75, no. 3 (summer/autumn 2001): 9–21.

Vitiello, Joëlle. "Le corps de l'île dans les écrits de Gisèle Pineau." In *Elles écrivent des Antilles (Haïti, Guadeloupe, Martinique)*, ed. Susanne Rinne and Joëlle Vitiello, 243–63. Paris: L'Harmattan, 1997.

Criticism and Background Studies

Alexander, Simone A. James. *Mother Imagery in the Novels of Afro-Caribbean Women.* Columbia: University of Missouri Press, 2001.

Anselin, Alain. *L'émigration antillaise en France: La troisième île.* Paris: Karthala, 1990.

Balutansky, Kathleen, and Marie-Agnès Sourieau, eds. *Caribbean Creolization: Reflections on the Cultural Dynamics of Language, Literature, and Identity.* Gainesville: University Press of Florida, 1998.

Bébel-Gisler, Dany. *Leonora: The Buried Story of Guadeloupe.* Trans. Andrea Leskes. Charlottesville: University Press of Virginia, 1994.

Bernabé, Jean, Patrick Chamoiseau, and Raphaël Confiant. *Eloge de la créolité/In Praise of Creoleness.* Bilingual edition. Paris: Gallimard, 1993.

Bongie, Chris. *Islands and Exiles: The Creole Identities of Post/Colonial Literature.* Stanford: Stanford University Press, 1998.

Bonniol, Jean-Luc. *La couleur comme maléfice: Une illustration créole de la généalogie des blancs et des noirs.* Paris: Albin Michel, 1992.

Bibliography

Britton, Celia. *Edouard Glissant and Postcolonial Theory.* Charlottesville: University Press of Virginia, 1999.

Burton, Richard D. E., and Fred Reno, eds. *French and West Indian: Martinique, Guadeloupe and French Guiana Today.* Charlottesville: University Press of Virginia, 1995.

Condé, Maryse, and Madeleine Cottenet-Hage, eds. *Penser la Créolité.* Paris: Karthala, 1995.

d'Almeida, Irène Assiba. *Francophone African Women Writers: Destroying the Emptiness of Silence.* Gainesville: University Presses of Florida, 1994.

Falloppe, Josette. "Une société en mutation." In *La Guadeloupe 1875–1914: Les soubresauts d'une société pluri-ethnique ou les ambiguités de l'assimilation,* ed. Henriette Levillain, 78–89. Paris: Les Éditions Autrement, 1994.

Glissant, Edouard. *Caribbean Discourse: Selected Essays.* Trans. Michael Dash. Charlottesville: University Press of Virginia, 1989.

Hargreaves, Alec G. "Perceptions of Ethnic Difference in Post-War France." In *Immigrant Narratives in Contemporary France,* ed. Susan Ireland and Patrice J. Proulx, 7–22. Westport, Conn.: Greenwood Press, 2001.

Hargreaves, Alec G., and Mark McKinney, eds. *Post-Colonial Cultures in France.* London: Routledge, 1997.

Lionnet, Françoise. *Autobiographical Voices: Race, Gender, Self-Portraiture.* Ithaca: Cornell University Press, 1989.

Makward, Christiane, and Njeri Githire. "Gisèle Pineau: Causerie à Penn State (avril 2001)." *Women in French Studies* no. 9 (2001): 220–33.

Murdoch, H. Adlai. *Creole Identity in the French Caribbean Novel.* Gainesville: University Presses of Florida, 2001.

Perret, Delphine. *La créolité: Espace de création.* Paris: Ibis Rouge Editions, 2001.

Rice-Maximin, Micheline. *Karukéra: Présence littéraire de La Guadeloupe.* New York: Peter Lang, 1998.

Rosello, Mireille. *Declining the Stereotype.* Hanover: University Press of New England, 1998.

———. *Littérature et identité créole aux Antilles.* Paris: Éditions Karthala, 1992.

Schor, Naomi. "The Crisis of French Universalism." *Yale French Studies* 100 (February 2002): 43–64.

Smith, Sidonie, and Gisela Brinker-Gabler, eds. *Writing New Identities: Gender, Nation, and Immigration in Contemporary France.* Minneapolis: University of Minnesota Press, 1997.

CARAF Books

Caribbean and African Literature
Translated from French

Guillaume Oyônô-Mbia and
Seydou Badian
Faces of African Independence:
Three Plays
Translated by Clive Wake

Olympe Bhêly-Quénum
Snares without End
Translated by Dorothy S. Blair

Bertène Juminer
The Bastards
Translated by Keith Q. Warner

Tchicaya U Tam'Si
The Madman and the Medusa
Translated by Sonja Haussmann
Smith and William Jay Smith

Alioum Fantouré
Tropical Circle
Translated by Dorothy S. Blair

Edouard Glissant
Caribbean Discourse:
Selected Essays
Translated by J. Michael Dash

Daniel Maximin
Lone Sun
Translated by Nidra Poller

Aimé Césaire
Lyric and Dramatic Poetry,
1946–82
Translated by Clayton Eshleman
and Annette Smith

René Depestre
The Festival of the Greasy Pole
Translated by Carrol F. Coates

Kateb Yacine
Nedjma
Translated by Richard Howard

Léopold Sédar Senghor
The Collected Poetry
Translated by Melvin Dixon

Maryse Condé
I, Tituba, Black Witch of Salem
Translated by Richard Philcox

Assia Djebar
Women of Algiers in
Their Apartment
Translated by Marjolijn de Jager

Dany Bébel-Gisler
Leonora: The Buried Story
of Guadeloupe
Translated by Andrea Leskes